VISION OF DEATH

Suzanne and Jessie stood in front of the enormous roller coaster. A short rope fence separated them from a series of gears and wiring. Jessie stepped over the rope, motioning Suzanne to follow her. The boy taking the tickets did not notice them as they disappeared back under the scaffolding. Jessie began running her hands back and forth over the cables Randal Clark had worked.

"Let it come naturally, Jessie." Suzanne spoke softly. "Empty your mind. Make it a blank screeen, like at the movies." She grabbed Jessie's hand, holding it tight.

Jessie's head tilted to the left. Almost immediately, little mewing sounds began coming from her lips. "No. Please, no." In her mind, she could see a single-edged razor coming toward the face of a girl whose features were frozen in terror . . .

FACE OFF

EMMA BROOKES

St. Martin's Paperbacks

This novel is a work of fiction. Names, characters, places, and incidents are either the product of the author's imagination, or are used fictitiously, and any resemblance to actual persons, living or dead, events or locales is entirely coincidental.

FACE OFF

Copyright © 1997 by Gladys Bale Wellbrock.

Cover photograph by Herman Estévez.

ISBN: 0-312-96216-9

Printed in the United States of America

St. Martin's Paperbacks edition/December 1997

10 9 8 7 6 5 4 3 2 1

For my sisters
Jo Ellen Bale Androes
Patricia Bale Cox
Helen Bale West
Barbara Bale Renick
Margaret Ann Wellbrock

Prologue

Rain drizzled down out of a partly overcast sky, making the night even darker. Even so, the tall, thin man standing under the tree outside the Sunshine Evangelical Free Church stepped back farther into the shadow of the branches when he saw car lights coming slowly down the street. He removed the cigarette from his mouth, cupping his hand around it to keep it lit, yet obscured from view. The car slowed, then turned left at the corner.

Inside the church he could once again hear singing. Surely it wouldn't be long now. Not that he was in any hurry. He had been following the girl for three days, trying to decide if she were the right one. No, actually, that wasn't true. He had followed her for three days because he needed time to work up his courage. *Shit, who wouldn't!*

He had finally located the perfect spot—an old abandoned office building on Brighton Avenue, scheduled for demolition. City crews would do a room-to-room check before starting any blasting. They were sure to find her body. He took a deep drag from his cigarette, blowing smoke out of the side of his mouth slowly. He felt important. It always gave him a *high* to kill—an extra little buzz, like he'd had too much caffeine or popped an upper. Still, this wasn't quite the same. Not the same at all.

Damn cops. Think they're so friggin' smart. Well, let

them try and figure *this* one out! He used the sleeve of his blue dress shirt to wipe dampness from his face, not certain if the moisture was coming from the light misting of rain, or sweat from the humid, muggy night.

The doors to the church suddenly swung outward, and he dropped his cigarette, grinding it to bits on the ground. There she was—part of the first group coming out. Her long blond hair was tied demurely back in a ponytail, and even from this distance, he could see her rosy cheeks and lips, devoid of makeup as always. Yeah. She was perfect. She was just friggin' perfect!

Chapter
One

Suzanne didn't move from the comfortable nest she had made on the couch. If she didn't answer the door, whoever was leaning on her doorbell would surely fade away into the night. It couldn't be anyone she knew. People who knew her knew better than to drop by unexpectedly.

"Miss Richards, are you in there? Please open the door, I need to talk to you." The voice sounded young, and unfamiliar to Suzanne.

"Go away!" Suzanne yelled. "Whatever you're selling, I don't want any!"

"Please, Miss Richards. I—I've come about my sister. I was told you could help me."

Suzanne laid the half-eaten bag of chips on the cluttered coffee table and rose, reluctantly, to her feet. Why the hell couldn't the world leave her alone? That part of her life was over.

She glanced around her small apartment. Stacks of papers and books were piled on tables and chairs. Empty take-out containers were scattered about, and three huge ashtrays were overflowing with stale cigarette butts. No way was anyone getting in here.

She left the chain on the lock and cracked the door. "Yes? What is it?"

"Miss Richards? Suzanne Richards?"

Suzanne nodded at the young girl standing in the hallway. She looked to be in her early teens. Fourteen, maybe fifteen. Her face was unfamiliar.

"Yes. I'm Suzanne Richards. What can I do for you?"

The young girl's eyes filled with sudden tears. "I want you to find my sister before she dies!"

Suzanne stared at the girl, then dropped her gaze and spoke softly. "I'm sorry. I can't help you. If someone told you I could, they were mistaken. I'm sorry." She started to close the door, but the girl put her small foot into the opening.

"Miss Richards, I rode a bus for sixteen hours and spent another four hours walking around looking for this apartment. My parents don't know where I am, and goodness knows they have enough on their minds right now without worrying about me. I've come a long way to talk with you, and I'm not leaving until I do." Her bold statement over, the girl sucked in a long, shuddering breath, and burst into tears.

"Oh, God! Will you stop that?" Suzanne tried to make herself heard. "You'll have the whole damn building on my neck!"

The young girl's wails continued until they reached a crescendo which threatened to shatter every piece of glass in the three-story brownstone.

"Okay! Okay!" Suzanne yelled. "Move your foot so I can release the chain, and I'll let you come in!"

The girl wiped her eyes on the sleeve of her blouse and looked at Suzanne, hesitantly. "Do you promise?"

Suzanne nodded, resigned. "I promise! Jesus! They'll probably have me arrested for child abuse if you keep that up!"

The girl managed a sheepish grin through her tears. "I *can* be rather . . . uh . . . annoying, when I put my mind to it, I guess. At least that's what Amy has always told me." She pulled her foot from the door jamb.

Suzanne slid the chain off, opened the door, and stood there bemused. "You *guess?* That's like saying you *guess* there is water in the Pacific Ocean!"

The girl slipped past Suzanne, and into the apartment, as if she were afraid Suzanne might change her mind at any minute and slam the door shut on her. Her large aquamarine eyes moved unabashedly around the small, dirty apartment, then fixed on the tall lady who still stood with one hand on the door, staring at her. Miss Richards was pretty, the girl decided. She had wide-set brown eyes, fringed with long lashes, thick eyebrows, and shoulder-length, dark brown hair, which needed combing.

"I need your help to find my sister, Amy. I know she is still alive, I just *know* it! The police have searched everywhere, and they say they can't be sure he even *took* her, but we all know he did, because Amy wouldn't just disappear without letting us know, and of course there was her purse and all, but the police say that just because they found the purse in his Dumpster, doesn't mean he kidnapped her, and even though we know they think he did it, they say they can't do anything and—"

"Whoa! Slow down." Suzanne closed the door to her apartment and walked over to the girl. "Let's start at the beginning. First of all, what's your name, where do you live, and shouldn't we call your parents?"

The girl flushed slightly as she dropped her canvas tote bag, wiped her hand across her jeans, then stuck it out toward Suzanne. "I'm sorry. You must want to shake my hand, right? You need to know if I'm on the level and not lying, huh?"

"*Are* you lying?"

"No! You'll see. Go ahead. Shake my hand."

Suzanne rolled her eyes toward the ceiling. "Ah, geez, is that what this is about? Do you believe everything you read in the papers?"

"I didn't read about you only in the paper. You were in a book I got at the library. *Amazing Psychics*. It said you were probably the best psychic in the United States, maybe even the world."

"Yeah, and that book also said that some boy in Austria could make himself fly. Did you believe that, too?"

"Well, no, I guess not." The young girl looked defiant. "But I cross-checked most everything that author said. I looked up old newspaper clippings, and even read about . . . about that guy they had to let loose because of your testimony."

Suzanne felt her knees go weak, and she slumped down on the couch. "If you know that, then you know why I don't offer my services anymore." Her voice broke, as she whispered hoarsely, "And you know that two twelve-year-old girls died because of me."

"That's not true! It wasn't *your* fault they let that jerk go. They had enough evidence to *hang* that guy, and the stupid judge let him off!"

Suzanne shook her head, remembering the anguish on Judge Carpenter's face when he handed down his decision—a decision that had cost him his career.

"You're wrong. The judge didn't have any other choice. Every piece of evidence the police had was obtained through my visit, my *handshake,* with Baxter Underwood. And guess what? There's such a thing in law as not having to testify against yourself, so all they could get him on was the traffic violation for which he had originally been stopped. If I hadn't entered the picture, sooner or later, the police would have gotten a lead and the case would have broken. As it was, he got off, and one month later—well, you know what he did to those two girls in Omaha."

"It wasn't your fault. You were only trying to help."

Suzanne forced herself to get on her feet. She had gone over the arguments a thousand times, back and forth. It wouldn't do any good to rehash them now. Her troubled eyes swept over the young girl, taking in the jeans and wrinkled white blouse, the wild mane of red hair, and the glistening eyes, once more on the verge of spilling over. Suddenly, she felt like a world-class heel. "What's your name, sweetie? Why don't we start with that?" As she called the girl by the pet name, a faint memory flitted in and out of her mind, surprising her. Someone—*who?*— used to call her sweetie.

"Jessie. Jessie Matthews. And please, Miss Richards, you've just got to help me."

"How old are you, Jessie? And where do you live?"

Jessie's shoulders slumped as if by answering Suzanne's question she was admitting defeat. "Fourteen. I'm fourteen years old and my home is on a dairy farm just outside Pueblo, Colorado."

"And you rode a bus from Pueblo to Kansas City without your parents knowing about it?"

A fresh deluge of tears washed over the girl's freckled cheeks. "Yes. I . . . I had a birthday two days ago. I used the money I got to buy the bus ticket. I tried to call you, but the operator said your phone was unlisted. Dad, he said that psychic stuff was all nonsense, and Mom, well—I knew she wouldn't go against Dad, and anyway, I *know* it's not nonsense, so I decided to come. I couldn't tell them. I knew Dad would never let me make a trip to Kansas City. Not after Amy."

"Are you saying Amy disappeared here? In K.C.?"

Jessie nodded her head. "Two weeks ago. Then the next day the police arrested a guy named Randal Clark and—"

Suzanne could feel the blood flowing from her face. "Oh, God, Jessie. Not the Kansas City Butcher! You aren't telling me that the authorities think your sister was one of *his* victims?"

Jessie's face changed from sorrow to anger, then to defiance as her jaw locked stubbornly. "*Not* a victim! Amy is alive! I would know if she were dead."

Suzanne averted her eyes, afraid Jessie would be able to read the skepticism she was feeling. How many times had she heard a mother or father, a spouse or sweetheart, say those same exact words? The truth was, they *didn't* know. They were operating only on hope. A hope that Suzanne invariably squelched when she found the body of a loved one.

"Jessie, I—"

"No, no, no, no, no . . ."

Suzanne stared in astonishment as Jessie stuck her index fingers into her ears and kept chanting. She continued until Suzanne walked over and pulled her arms down. "What the devil are you doing?"

"I didn't want to hear what you were going to tell me. You were going to say that Amy is dead, weren't you? You were going to say that *everyone* always thinks *their* missing person is alive, but that you mainly find them after they are dead!"

Suzanne eyed Jessie strangely. "How did you know that was what I was thinking?"

"I, well—" Jessie stumbled over her words. "The truth is, I had been reading about you even before Amy was missing. I've always sort of just *known* things. Not *big* things, like you, only small, unimportant things for the most part. But I wondered about it and started reading everything I could find about—about people like us." She looked down at her feet, self-consciously. "Not that I would presume to think I was anywhere near as good as *you* are! I don't have your *special* ability at all. But maybe I could help you a little. Maybe between the two of us, we could find Amy."

With that short statement, Suzanne knew more about Jessie than probably her own parents knew. She knew about the terror the girl had gone through as she tried to figure out what made her different from all her friends. She knew about the bad dreams, the sickening feeling in the pit of her stomach when something she had only thought about, had come to pass. The feeling that somehow she had *made* the event happen—had caused it. No one, not a parent, not a teacher, not a member of the clergy, could understand and counsel a young psychic just coming to grips with his or her talents. And no one but another psychic could know the pure hell of those early years.

Her own hell had begun when she was only five years old. Her beautiful, soft-spoken mother had died that summer—a horrible, violent car crash had ended her life. Her father, blaming her, had barely spoken to Suzanne over the next three years. Then one day she had come home from school to find her father in the bathroom of their cramped, dirty apartment, his face blasted away by a twelve-gauge shotgun.

"It's your fault, little lady, don't you ever forget that! Your momma would never have been going to visit your aunt Alma if she weren't afraid of your devilment! She said she just had to get away from you for awhile—away from your witchcraft!"

"Daddy, Daddy—don't be mad at me. I told Mommie something bad was going to happen. I told her. I told her!"

"You made it happen! Just like you made Zero run into that truck. Jean was right about you. You're no good! A spawn of the devil!"

For three years as they moved from city to city, state to state, she had lived with a father who would not look at her, would not touch her, and who screamed "devil" at her when anything went wrong in his life. If he lost his job, it was because Suzanne had put a hex on his boss. If the car broke down, Suzanne had made it happen. By the time she was eight years old and stood staring at the bloodied body that was once her father, Suzanne figured her life could never get any worse than it was at that moment. She had been wrong.

"Don't you believe me, Miss Richards?" Jessie's words jarred Suzanne back to the present. She quickly reached out and drew the girl to her, holding her tight. "Yes, sweetheart, I believe you." She spoke the words softly. "I'm sorry for you—it's a terrible burden to bear—but I believe you."

Jessie extracted herself from Suzanne's hold and looked at her, puzzled. "I don't think it's such a terrible burden! If it will help me find Amy, then it's worth anything I would have to go through. Besides, my mother told me she wasn't sure about all this psychic stuff, but if it were true, then it was a special gift, and it just meant God smiled a little wider on me than on most folks!''

''Your mother sounds very wise.'' Suzanne spoke the words honestly, trying to push away her father's harsh words. Funny though, she could never remember her mother being frightened of her. Of course, she couldn't really remember her mother at all, anymore. All of her memories were shrouded with the bitter denouncements she had endured from her father. She tried never to think about or remember anything from that terrible time.

Suzanne shuddered, shaking her head quickly as if by doing so she could dismiss the thoughts which had inexplicably been leaping into her mind since the arrival of the girl.

''Okay, Jessie, let's sit down and start all over again.'' Suzanne began sweeping debris off the couch.

''Maybe I should call home now,'' Jessie said. ''If Mom or Dad called my friend Nicole and found out I wasn't there, well, it would be just awful for them.''

''So you did think of them at least a little before you took off?''

Jessie's chin raised defiantly. ''Of course! I made plans to stay in the city with Nicole after school. If everything went right, Mom and Dad wouldn't miss me until tomorrow after school when I didn't get off the bus.''

Suzanne handed Jessie her portable phone, then sat listening to the one-sided conversation.

—''Momma, this is Jessie. Now, don't get excited, but I'm in Kansas City to look for Amy.

—No, Momma, I'm not at Nicole's.

—No, Momma, I skipped school and took the bus to Kansas City.

—Yes, Momma, I'm okay.

—No, Momma, I'm with Suzanne Richards, that psychic I told you about.

—Yes, she is real nice, and Momma, guess what? She's going to help us.''

Jessie took the phone down from her ear and looked at Suzanne. ''She's trying to explain to Daddy. I can hear him yelling. By the way, you *are* going to help us, aren't you?''

Suzanne managed a wry smile, nodding her head, resigned. Already she could feel a special pull toward the young psychic. She wouldn't refuse her.

Jessie quickly put the phone back to her ear as she heard her father's voice, calling her.

—''Yes, Daddy. Yes, I know it was dumb, but it was all I could think of to do.

—I know, and I'm sorry for that.

—Daddy, I'm not in any danger.

—Da—

—But—

—Yes, Daddy.''

She handed the phone toward Suzanne. ''He wants to talk to you.'' Her voice dropped to a whisper. ''You have to convince him to let me stay!''

''I . . . I don't know much about dealing with fathers,'' Suzanne whispered back, taking the phone.

''Hello. Mr. Matthews?''

''Yes, this is Jake Matthews. Miss . . . Richards, is it?''

''Yes. Suzanne. Suzanne Richards.''

''I'm sorry for our Jessie intruding on you like that. If you could just make sure she's all right until we can get there, we would really appreciate it.'' Suzanne could hear a mixture of anger and worry in the man's voice as he spoke. ''We'll check on flights, but if we can't get one right out, then we'll start out in the car. No matter what, we'll be there in ten, twelve hours. Would you mind watching after her until then?''

''Mr. Matthews, listen to me,'' Suzanne answered. ''There is a chance, albeit a slim one, that I might be able to help find your Amy. Why don't you give Jessie and me a few days? Let us see what we can find out. I'll take really good care of your daughter. I promise.''

''I'm sorry, Miss Richards. I'm sure you believe in that stuff, and mean well, but I've already lost one daughter. I don't intend to lose another.'' Suzanne could hear the anguish in Jake Matthews's voice as he spoke.

Jessie suddenly reached up, covering the mouthpiece of the telephone with her hand, and spoke excitedly to Suzanne.

"Tell him the cow he is looking for is in the ravine just north of the old river road. Tell him she is giving birth and is in trouble—that the calf needs pulled."

"What?"

"Do it! Just do it!"

Suzanne took a deep breath. "Uh . . . Mr. Matthews, this is going to sound strange, but the cow you are looking for is . . ." she hesitated, looking quickly at Jessie.

"In the ravine just north of the old river road," Jessie whispered.

"In a ravine north of the old river road. She is trying to give birth, but is in trouble."

"The calf needs *pulled*," Jessie whispered. "Tell him the calf needs pulled."

Suzanne rolled her eyes and flung one hand up in question to the girl.

Jessie nodded, impatient. "He'll know. Just tell him!"

"Mr. Matthews, the calf needs pulled," Suzanne said quickly.

She glanced at Jessie, whose forehead was wrinkled in concentration.

"Twins!" Jessie whispered excitedly. "Tell him Sally is having twins and he needs to get to her!"

Suzanne relayed the message, feeling more foolish by the minute. By the time Jessie's mother came back on the line, she was certain the Matthewses would contact the police to retrieve their daughter from the madwoman. Instead, the voice she heard was more hopeful than skeptical.

"Jake has gone to check, Miss Richards. How did you know he had been looking for Sally for the last four hours? She is our best Holstein, but what with all the horror over Amy's disappearance, we haven't paid much attention to the farm lately. Then tonight Jake realized Sally hadn't come in for the milking and he began searching for her."

Surprise registered on Suzanne's face, and she looked at Jessie with new respect. She covered the mouthpiece with her hand. "Do you want me to tell your mother it was you?"

"No!" Jessie whispered. "Let them think it was you. Then maybe they will let me stay."

Suzanne removed her hand and spoke with a confidence she didn't feel. "I'm glad I could help, Mrs. Matthews. And won't you please reconsider letting Jessie stay with me for a few days? I realize you don't know me, but if there is even the slightest chance we could get a line on Amy, wouldn't it be worth the gamble?"

She could hear the woman's muffled sobs as she answered. "I'll talk to Jake when he gets back, Miss Richards. We sort of lost hope after the police told us they suspected that beast Clark of taking her." Her voice broke. "He . . . my God, he dismembered those other girls. I just can't bear to think about it. Our Amy. Our dear, sweet Amy."

Suzanne wanted desperately to give the woman some hope, but knew she dared not. The chance of Amy still being alive was slim to none, and she knew it.

"Mrs. Matthews, I'm going to leave you my telephone number. You talk it over with your husband, and whatever you decide, I'm sure it will be the right decision. In the meantime, Jessie is fine here with me. I won't let anything happen to her. You have my word on that."

Jake Matthews followed the newly painted white fences which encompassed the ranch house, barns, and pasture. His land didn't end with the fences, but continued for miles of open range. How Sally had managed to get out with the other cattle, he didn't know. Probably that young kid from town he had hired to repair the fences, who thought it too much trouble to get back out of his sports car and lock the gates after he went through them. He should have fired the lad that first day, anyway. Whoever heard of running a fence line in a candy-apple Trans Am? And every time

Jake came across an open gate, the kid always had the same answer. "I knew I was coming back through in a few minutes. I didn't see no need of wasting time closing it." And Sally, dang her contrary hide, she always did try to get off by herself when she was birthing. If she was ready to drop, then she would certainly have taken advantage of an open gate.

The main trouble was, these last two weeks had simply been one big blur for Jake, ever since the Kansas City police had called, informing them that Amy's purse had turned up in a Dumpster outside the apartment of that Randal Clark. The bastard had enough evidence in that apartment to link him with the deaths of eight young girls. The police said there wasn't any doubt that he was the infamous Kansas City Butcher. Even so, Clark wasn't admitting a thing.

Quick, hot tears filled Jake's eyes, and he brushed them away, angrily. The police were still searching for Amy's body. They offered no hope that she would be found alive, and insisted there was no reason for him and Martha to come to Kansas City just yet. He wanted to believe, but Jessie's insistence that Amy was still alive didn't make it so.

Amy and Jessie. The lights of his life. So different, yet both devoted to one another, and to this land he and Martha had toiled over to make a success. He could not have asked God to send him any two more precious daughters. Amy, with her love of books, of drawing, her music. He could still remember the joy on her face when she received the letter saying she had gotten the job of design artist at Hallmark Cards in Kansas City. "Don't worry, Dad," she had said, hugging him. "I promise to call home twice a week and write you almost every night!" Amy, with her mother's blond good looks and quiet reserve. Still waters running deep.

Now his Jessie was another story altogether. He could picture her racing Higgins, her stallion, over the fields, her long red hair flying in the wind. Jessie had never known a moment's fear in her short life. She was a whirlwind of activity, and it was this trait that worried Jake when he thought of her alone in Kansas City. Jessie wouldn't be cautious. It was completely against her nature. He should have paid more attention when she first started talking about that Richards woman. God knows when she got something in her head there was usually no stopping her. But to travel all the way to Kansas City alone! He shuddered to think what might have happened. And for what? So some kind of lamebrained gypsy could look into a crystal ball and tell them where Amy was? Jake suddenly felt foolish for running out in the dark because this woman almost six hundred miles away said she knew where his cow was. Knowing Jessie, she had probably told that Richards woman to tell him that story to get him out of the house so Jessie could work on Martha.

All of Jake's common sense told him to turn his Ford pickup around and head back to the house, yet he continued on, following the river road. Up ahead, the headlights picked up the ravine which ran for about a quarter of a mile along the road. He stopped and looked down along the north side of the deep ravine. He had traveled this road a dozen times during the hours he had spent looking for Sally, but had seen no evidence of the cow. He got out of the pickup and walked along the grassy edge, shining his flashlight down among the brush. He heard a long, ragged lowing sound and quickly scrambled down the ravine. Sally was on her side, almost hidden back among the trees. He could see one small leg protruding from her body.

Chapter
Two

Detective Harry McDermott pulled his Ford Crown Victoria onto Broadway and headed for the downtown area. Maybe word on the street would give him a starting place. Right now he was up to his ass in speculation, and with at least three young ladies still missing, he was feeling the weight of the investigation. The investigation that was the largest single investigation in K.C. history. The investigation that he, personally, had been heading up for eighteen long months. To make it worse, instead of sitting back and crowing at the arrest of Randal Clark two weeks ago, Harry was squirming like a dog with an itch it couldn't quite pinpoint to scratch. Some little bug was just biting away at him, making him nervous as hell.

He turned to his partner in the seat beside him. "Damn it, Jim, what's the matter with Clark? He acts like he plans on being released any minute. Our guys found enough shit in his apartment to hang him ten times over, yet he just looks at us calmly, like he hasn't a care in the world. I can't figure him. I just simply can't figure him!"

Jim Stahl shrugged his shoulders indifferently. "Harry, you gotta quit taking everything so personal. I'm telling you, you won't make it if you don't quit that shit."

"Yeah, yeah," Harry answered. "How many months now until retirement, Jim? You planning on coasting out, or what? Am I supposed to cover my own damn backside if we run into trouble?'' Harry turned and grinned at the sixty-three-year-old man sitting beside him. His hair, what he had left of it, was gray, and his face was lined deeply from countless nights of lost sleep during his forty-three years of police work. Not for a minute did Harry think his partner wouldn't be there when the chips were down. Jim Stahl would go at his job full force right up to his last hour of duty. He was just that kind of man.

''I'm sure as hell not planning on getting myself shot up, if that's what you mean.'' He glanced down at the date on his watch. ''Not with two months, four days to go. And I'll be damned if I'll lose sleep over three girls who are probably scattered all the hell over Johnson County!''

''Right.'' Harry nodded. ''And last night when I talked to Ruth, she must have been dreaming when she said you were in at the kitchen table working with a Magic Marker and a K.C. map trying to see if there was any pattern to where Clark dumped the bodies, hoping to figure out where the last three girls are.''

''Huh!'' Jim grumbled. ''You'd think after being married to a cop for over forty years, Ruth would have learned to keep her mouth shut!''

''Well, you old fart! No one but a bloody saint would have put up with your sorry ass for that long!''

Jim had the grace to look sheepishly at his partner of sixteen years. ''Can't argue there. I know how luck—'' Jim swung his head sharply to the right. ''There, Harry! There's Willie now.'' He sat up straight and pointed to a thin, dark man leaning against a street lamp.

Harry hit the siren. ''I'll get the cherry top,'' he said to Jim. ''Make us more official.'' He quickly reached out the car window and attached the flashing signal light to the roof of the car.

Willie Rodriguez started to run, his stiff leg swinging out awkwardly in the attempt.

Jim jumped from the still-moving car and yelled after him. ''Hold it, Willie, or I'll shoot.''

Harry swerved the car into the curb, exiting the vehicle

just as Willie came walking back, arms high in the air and speaking rapidly. "Don't shoot! Don't shoot, man!"

"You know the routine," Jim said. "On the hood!" He grabbed Willie by the shirt and pushed.

Willie quickly placed his hands on the hood of the police car and spread his legs. "Shit, guys. You don't have to make it look *that* damn real, do you?"

"Didn't want to blow your cover, Willie me boy!" Jim smiled wryly at the skinny Mexican. "What have you got for us?"

Willie stole a quick look around. "You wanted something on Randal Clark? The one they call the Kansas City Butcher?"

"Yes," Harry answered impatiently. "What do you have?"

Willie sniffed, running a bony finger back and forth under his nose.

"Word on the street is he ain't the one."

"Ah, shit!" Harry had to control himself not to yell. Willie was one of their best informants. He had really counted on a solid lead when Chief Caswell had told him Willie had called and wanted to see Jim about Clark. "What are you talking about? We have him nailed every way but Sunday. His apartment even had body parts in it!"

"I don't know, man. I'm only tellin' you what I hear. They say some guy stayed at Clark's pad once in a while. They say maybe *he* done it."

"*They*, who are *they*?" Jim barked. "Just who is feeding you this line of horseshit, Willie?"

Willie shrugged, knowing Jim didn't mean anything by his remark, and knowing the detective trusted him completely. "Everyone, man. Hit a few of the other boys. They'll tell you the same, Jim, I swear. And another thing, this guy, he ain't got no prints." Willie held up his fingers. "Burned off, so they say. Smooth as a baby's bottom!"

Chapter
Three

Suzanne walked over and sat beside Jessie on the cluttered couch. "We need to talk."

It was a statement, not a question, so Jessie popped the last of the bologna sandwich into her mouth, took a long draw on the can of Diet Coke her hostess had provided, and looked expectantly at Suzanne. Her father had phoned less than an hour ago, grudgingly giving his approval to her staying with Suzanne for a few days. The two newborn calves were doing fine, thanks to Jake's arriving when he did, and even Sally had pulled through the ordeal. The miracle of it had not been lost on Jake. When he talked to Jessie, she had heard the hope in his voice when he gave his permission for her to stay. "All right, baby. I suppose if there is a chance that lady can find Amy, we have to take it. But you be careful, you hear me?"

Once the decision to stay had been made, there seemed to develop a certain reserve between the woman and the girl. Suzanne had tried to figure out a hot meal she could actually prepare for Jessie, but had to admit defeat. When Jessie emerged from the shower, Suzanne had thrust the sandwich at her, apologetically. Now they sat on the couch, an awkward silence between them.

Suzanne reached over and took Jessie's hands in her own. "I promised your father I would take good care of you, and that includes your mental health. You have got to understand that this might not turn out the way you want it to. Even *if* we find Amy, the odds that we'll find her alive aren't good.''

''The odds weren't good that I would make it all the way from Pueblo to Kansas City and find a lady I had only read about in a book, who had no address or telephone number listed. But here I am sitting on her couch! And I don't believe in preparing for the worst. If that's what you expect, that's probably what you'll get. Me, I always expect the best. Haven't you ever heard about the power of positive thinking?''

Suzanne snorted loudly. ''Jessie, my girl, I am about the most negative person on this planet. We might just as well clear that up right now. I don't have much faith in anything anymore, including myself. If you want a Pollyanna, you came to the wrong place.''

Jessie brushed long strands of damp, frizzled red hair from her face and grinned at Suzanne. ''That's okay. I'm enough of a Pollyanna for the both of us. And who knows, maybe some of it will rub off on you. Now, how are we going to get you into the jail to see Randal Clark?''

''Jessie, I can't possibly do that. Do you want to take a chance on Clark going free because I interfered?''

''Well, no, but—''

''No buts! It's out of the question. Understand?''

Jessie jumped to her feet, swinging her arms up in a dramatic gesture. ''Aren't you even going to *listen* to me? I'm not stupid, you know! All the way here, I worked on a plan. I knew you couldn't just go in there and see him, because of what happened with Underwood. But . . .'' Jessie stopped, then finished in a rush. ''What if you dressed up like a nun and went to see him?''

''What?'' The words exploded out of Suzanne's mouth. ''Are you nuts?''

''Now wait a minute,'' Jessie said reasonably. ''Don't get excited. Let's think about this. When the police called Mom and Dad they said Clark's apartment had several rosaries and statues of saints in it. They were checking to see if Amy was Catholic, to see if they could get any kind of a pattern established with the women he has killed, but as near as I can tell, they drew a blank and that means *Clark* must be the one who is Catholic and since *you* lived in a convent for a while when you were young, I figured you should be able to pull this off.'' Jessie took a deep breath. ''Well, what do you say?''

Suzanne arched her eyebrows. ''What do I say? I say it is a little hard to follow your conversation. Have you ever heard of a run-on sentence?''

''Is that anything like running off at the mouth?'' Jessie asked, an impish grin playing across her face.

Suzanne nodded. ''Exactly!''

''Okay, then.'' Jessie's face lost the grin and turned serious. ''This is the way it is. Amy is alive. I've lived with this psychic stuff enough to know I can't be mistaken about that.''

''How do you see it?'' Suzanne asked quietly. ''Death, I mean. Is it horrible for you?''

Jessie gazed down at her hands, remembering the visions she had of her aunt Vera's death. For hours she had watched as the mental picture of her favorite aunt got darker and darker. She was somewhere in the Bahamas, scuba diving with a group of school teachers on vacation. Amy had tried to reach her by phone—to warn her—but had been unsuccessful. She had confided in her mother then, and told her of her concerns. Her mother had nodded, accepting what this youngest daughter of hers was saying without question, then contacted the tour group and left word for Vera to call as soon as she returned to her motel. Unfortunately, perhaps inevitably, Vera never came back to the motel. A sunken ship they had been exploring, after years of stability, had suddenly shifted, pinning Vera and another teacher under the hull. Both women, novices at scuba diving, had panicked, not giving the instructor time to get to them.

''You don't have to talk about it,'' Suzanne said. ''I know how rough it can get. Believe me, I know.''

''No. It's okay. It's sort of neat to have someone to talk

to—someone who really understands what I'm saying. I tell Nicole, she's my best friend, just about everything, because sometimes I think I'll just bust if I can't talk about it, but I know she doesn't really believe me always. I told her about Aunt Vera, though, and she was really spooked when she found out about the accident.''

''What happened?''

''It was the first time anyone close to me had died,'' Jessie said quietly. ''Even my grandparents are alive. So at first I wasn't certain what I was seeing. But the vision was similar to what I had seen when different animals of mine on the farm had died. First I sort of *see* them in my mind, then the image begins to get darker and darker. Momma and I tried to reach Aunt Vera in the Bahamas, but we were too late. She died in a scuba diving accident.''

''I'm sorry. You know it wasn't your fault, don't you? That's the hardest lesson a psychic has to learn.''

Jessie nodded with an assurance that belied her young years. ''That's what Momma said. She said it over and over until I believed her.''

''I think your mother sounds pretty special.''

''She is. I don't really know if she believes in all this psychic stuff, but she knows I can do some pretty weird things, so she tries to keep my head on straight through it all. We had a Border collie named Jo-Jo who got run over, and I knew something was wrong and went to find him. Momma loved that dog almost as much as she did Amy and me. When I said something had happened to Jo-Jo, Momma just went to the phone and called the vet. I sort of guessed she must have believed in me, to call the vet before I even went looking for him.''

''Get down, Zero! Get down! Bad doggie! You're going to ruin my new dress!'' Suzanne heard the child's words. Her words. Then her father screaming at her. *''You've killed him, you little devil! You sent him into the road didn't you? Just because he jumped on your dress!''* She could still see her father coming toward her, fury on his face. She had tried to run, but he grabbed her and tore at

the pretty new yellow dress her mother had sewn for her.

"You think this dress is so God-damned special? Well, how do you like this?" And he had ripped it from her body, tearing it into a dozen pieces.

The next day her mother had left to go visit her sister Alma, and it was the last time Suzanne had seen her.

She had begged her mother not to go. She knew something awful was going to happen. When Roy came to her with news of the horrible car accident, she hadn't even been surprised.

"Miss Richards? Are you all right?"

Suzanne shook her head, trying to erase old memories. "Yes, I'm sorry, Jessie. Once in a while when you speak of events that have taken place in your life, it reminds me of my own childhood." She rubbed her hands across her face as though just waking up from a bad dream. "So what happened to Jo-Jo? Did he survive?"

"Oh, sure. He still goes out to bring in the cows every evening. Out of habit, mostly. Momma says to let him keep doing it, even if he is so old now that he can barely make it. She says if we took his job away, he'd probably just curl up and die."

Like me, Suzanne thought. *I'm twenty-seven years old, and feel like I just want to curl up and die. The only thing I ever did that was worthwhile was taken from me.*

Four hours later, Suzanne lay in bed listening to Jessie's even breathing coming from the couch. She kept her eyes closed tightly, but sleep wouldn't come. She couldn't even relax. Seeing Jessie, talking to her, had given rise to a host of memories which were flooding through her mind.

She could still remember as though it were yesterday the first time she found a missing child. A dead missing child. Her best friend's little sister.

When Jennifer had called and told her Peggy Ann had disappeared and the police were looking for her, Suzanne had rushed immediately to her friend's house. Peggy Ann had been like a little sister to her, also—always tagging along and making a nuisance of herself as only an eight-year-old can do.

There had been four of them hanging out together that summer. Lewis Martin, Jennifer's cousin, whom Suzanne had an enormous crush on; Bobby Steeples, who lived next door to Jennifer, and the two of them. It had been the best summer of Suzanne's life. They had biked, and swum, gone to all the new movies, and laughed the summer away, as only eighteen-year-olds just starting to find their way in life can do.

Bobby had just arrived with a group of searchers when Suzanne came running up the walk to Jennifer's home. "Have they found her?" she shouted to Bobby. He shook his head, weary from the long hours he had spent tramping the fields. Suzanne went up and put her arms around her friend. "What can I do to help?"

"Just go be with Jenny and her family. They are going nuts. Peggy Ann's been gone for over nine hours now. We have looked everywhere we can think to look." Then, knowing she would want to know, knowing how she felt about Lewis, he had added, "Lewis is in the house, I think. The group he was with was just ahead of us. We all came back to get something to eat. I'm sure he will be glad to see you."

Suzanne entered the home that had become almost like her own over the last months. Ten or fifteen people stood around in the living room, trying to console one another and offer support to Jennifer's family. Jennifer saw her and rushed over, dissolving in tears. Suzanne wrapped long arms around her friend and held her tight. Out of the corner of her eye, she saw Lewis coming toward them. She held out an arm so that he could join in the hug.

The moment Suzanne touched Lewis, cold shivers of fear washed over her. She suddenly knew what had happened to Peggy Ann. Slowly she dropped her arm and began backing away from her friend.

"You killed her! My God, Lewis, you killed her!"

"Are you crazy?" he yelled at her. "I've been out looking for her all day. Just ask anyone."

Suzanne slowly shook her head, then she turned to Jennifer's father. "Peggy Ann's in the trunk of his car! She's been there all along. He raped and choked her. Oh, God! I'm sorry. I'm so sorry!"

Lewis had tried to run at that point, but many hands grabbed onto him, holding him down as they searched his pocket for car keys.

Afterward, the police had questioned her for hours on end, not believing she hadn't known about Peggy all along. Even when Jennifer assured them she, herself, knew about Suzanne's psychic powers, they still hesitated to believe her story.

Finally, a detective had entered and handed her a can of pop. As she took it from him, her hand brushed against his. Instantly, she grabbed hold of his hand, holding it tight. She looked up at him, speaking softly. "You are worried about your son, aren't you?" Without giving the officer time to answer, she went on. "You had a fight with him earlier this evening. He's been getting in a lot of trouble lately, and you suspect he's taking drugs. You hit him, sir. Then he ran out of the house. David. His name is David, and you are afraid you were too rough on him. You came in to ask if it would be all right if you left early to try and find him."

Detective Sands pulled his hand from Suzanne's grasp and sank down in a chair. He looked at the other three officers in the room. "She's right. She's absolutely right. And even my wife doesn't know about that fight. I've never hit David before, not even when he was little. But I lost it today. I just lost it."

"Oh, Christ, Sands," Detective Charles Botello said. "She's the same age as your boy. She probably knows him or heard about your fight from a mutual friend. You surely aren't going to buy into this crap, are you?"

Suzanne pushed away from the table and stood up. She moved across the room and placed her hand on the officer's arm. "Really, sir, you had better quit fooling around with . . . Millie, isn't it? Your wife, Barbara, is a very nice person, but she is going to kill you if she finds out." She moved to another detective. "And you, Mr. James. Your wife is about to give birth to your first child. Oh, and I see you already know it's going to be a boy. You've even decided on a name. Winston, isn't it? After your grandfather?"

"Suzanne," Detective Botello spoke, promising himself to break off his affair with a waitress named Millie just as fast as he could get to a phone. "I want to apologize for putting you through the last several hours. As far as I'm concerned, you're free to go home now." He raised his eyebrows at the other officers in the room. "I assume that's all right with everyone? Or do we want to wait until she blurts out all our histories?"

Detective Sands stood and offered his hand to Suzanne. "Well, I don't know about these other gentlemen, but I want to thank you for your help. And please understand why we hesitated to believe your story. As police officers, we are bombarded daily with nuts claiming to have knowledge about a crime due to some dream or vision they had, and we are forced to follow up on what they tell us. We just get so sick and tired of wasting man-hours on this kind of—as Charlie said—*crap*, that we aren't open to the *real* thing when it comes along. I for one am stunned at your ability. I've never seen anything like it. Would you perhaps be willing to help us out on occasion?"

Suzanne nodded her head, not knowing at the time that Sands's innocent question would embark her on a journey through some of the most incredible moments of her life, then plunge her deep into hell.

Chapter
Four

What had started out as a reasonably pleasant May day, was rapidly turning into a scorcher. The hot sun beat down mercilessly on Suzanne's old gray Cutlass. Even with both windows open, the heat was stupefying.

"I'm sorry, Jessie, I've been meaning to get that air conditioner fixed. I guess I just forgot how Kansas City temperatures can change fifty degrees in the matter of a few days, and sometimes a few hours! It seems like only last week I was still wearing sweaters."

Jessie hung her head out the window of the car. Her long, red hair billowed in the wind, then snapped back, stinging her face. "You know what I think?" she said. "I think you need to get organized!"

Suzanne grinned. "No kidding."

"No kidding," Jessie parroted. "All you could find for breakfast was some crummy stale crackers, you didn't have anything clean to wear, your apartment is—well— let's just say, bulldozer material, your air conditioner's broken, and there's about an inch of crud on your car. You need to get a plan. You seriously need to get a plan!"

With one hand Suzanne shook out the last cigarette from a crumpled package of Winstons. "Hey, kiddo, I'm the one helping *you* out, remember? I would have been perfectly content to get up this morning, drink black coffee, put on my sweats and loll around the house. I didn't know I was going to be entertaining Martha Stewart!"

Jessie pulled her head back inside the stuffy car. "Now, that's not what I mean at all, and you know it. It's just that it seems to me you're sort of, I don't know, *hiding out* from the world, or something. How long have you been ordering in fast food? And I bet you haven't been to the grocery store in a month."

Suzanne kept her eyes on the road as she fished through her bag for a lighter, found one, then lit the slightly bent cigarette dangling from her mouth. "Guess I'll have to go now," she muttered. "That's my last cigarette."

"Come on, come on," Jessie persisted. "How long has it been since you went to the grocery store? Or better yet, how long has it been since you were even out of your apartment?"

"Okay, okay! I haven't been to the store in over a month, and I haven't been out of my apartment since about a week ago when I ran down to the Stop and Plop for cigarettes and lunchmeat." She turned to Jessie. "Are you satisfied?"

Jessie nodded, deciding to drop the subject. "Is there really a place called the Stop and Plop?"

Suzanne's laughter filled the car. "No, no. That's only my little pet name for convenience stores—*all* of them."

Jessie's reaction was one of surprise. "Do you know that's the first time I've heard you laugh? You should try it more often!"

"And you, my young friend, should try minding your own business a little more often!" The smile on Suzanne's face told Jessie her words weren't meant to be harsh. "And instead of sitting there giving me all this grief, why aren't you planning out what I'm going to say to get in to see Clark? After all, this is *your* idiotic scheme. I can't believe I let you talk me into this. If I get thrown in jail, have you figured out what *you* are going to do?"

"Oh, they won't throw a *nun* in jail. Besides, no one will pay any attention at all to you, I'll bet. Who would think to check up on a nun?"

"You'll forgive me if I don't hold with your strong

sense of optimism. The way things have gone for me lately, they'll not only put me in jail, but they'll move me in as Clark's cellmate!''

Jessie couldn't help grinning. "Well, isn't that just what we want?"

Suzanne threw the cigarette butt out of the car window. "Easy for you to say, kid. Easy for you to say."

"That's it, guys." Sidney Hollings flung one arm up in the air, his thumb pointing skyward. "We're all set." He looked at his watch. "Take the floors assigned to you and give them a final check. I want everyone back here in fifteen minutes. We need to blow before the winds get any stronger."

Eight men in hard hats began walking back toward the old eight-floor office building. They had checked it as they finished setting the charges, but each man knew how easy it was for a homeless person to sneak in when they weren't looking, or a child to wander in looking for a place to play.

Michael Thatcher was new on the job. In the three months he had been working for Hollings, the man had yet to trust him to sweep a room. He had watched as the other men painstakingly opened every closet, checked under debris, and did everything they could to ensure no one was trapped when the building imploded, but as yet, he had not been trusted with an unsupervised sweep.

He stood waiting for Hollings to join him and was surprised when the man nodded toward the building. "Go on, Thatcher. This is your baby. First floor."

Michael unhooked the flashlight from his belt. "Yes, sir!" He trotted toward the building.

He could hear the other men as they called out warnings on the floors above him. He opened the first office door and walked in. It was a small alcove, only one small rest room to check. His voice bounced back at him as he called out, "Anyone in here? The building is coming down, you must exit the premises before she blows."

He worked his way slowly down the offices on the west side, then crossed over to begin the larger rooms on the east. Michael's flashlight picked up splashes of red stain on the old hardwood floor, and he could feel the hairs on the back of his neck stand up. "What the devil—" The severed hand was placed between the door and the door jamb, and at first Michael thought the other men were setting him up—trying to give the new kid on the block a little scare. He pushed the door open with his foot. He could see body parts scattered over the room. He let out a loud scream as he backed slowly out of the room, then turned and puked all over the hallway.

The McFadden Costume Shop was located on the lower three floors of an old brick building which used to house the largest magic show inventory in three states. As the great magic show era waned, the owner had begun renting out floors to other businesses. Now it housed the only two that had survived—the McFadden Costume Shop and Merlin's Magical Kingdom.

Suzanne and Jessie walked up to the old man behind the counter just inside the main door. "Excuse me, sir. My name is Suzanne Richards and I called this morning about renting a nun's habit. Did you find one?"

"Yah, yah, I set it back for you," the old man said in a soft Irish brogue as he eyed Suzanne carefully. "I'm wondering, though, if you won't be a wee bit tall for it? We may have to let the hem down some. How tall are you now?"

"About five foot eight in my bare feet," Suzanne answered. "And we really don't have time to wait for alterations. Don't you have any longer habits?"

The old man shook his head. "No, not in the order you want." He smiled warmly at Suzanne. "You see, lassie, there is a play going on at the New Theatre Restaurant about nuns. They've near wiped me out! I just have the one, but it will only take my wife five minutes to let the hem down. Now wouldn't you be having that much time?

And besides,'' he said with a wink, ''it will give me just a wee bit longer to gaze at two lovely young lassies, now, won't it?''

''Well, you old charmer!'' Suzanne laughed. ''How could we possibly say no to you after that wee bit of blarney?''

The old man made an elaborate bow then extended his hand. ''The name's McFadden. Patrick Irl McFadden. And I have been accused, on occasion, of kissing the Blarney Stone. However, now, 'tis no blarney that I have before me two fine looking colleens. And *you*, lassie''—he reached across the counter and gestured toward Jessie's red hair—''you look like you could have stepped right out from County Cork! That's a grand head of hair you have there, now!''

Jessie could feel her face getting warm as she mumbled a thank you and thought to herself that she could hardly wait to tell Nicole about her ''grand head of hair.''

Mr. McFadden gathered up the costume. ''Nellie will have this for you in no time. She's a whiz, she is, and a darlin' woman to boot.'' He disappeared into a back room.

''Well!'' Suzanne pointed to the large sign hanging prominently on the west wall which said, In Business Since 1945. ''I guess we know how Mr. Patrick Irl Mc-Fadden has managed to stay in business for over fifty years, don't we?''

Jessie grinned and nodded. ''I know *I* sure wouldn't go anywhere else to get costumes. After all, no one else has ever told me, 'That's a grand head of hair you have there, now.' About all *I* ever hear it called is a *wild mane!*''

Suzanne went over and fingered Jessie's hair. ''Your hair is beautiful, Jessie. There are women who would kill for all those natural curls, and did you know that only about five percent of women have red hair—*real* red hair, that is?'' As she said the words an image of another woman flitted across her memory. Another woman with red hair. Who? Her mother? She couldn't remember.

Mr. McFadden opened the back door and motioned for

Suzanne. "Would you like to try it on now, lassie? Do you be knowin' how it all goes together, or do you want my Nellie to help you now?"

Suzanne turned to Jessie questioningly. "I guess I could just as well get dressed here, don't you think? It would save us going back to the apartment." She went into the back room and met Nellie—a fine-boned, white-haired, wisp of a woman whose beauty had only slightly faded over the years.

Nellie extended a frail looking hand when Patrick introduced the two women, but then surprised Suzanne by grasping her hand firmly and shaking it. Her years of seamstress work had toughened the muscles in her arms and hands. Any frailness about Nellie McFadden was only in the eyes of the beholder.

"Are you going to be in a play, dear?" Nellie asked.

"No, no. I'm just, well, yes, I am." Suzanne stumbled over her words, forgetting the carefully crafted lie she and Jessie had devised—something about a costume party.

"And what play would that be now?" asked Nellie. *"Nunsense?"*

"Yes . . . yes, that's it," Suzanne answered.

Nellie put down the black habit and looked squarely at Suzanne. "Now, child, Patrick and I have done all of the costumes for that show. We know every actress and every understudy. What is it you really need with a nun's habit? You aren't going to be up to any mischief with it now, are you?"

Suzanne dropped her eyes. "No. No, of course not." For some strange reason she couldn't seem to lie to the old woman. "I need some information from a man in jail. We, Jessie and I, we think he knows where Jessie's sister is. But you mustn't tell anyone. Please! If anyone knew we were going to see him, it could result in the charges against him being dropped. Don't ask me how I know this. Just trust me that I know."

"All right." Nellie nodded her white head, making her

mind up quickly. "I'll keep your secret, dear. 'Tis a fine honest face you have."

Suzanne stepped into the long black habit, then attached the collar. "This is how it goes, doesn't it?" she asked.

Nellie smiled. "Yes, dear. And do you know what order to say you're from if you are asked?"

Suzanne thought of the convent where she had stayed for awhile when she was young. "How about the Doors of the Blessed Sacrament? Do they still wear the traditional habit, or have they gone modern, too?"

"That will work, I think. But if you run into a priest, you had better duck into the nearest bathroom. I'm afraid you couldn't fool one for very long." She stuffed Suzanne's hair up under a white cap. "This is called the coif. It's always worn under the veil. It's tight, I know, but you need it." She finished dressing Suzanne's head, then turned her toward a large standing mirror.

"Oh, my! I *do* look like a nun, don't I?"

"Wasn't that the point?" Nellie asked, smiling. "Now, where's your rosary? I'll attach it to the belt."

Suzanne thought of the small jewelry box full of rosaries which had belonged to Miss Emily. It had been months since she had even had them out. "I didn't bring one with me," she answered. "Do I really need it?"

Nellie smiled. "Yes, dear, you really need it. Just a moment" She crossed the room and retrieved her purse from a cupboard. She pulled out a small, beaded bag from which she took a beautiful jeweled rosary.

"Oh, no," Suzanne said. "I couldn't possibly!"

Nellie nodded emphatically. "Yes, you can. There has to be a rosary hanging from the belt. Sure and if the duty officer is Catholic he'll know you aren't a real nun, and that's for certain, dear." She fastened the rosary to the belt. "There! Now you look a proper nun!"

Chapter
Five

Amy awoke with a start and checked her watch. Ten o'clock. How long had she slept? Was it ten in the morning, or had an entire day slipped by her?

There was only one way to tell, and even though she knew she should be used to it by now, she still had to steel herself to turn off the light. The horror of what it would be like if the lamp failed to turn back on, was always lurking in her mind.

Still, she needed to know. She had to know. It was her only link to the world. Her only hold on sanity.

She pushed against the rough cement floor to come to a sitting position. A wave of dizziness hit her and she steadied herself by reaching out to the wall. How many days had it been since she had eaten? Why hadn't she saved a few of the granola bars? Why hadn't she rationed them out?

She remembered her cotton undershirt and grabbed for it, stuffing a small section into her mouth and sucking. Good. There was still some dampness left in it.

Even though the cement was rough against her knees, she crawled over to the small lamp and spoke aloud. "Please, God! Let the light come back on. Just please let the light come back on." Her hand shook as she turned the small switch which plunged her prison into blackness.

A few feet away from her, Amy could see the small shaft of light coming from the pipe inserted in the ceiling.

Daylight! Quickly, she turned the switch to the lamp, and the room sprang back to life. She reached up to the poster with the pictures of monkeys on it and, using her fingernail, scraped another long line. Twelve days! My God, she had been in this hole for twelve days!

The man had left her six granola bars, a jug of water, and a Folgers coffee can with a roll of toilet paper inside. She had eaten the last of the bars four days ago, and since then had been tempted to finish off the wrappings.

Her water had run out as well, but luckily the previous evening she had seen a small puddle of water forming on the floor under the pipe, and realized it must be raining. She had thrown herself flat on the floor and sucked up the water, then held her undershirt under the pipe, trying to dampen her shirt so she could wash off her face and body.

Amy looked around the small, cramped room. "The water jug! You dummy! Put the water jug under the pipe!" She stood and walked on unsteady legs over to the plastic water bottle. The opening was small, but maybe if she positioned it just right, it would catch the drips. "If it ever rains again! If I don't die first!"

She had been talking to herself since the third day of her confinement. Some of the time she talked to God, some of the time to her parents or Jessie, but mostly, she just chatted to herself, trying to keep a hold on her sanity.

For the first several days, she was more frightened of the man and the things he said he was going to do to her when he returned. She had cried, losing precious moisture from her body. She was sorry now that she had wasted tears on him.

Her greatest fear was the light failing. She could even face death now, if only she could do it with the light on. What was the life expectancy of a light bulb? Should she be trying to conserve by turning the light off for periods of time? No. Amy knew she couldn't do it. To be buried in this room was bad enough. She would go completely crazy without the light.

Her other fear was that the pipe would become blocked

and she would slowly suffocate in her prison. Sometimes she stood on her tiptoes and placed her mouth over the pipe opening in order to get a really good breath of air. Or maybe that was only her imagination. It was hard to tell anymore what was real and what was not.

"Jessie! Why haven't you found me?" She yelled the words. "I know you can do it, Jessie! Please. Please come for me." Even as she spoke the words, she knew it was hopeless. Jessie was hundreds of miles away in Colorado. And even if Jessie realized she was in trouble, she wouldn't have any idea where to look for her. The man had drugged her, so even if Jessie could pick up on her thoughts, Amy couldn't direct her. She had awakened in this hole, located God knows where, and the only sound she had heard for twelve days was her own voice getting more and more desperate, more and more weak. For the first few days of her imprisonment, she had screamed until her throat was raw and bloody, hoping someone would hear her. Finally, she had quit screaming.

Suzanne and Jessie pulled into the parking lot of the police station at 1125 Locust.

"I need a cigarette," Suzanne said. "We should have stopped before going for this costume."

"Oh, sure! And why don't we get you a can of beer to hold in your other hand?" Jessie answered. "I'm sure no one would suspect a thing, right?"

"Oh, come on. Give me a little credit. I'm just grousing. I wouldn't really smoke a cigarette while wearing this habit. Sister Mary Elizabeth would skin me alive, and somehow I just know she would find out!"

"Who is Sister Mary Elizabeth?"

"That book you read mentioned I had spent some time at a convent, right?"

"Right. When you were little."

"Not too little, I was eight years old when I first went there. It was really an orphanage run by a group of nuns. I lived there for almost two years, but during those two years, I was often in the company of Miss Emily, a spinster lady who was the sister of the nun who was in charge of the orphanage, Sister Mary Elizabeth. Miss Emily wanted to adopt me, but back in those days single women were not allowed to adopt. And anyway, Miss Emily was in her fifties, which would rule her out altogether.''

''So what happened?''

''I'm not certain. No one adopted me for two years. I was tall for my age, gangly and clumsy. Not too many people want a kid that's already half-grown. Then one day Miss Emily came to pick me up and she said I was going home with her. For good. She said Sister Mary Elizabeth spoke with the bishop and special permission was granted. All I cared about was that I was going to live with Miss Emily. I loved her, and there wasn't a doubt in my mind that she loved me. We were happy together until her death four years ago.'' Suzanne didn't mention the horrible nightmares where she awoke screaming and Miss Emily would hold her, rocking back and forth, crooning comforting words, trying to help her forget whatever demons had been unleashed in her early childhood. She was in high school before the nightmares finally went away.

''What about Mary Elizabeth? Is she still alive?''

''Yes. She retired a few years ago and lives in a retirement home in Michigan. I go see her whenever I can. She's almost ninety now, and getting frail.'' Suzanne used the sleeve of the habit to wipe perspiration from her face.

''I'd better get going. I'm going to be soaking wet before long.''

In front of the station there was a statue of a police officer holding a baby. Suzanne looked up and gave a small salute. ''Wish me luck.''

Almost the minute the car was empty, Jessie's head snapped back and her hands began trembling. She grabbed hold of the car seat to steady herself, then squeezed her eyes shut tight. ''Amy! Amy, is it you?'' she whispered the words.

The scene began unfolding in front of her. She could see animals prancing around. Monkeys. And a man with a beard. But the images were spinning. Going too fast for her to see them plainly. A seat. She could see people in some kind of seat, with their arms in the air as though someone were holding a gun on them. Then she heard Amy's voice, as clear as if she had been speaking to her from the backseat. "Jessie! Come for me! Please!" Then the images began to fade, as they spun faster and faster.

"No!" Jessie screamed. "It isn't enough!" She put her hands to her forehead in concentration, but it was gone. "No!" She doubled up her fists, smashing them into the car seat. "Amy! I need more! Please, Amy! Stay with me!"

Thirty miles away, dizziness finally overcame the girl in the cement box, and she sank to the floor, unconscious.

Chapter
Six

Chief of Detectives Edward K. Caswell had two habits which drove his men crazy. He constantly cracked his knuckles, and he made little sucking noises with his mouth, as if he were trying to dislodge a stuck piece of food from between his teeth. Sometimes, between the sucking and the cracking, it was hard to concentrate on the man's words.

Harry McDermott was doing his best to follow along. Chief Caswell had listened stone-faced to Harry's report of what he'd heard from Willie, then uttered one word. Sonofabitch. When Caswell said it, it came out as one word and it could mean anything from "congratulations" to "get the hell out of my face." Harry gathered that this time it meant merely, "Sonofabitch!"

"And on top of everything else the families of the three missing girls are coming down on us hard. I just found out two of the mothers are going on *Noontime with Nora* to-morrow."

"What will that hurt, Chief? We need to get the public involved. God knows where he left those bodies. Everyone in K.C. needs to be on the alert."

"Right!" Caswell raised his hand to quiet him. "Don't say it. It's the public's right to know, right? Sonofabitch, but I get tired of the public's right to know. Do you have any idea how many leads will come through this office once those ladies hit that talk show? About five hundred in the first hour alone!'' Caswell ran long fingers over his closely cropped gray hair. ''And city hall thinks we need to cut back on manpower. Sonofabitch!''

''How should we handle Willie's little bombshell? Do you think there's any chance Clark's attorney started the rumor about us having the wrong man? Nordyke is just about that much of an asshole.''

''No. Christ, no! Andrew Nordyke doesn't want Clark back on the street any more than *we* do. He's just making the usual rumblings, but hell—he has three daughters all in about the same age group as the ones Clark's been killing. I can't imagine him wanting Clark set free, and I sure as hell don't think he would phony-up evidence to see that happen.''

''Well, I've certainly seen him do some fancy legal footwork to keep his clients from doing any time in jail. Wouldn't it be a feather in his cap if he could free Clark, the worst serial killer Kansas City has ever seen?''

Caswell shook his head. ''That's just it. You don't want to be the one responsible for setting a cold-blooded killer like that free. It would ruin Nordyke, especially if Clark was released and killed again. No. As long as Nordyke is convinced of Clark's guilt, it wouldn't be in his best interests to see him get off. Which doesn't mean, of course, that he wouldn't do his best to defend him.''

''Well, then what? You were in Clark's apartment. Did you see any sign of a roommate? I know I sure as hell didn't. But yet Rodriguez seemed mighty sure of his facts.''

From the back of the room Jim Stahl spoke for the first time. ''I've got to tell you, Chief, Willie Rodriguez is my best informant. We go back a long ways—a hell of a long ways. He might try to jive one of the other boys, but he wouldn't me.''

Chief Caswell nodded. ''I know, Jim. If Willie told you it's the word on the street, then by God, it's the word on the street.''

* * *

The year was 1973 when Jim Stahl, along with his wife, Ruth, and their two teenage sons, moved to the Kansas City area from Chicago. He had only been on the force a few days, and even though he had entered the K.C. precinct with nearly twenty years' experience in police work, he was being tested by the local boys to see if he measured up.

The call had come through about midnight. A worker at the Kansas City stockyards was unloading cattle when he heard faint yelling from one of the cars. He didn't know what to do. The train had come from New Mexico, and if it was carrying illegal aliens, most of them were surely dead by now. On top of that, the latch to the boxcar had been welded shut and he would need help getting into the car.

Jim's car was the second on the scene. By the time he got there, two officers were helping young Mexican men out of the boxcar. A third officer was chasing after a slightly older man. As Jim watched, the officer easily overtook the man, then swung his baton at the man's legs. Jim could hear the crack as the Mexican's thin leg broke.

"Hey!" Jim yelled as he ran up. "What the fuck do you think you're doing?"

"This isn't any of your business," the officer snapped. "Get back there and help unload the rest of those damn wetbacks." His baton again cracked down on the Mexican.

"The hell I will!" Jim yelled as he threw a punch which connected solidly with the officer's chin. With one hand he grabbed the officer's baton and hurled it back toward the police car. With the other hand he gathered the top of the officer's shirt into a wad, then lifted him into the air, tossing him away. "Get the fuck out of here!" Jim screamed. "And call an ambulance, or I'll have your badge, asshole."

Jim dropped to one knee and spoke softly to the man. "Do you speak English, señor?"

"Sí, sí." The man nodded. "I speak very good English."

"My name is Jim Stahl. Officer Stahl. I'm so sorry for what the other officer did."

The man nodded again. "My leg, I think she is broken, señor."

"Don't worry. I'll get help for you. I'll see that you get to the hospital. What is your name?"

At first Jim thought the man wasn't going to answer, but then he said, "Willie. Willie Rodriguez. I come to this city because my father, he is dying and calling for me. I must go to him."

By the time the ambulance arrived, several more police cars had arrived on the scene. The officer who had broken Willie's leg came over to Jim and in front of a force of twenty or so of his buddies said, "You've been in town three days and you think you can *have my badge?* That asshole was an illegal running from the law. I was perfectly within my rights to stop him. You and me aren't finished, yet."

"Oh, yes, but we are," Jim had answered him coldly. "I can't abide a sniveling coward who uses his uniform to hide behind when he wants to pull a bully act. And you don't need to worry about my having your badge. Just remember if I see or hear about anything like this again, I will personally beat the living shit out of you."

The next day when Jim reported for duty, he could tell by the slaps on his back and the handshakes, that he wasn't the only officer who had been sickened by the events of the previous night.

Three days later, before his leg had properly been set, Willie Rodriguez disappeared from the hospital. Six months later Jim ran into him again, hustling anything he could on the streets, and dragging a gimp leg along.

As an officer of the law, Jim knew he should report Willie as an illegal to be deported. But by then he knew that Willie had kept seven young Mexican men alive in the hot train car by shinnying out of a tiny space in the ceiling and going for food and water whenever there was a train stop. He was the only one small enough to do it, and at any point could have abandoned them, disappearing into the countryside.

Besides, Jim figured, Willie was left with a crippled leg because one of his own kind wanted to flex his muscles. Screw it. He wouldn't give him up.

Willie was still eyeing him warily when Jim stuck out his hand. "Good to see you again, Willie. How's it going? Did you get to your dad in time?"

Relief and admiration played across Willie's features. "Sí. I was with him two weeks before he died."

And with that, a friendship had developed between the two men. Several years later, when amnesty was granted to many of the illegals, Jim had made it a point to see that Willie got his papers.

Now, Jim was sixty-three years old and Willie had passed fifty, but they still looked out for one another and both men trusted each other implicitly. That was what worried Jim. Willie kept his ears to the pavement. He could weasel in and out of places without anyone ever realizing he was there. After talking with Willie, Jim felt in his gut that the story of the Kansas City Butcher wasn't over yet.

There was a light staccato beat on the door to Caswell's office. Jena Karnitz, a first-year detective, stuck her head in. "Chief, you won't believe this, but we have a murder on Brighton Avenue. Same MO as the butcher—body parts scattered about."

"Sonofabitch!" Caswell exploded.

"And, Harry . . ." Jena's tone indicated that there was a marked difference between how she viewed the nearly sixty-year-old, graying, potbellied, married chief, and the thirty-seven-year-old, unmarried Harry, who was six foot four inches of lean muscle. "There's a nun here who wants to see Clark. Shall I let her go back?"

Harry nodded. Right now, the last thing he had time for, was Randal Clark's religious needs.

"Get the ME on the phone, Jena—Davis, if he's available, and get him over to Brighton. Jim, let's roll. This has got to be a copycat, but we won't know for sure until

Davis checks. Good thing there are a few little facts that the copycat couldn't know. Maybe that will keep Nordyke off our asses.''

Chief Caswell's office was located down a narrow hall, just slightly off the main activity room. When Harry hurried past Jena out the door, he saw the nun standing off to the side, and thought to himself that if the nuns who had drilled catechism into him in his younger days had looked anything like this one, he might have learned his lessons. She was tall, with thick eyebrows and lashes, and a complexion which was flawless, except for the film of sweat covering it. There was just something about the woman that caused Harry to slide to a stop. "You wanted to see Clark?"

Suzanne nodded, dropping her eyes demurely. "Yes, sir."

Harry glanced at Jena. "Fix her up with the phones for a few minutes, then."

"The phones?" Suzanne questioned.

"Yes," Jena said. "We have a two-way phone where you can speak to Clark through a glass window."

"Oh, but that won't do!" Suzanne protested. "I need to touch Clark." Her mind searched for a logical reason for the request. "I need to anoint him. You know, the anointing of the damned. His forehead. I'll just need to touch his forehead long enough to make the sign of the cross."

"All right," Harry said, giving in to her easily. "Jena, see that—" He turned to Suzanne. "What was your name?"

"Sister Mary Elizabeth."

"Jena, see that Sister Mary Elizabeth has a few minutes with Clark." He reached out and took Suzanne's hand in his own large one. "It was nice to meet you, Sister. Why don't you wait in Chief Caswell's office while Jena arranges things?"

Suzanne entered the office, puzzling over her handshake with the handsome detective. Why hadn't she picked up a reading from him? Rarely did she ever come in physical contact with someone without immediately knowing more about the person than she had any right to know. It had all but killed her love life. Yet she hadn't received anything from this man.

Outside in the hall, Harry motioned for Jena and Jim to follow him farther away from the closed door.

"Set up a tape recorder before you bring the two of them together. I don't know who the beauty in the black habit is, but she sure as hell isn't a nun."

"How so?" asked Jim.

"For one thing, there is a faint smell of tobacco about her, and that deep, husky voice sure sounds like a smoker to me. But for clinchers, I know for damn sure that there is no such thing as the *anointing of the damned*. She just said the first thing that popped into her head when she learned there would be a glass partition between her and Clark. So just play along and see what she wants. But keep a close eye on her and search Clark the minute she leaves. For some reason, she wants to be physically close to Clark. Find out why, then hold her here until we get back. Oh, and you'd better make sure she doesn't have any weapons on her."

Jena raised perfectly arched eyebrows at Harry. "And just how would you suggest I do that?"

"Send her through the metal detector, officer," Jim interrupted. "Just go through yourself, and she will follow. She doesn't need to know a thing."

The instant Officer Karnitz took her by the arm to guide her into the meeting with Clark, Suzanne knew she was in trouble. The young woman's thoughts were a jumble of wondering who the woman in the nun's habit really was, if someone named Harry was ever going to ask her out, and what she was going to say to the nun to keep her at the police station.

Damn, Suzanne thought wildly. *They plan on keeping me here when I finish with Clark!*

She followed the officer into a room where a man sat alone at a table, his hands and feet cuffed. Two police officers stood by each of the doors.

The first thing that struck Suzanne was how ordinary the man looked. He wasn't anyone she would have even noticed in a crowd. His features were fine, but his complexion suggested he spent a lot of time out of doors. It was ruddy, lined, and weathered. There was nothing on his face to suggest he was a killer who had slaughtered God knows how many young girls, scattering their bodies across the city. He was someone Suzanne would have stopped on the street to ask directions of, or spoken to in a grocery line.

Clark's eyes moved lazily in her direction, looking her up and down. The bright blue of his eyes startled her. Brown eyes would have fit his face better. Somehow the blueness unnerved her, making her look away.

"You may sit there across from him if you like, Sister," Officer Karnitz said. "We'll give you ten minutes, that's all."

Suzanne bowed her head slightly at the officer. "Thank you." She began walking toward Clark, trying to avoid his eyes. She pulled out a chair and sat down, then reached across the table and put her hand on his arm. "Bless you, my child."

The minute Suzanne's hand touched Clark a shock wave went through her body. Cold, hard fear clutched at her, as she felt the room spinning. Quickly she drew back her hand.

"So, Sister. What do you want with me?" Clark spoke. He laughed, a deep, throaty laugh which sent chills down Suzanne's spine. "Are you here to save my soul?"

Suzanne steeled herself and again reached across the table, placing her hand on Clark's arm. The images came rapidly, like a child in charge of the clicker at a slide presentation. Too fast to see the picture clearly. With her free hand, Suzanne grabbed the edge of her chair, squeezing hard, trying to gain control and slow the images.

Click. A young girl on the ground, Clark standing over her. *Click.* Clark brings an ax or meat cleaver down on the girl. *Click.* A close-up of the young woman's face, which seems to be covered with thick makeup. *Click.* Another girl, more heavy makeup.

Click. Suzanne saw a road—a winding, gravel road, which turned into a river of blood as she watched. The blood flowed down, covering tall brush and large sunflowers.

"Hey, what's the matter with you, Sister?" Clark's voice jolted Suzanne back to the present. "You some kind of nut or what?"

Suzanne watched as Clark unpried her fingers from his arm. "You trying to break my arm, Sister?"

Suzanne knew she had to go for broke. She stood and reached across the table, placing her thumb on Clark's forehead. "Will you receive the blessing, my son?"

Clark looked up at her, nodded and started to speak. Suzanne whispered in a rush. "Where is Amy Matthews? What have you done with her?"

An enormous black cloud descended around Suzanne. Cold icy fingers of fear jabbed at her from the darkness. *No! What is happening?* She could feel another presence. An evil entity. Besides Clark. She could feel herself trembling, gasping for air. *Let me through! I need to know!* But she couldn't penetrate the darkness.

Then all at once she was struggling. Trying to escape, trying to reach the air. She could see shovels of dirt coming down on her, choking her. Then it was Amy. The dirt was coming down on Amy, covering her. She realized her thumb was burning white-hot and she pulled it down from Clark's forehead. Immediately, the spell was broken, and she sat down heavily in the chair.

Jena Karnitz came running over. "What's the matter? What happened? Are you all right?" Her eyes took in Suzanne's white face and shaking hands. "Maybe you had better come lie down for a few minutes."

"Get her away from me!" Clark screamed. "What are you guys trying to pull on me, anyway?"

Suzanne stood, grabbing on to Jena for support. "Maybe I had better lie down for a few minutes. I do feel rather faint."

"There's a small couch in the coffee room," Jena said. "Will that be all right? Can you make it?"

"Yes. Thank you. Thank you so much. You're very kind."

Officer Karnitz guided Suzanne into the coffee room and indicated the couch. "Is there anything you need?"

"Well, yes, actually. I have some pills in my purse, but I left it in that other office where you had me wait. Would you mind getting it for me?"

"Not at all," Jena answered. "I'll be right back."

The minute the door closed, Suzanne headed for the open window she had noticed when they entered the room. She cranked it farther open, then hoisted herself up and fell not so gracefully through it to the ground outside.

She stood up and ran for the parking lot then jerked open the door to her car. "Come on, come on!" she said as the motor sputtered and refused to kick in.

"What is it? What's the matter?" Jessie yelled. "What did you find out?"

"Just a minute, Jessie. They know I'm not a nun and they are going to be after me any minute."

"You mean we're busting out?" Jessie asked in astonishment, with just a mixture of glee.

The engine finally turned over. Suzanne sped quickly out of the parking lot, entering the traffic on Locust Street. She cranked her head around to see if anyone was following. No. They had made it.

Jena Karnitz searched once more for the missing purse. She didn't like the way the nun's face had gone from beet red to white, nor had she ever seen anyone tremble like the nun had done. There was no question in her mind but that the nun needed her pills.

Where the hell was that purse?

Suddenly, the picture of how the nun looked when she entered the police station leaped into Jena's mind. Damn it all to hell! She hadn't been carrying a purse!

Jena rushed to the coffee room and wasn't even surprised when it was empty.

Chapter
Seven

Suzanne began taking off the veil and band, tossing them into the backseat. Just in case a bulletin had gone out to stop a nun, she thought it wise to at least get the headwork off. She pulled off the coif and shook out her damp hair.

"Will you please tell me what you found out now?" Jessie pleaded. "And then I have something to tell you."

"I'm sorry!" Suzanne said in exasperation. "I've just never been *running from the law* before. I can only think of one thing at a time, and right now all I want to do is get as far away from here as possible."

"You don't look so hot to me," Jessie said. "Why don't you pull into that parking lot so you can finish taking off that nun's outfit, and maybe get some water or something."

Suzanne didn't argue. She quickly crossed two lanes of traffic and pulled into a discount store's parking lot, bringing her car to a stop between two vans. With shaking hands she finished pulling off the heavy black habit, stripping down to damp shorts and shirt.

"Wait right here," Jessie said as she jumped from the car. "There's a pop stand over there. You look like you need something to drink."

Suzanne watched as Jessie ran over and purchased two drinks. *How am I going to tell her?* she thought as she watched Jessie running back to the car, spilling pop as she ran. *How can I tell her that Amy is dead? Dead and buried?*

"No, she isn't!" Jessie said as soon as she got back to the car. "Amy isn't dead. She called to me. I heard her as plain as day."

Again Suzanne was surprised by the degree of psychic ability the young girl had. "I wish you would quit reading my thoughts. It's rather unnerving you know!"

"Okay, if you want me to stop, I'll try. I'm not certain I can, though. This is the first time I've ever been able to read another person's mind. Sometimes your thoughts just zoom into my head without my really even thinking about it. I wonder why?"

"I suppose because we both have a great deal of psychic ability. From everything I've read, when both lines are open, the transmission is better. But then, I'm much like you. When I touch someone the images just slam into my head and by then it's too late to stop them."

"What did you find out? What makes you think Amy is dead? She isn't, you know."

Suzanne stared out the windshield of her car, remembering every detail of her encounter with Clark. "I don't know exactly what happened, Jessie. Something new. Something strange. It always unnerves me to read a killer, but this was different. I couldn't get completely into his mind. I was terrified. It was like I knew I would die if I went any further."

"Well, what *did* you find out? What makes you think Amy is dead?"

In halting words, Suzanne told Jessie everything she could remember that had happened. When she finally came to the part where she had seen Amy lying down, with her eyes closed, and dirt being piled on top of her, Jessie interrupted.

"How are you sure it was Amy you saw? Couldn't it have been one of the other girls?"

Suzanne's hand reached across the seat and found Jessie's. "This girl looked exactly like the picture you showed me of Amy—porcelain complexion, long blond hair, almost angelic looking. Besides, I knew it was Amy. I would have known it was Amy even if you had not shown me the picture.'' Suzanne remembered something else. ''And she was wearing a gold chain with a tiny white, maybe ivory, cross attached to it.''

Jessie's hands flew to her neck and she pulled out a chain from under her clothing. She pushed the ivory cross up to Suzanne. ''It *was* Amy, then. Aunt Vera bought us each one of these when she visited Alaska.''

Suzanne looked at the identical cross she had seen in her vision. ''I'm sorry, Jessie. So sorry!''

''For what? I'll agree that you saw Amy, but you must have misinterpreted what you saw. That happens all the time with people like us. You know that.''

Suzanne wondered how she was ever going to be able to explain to Jessie that her abilities were not the same as most psychics. What she saw unfolding in her visions had already happened in most cases. And she was never wrong.

''Jessie, the reason my psychic impulses are so much greater than other psychics', is that I receive some sort of an electrical current when I touch a person. Any person. If that person has been involved in a crime, then the images are always clear and accurate. I have been brought in by dozens of different police forces to help in really bad crimes, especially where there is someone missing. And, sweetie, I've never, ever been wrong. Not once. I don't have to try to interpret my visions, as most psychics do. It's like I go into the mind of the killer and see everything through his eyes. I know *how* he killed, I know *where* he killed and where he hid the body, and I can even sometimes tell *why* he killed. If I spend enough time with the killer, I can almost retrace his steps, right down to where he ate lunch or went to the bathroom.''

''Is that what got you in trouble with Underwood?''

''To be perfectly honest about it, I didn't do anything with Underwood that I hadn't done a hundred times before. Only Underwood happened to have a seemingly endless supply of money. He had a team of attorneys working for him who zeroed in on everything they could possibly find to get him off. When they discovered me, and my part in helping to find the bodies, they researched every case I had ever been involved in—every word I had ever spoken in interviews—every word that had ever been written about me. When they learned I *get into the mind* of the killer, they used that to say it was, in effect, forcing a defendant to testify against himself.''

Although it had been almost a year ago, Suzanne vividly remembered her first encounter with Underwood as though it were yesterday. She was living in Omaha, the city that had been home to her and Miss Emily. She was still living in Miss Emily's house, which she had inherited from the old woman at her death.

She was on her way to the funeral of one of the victims. She was going to work the crowd, moving from person to person, brushing up against them, shaking their hands, touching them in some manner. It was something the police had her routinely do, in case the killer attended the funeral of his victim. It was a fact that killers, especially serial killers, enjoyed going to the graves of their victims, and often attended their funerals. It was the perfect opportunity for Suzanne to try to do a reading.

On this morning, she was riding to the church in the backseat of a police car. In the front were detectives Sands and Botello, two of the officers who had grilled her mercilessly about the death of Peggy Ann years before. Over the ensuing years, she had become good friends with the officers, attending David Sands's wedding, where it was obvious any enmity between father and son had long since been forgotten, and becoming godmother to Charles and Barbara Botello's baby girl, where it was also obvious a waitress named Millie had been long forgotten.

They had just turned the corner at First and Broadway, when a long white Cadillac shot out from an alley, forcing them to slam on their brakes. Neither Sands nor Botello wanted to take the time to issue a traffic ticket, and would have ignored the incident, except that Underwood, unaware that the unmarked car in back of him contained police officers, proceeded to run two lights.

Sands and Botello exchanged glances. "Shall we nail him?" Sands asked.

"Hell, yes!" Botello answered as he rolled down the window and attached the cherry top. "We still have plenty of time."

To this day, Suzanne didn't know what had made her get out of the police car. She watched as the short, stocky man behind the wheel of the Cadillac got out of his car and spoke to the officers. It looked like a routine traffic stop, nothing that should even interest her. Yet she sat in the car watching the man, getting more and more uneasy. Finally, she had exited the car and walked over to where the three stood. Sands and Botello were surprised, but had worked with her enough not to question anything she did. Suzanne reached over and extended her hand for the man to shake. She had found over the years that most people readily accepted a handshake. It was the quickest, easiest way to do a reading. Baxter Underwood was no exception. He shook her hand.

The gruesome images of young bodies crashed into her head with the force of a jackhammer. Suzanne heard herself gasping as the scenes flashed through her mind. Underwood pulled his hand from her tight grasp, realizing too late who she was.

"He's the one." Suzanne turned to Sands and Botello. "He just dumped the body of another little girl in that alley he was coming out of back there. Her little panties are in the trunk of this car."

And yet the courts hadn't been able to convict. The search of the trunk had been ruled illegal because there had been no probable cause other than the word of Suzanne. The body had been found because Suzanne *invaded* Underwood's mind—clearly a case of forcing Underwood to testify against himself.

So Underwood had walked, only to kill again within

weeks of his release. One of the twelve-year-old girls he raped and murdered was the only daughter of his lead attorney. It was like he was giving notice that this time around, he had better be put away.

The newspapers had crucified her, the police force, and Judge Carpenter. Part of the problem for Suzanne was that she was on the police payroll. Underwood's attorney argued successfully that as part of this force, she was bound by the same letter of the law as the officers. Had Underwood been Mirandized? No. Had he been advised his very *thoughts* were going to be used against him? No.

All at once the same newspapers that had thought Suzanne was an angel in disguise, thought she was a monster. Why would Suzanne take money for such a God-given talent? Why had she placed the investigation in jeopardy by jumping in before all the facts were known? Every time Suzanne picked up a copy of the *Omaha World Herald,* she felt a little of her life drain away.

Damn it! She hadn't *wanted* to take money for helping the police, but what was she supposed to do? She spent most of her time traveling across the country, using her skills to find missing persons, and aiding different police investigations. When she'd first started working for the police, she had refused all offers of payment—considering it a prostitution of her talents. But the day came when she realized she was working full-time and had nothing coming in each month except the small trust fund Miss Emily had established for her. She had to eat, for Christ's sake!

But they continued to crucify her. Suzanne didn't even stay in town for the trial of Baxter Underwood on the new murder charges. She sold Miss Emily's house, loaded up what possessions she could get in a Ryder truck, hooked her Olds to the truck, and slunk out of town, her tail between her legs. She hadn't even decided on a destination until the attendant at the Ryder place said he had to know where she was going before letting her have the truck. The people in line in front of her had been moving to Kansas City. She decided that was as good a place as any.

She had now been in Kansas City ten months. And she knew a grand total of six or seven people, who knew *her* well enough to let her alone. They thought of her only as an eccentric recluse, and knew nothing of her past history. She did research for a television conglomerate, working out of her home, away from people. Fortunately, between the sale of Miss Emily's house and the trust fund, she didn't have to make much money to get by.

Occasionally, a reporter would track her down, hoping for a story. When this happened she would just slam down the phone, or shut the door, insulating herself from any more misery.

She had read in the *Kansas City Star* that Baxter Underwood had been convicted for the deaths of the two twelve-year-old girls. That was all she wanted to know about that whole terrible time.

Jessie was right. She had been "hiding out" from the world. Maybe it was time to come out of hiding.

Chapter
Eight

"**H**as a criminalist been notified yet?" Harry asked the young officer standing outside the office building on Brighton Avenue.

"Yes, sir. Everyone's been called, even the ME," Patrolman Williams answered. "We were just up the street on traffic detail when these men hollered. We came over and secured the area."

"Stanley Davis is the ME we wanted. Is that going to be a problem?"

"No, sir. That's who the station said you requested. I believe they caught him in his car not far from here. We were told he'd be here in about fifteen minutes."

"Good." Harry glanced around at the men in hard hats. "What's the story? Who found the body and what were these men doing?"

"The building was going to be razed, sir," Williams answered. "They were doing a final run-through when one of the men discovered the body—or what was left of it."

"Pretty bad?"

"Yeah. Both legs and feet, both arms and hands—the head. Just like all the others."

Hopefully not like all the others, Harry thought.

"I assume your partner is in with the body?" Jim asked.

"Yes, sir. And we haven't allowed anyone in, but a Mr. Hollings wants to speak with someone as soon as possible.

He wants to know what they should do about the explosives they have set.''

"Not yet," Jim said. "Tell him we'll talk with him later. Right now, no one comes in who's not official. Got that?"

"Yes, sir."

Harry and Jim walked into the old office building and followed the trail of puke down the hallway to the open door.

"Looks like somebody wasn't prepared for what he found," Jim said.

The second officer was standing just outside the door. By the looks of him, Harry guessed he had contributed to at least part of the mess in the hallway. Harry couldn't say much. The first young girl he had found butchered like this had emptied his own damn stomach. He nodded at the young man. "Go get some air, officer."

Jim went first into the room, stepping carefully over the severed hand, checking behind the door before pushing it open. The scene was as gruesome as all the others had been. If this were a copycat killing, the perpetrator had a blood lust the same as Clark.

Body parts littered the small office room. Jim went over and looked down at the naked torso of what had once been a lovely feminine form. He knelt down, looking closely at the skin around the stomach and pubic area. He could see several evenly spaced dried splatters of what looked like semen. "Damn," he swore softly.

"What is it?" Harry asked as he entered the room. "Don't tell me—"

"Yeah," Jim said. "Looks like."

"Shit. Have you checked the head?" He looked around the room, spotting the decapitated head of the young girl sitting a few feet away, looking as though she had merely sunk through the floor, until only her head was showing. It was Clark's personal signature.

Harry went over and knelt beside the head. His stomach churned as he realized the significance of his find. He turned to his partner. "Makeup on an inch thick, right eyebrow shaved, then penciled in. Damn it all to hell!"

"I heard Amy call for me. That much I know," Jessie said stubbornly. "I have never had a psychic experience that strong. And no, I didn't fall asleep in the car and dream it!"

Suzanne looked squarely at Jessie, squinting her eyes in mock anger. "Reading minds again, are we?"

Jessie tossed her long red hair. "Well, it looks like I have to do *something* to make you believe me!"

"All right. Start at the beginning and don't leave anything out. I guess it *is* rather presumptuous of me to insist *my* reading is the accurate one." Suzanne pulled her legs up onto Miss Emily's worn couch, crossing them Indianstyle to match Jessie's. "Maybe there is another explanation for what I saw." As she said the words, she hoped the answer wasn't that Jessie heard Amy call out for her right before she died, and that she, herself, saw the actual killing.

"Okay, I'll tell you everything, but part of it doesn't make sense." She spoke the words defensively, defying Suzanne to doubt her.

Suzanne felt small, petty. Who the hell did she think she was to be questioning this young girl's psychic ability? What must Jessie be thinking about her?

"I'm sorry, sweetie," she said. "I can be arrogant and obnoxious, can't I?"

"Oh, you're all right," Jessie said. "I know you're only trying to keep me from being hurt."

Suzanne smiled. "Okay then, why don't you start at the top and tell me everything you can remember?"

"The first thing I heard was Amy's voice calling to me. I heard it as plain as day, really I did. She said, 'Jessie, please. Please come for me!' That was all. But then I started getting a whole lot of images." Jessie stopped talking, lost in remembering.

"Such as?" Suzanne gently prodded.

"Monkeys. I know it sounds weird, but I saw monkeys. There was a man with a big beard, and a bunch of people with their arms in the air—like someone was holding a gun on them."

"Did it seem to you the monkeys and people were with Amy?"

Jessie shook her head. "I don't know. I couldn't tell. They were spinning around, flashing by so fast I was having a hard time making out the images."

"What about the background? Do you remember anything at all about that?"

Jessie knitted her forehead in concentration. "The people with their hands in the air were sitting in seats—double seats of some kind, maybe like on an airplane."

"Think back, Jessie. Was it nighttime or day?"

"Day, I think. Yes. Yes, I'm sure of it. There were clouds in the background. Big, fluffy clouds."

"Close your eyes, Jessie. Concentrate hard and let your mind act as a camera. You want a wider view. The camera is going to pan around past the people with their arms in the air. Try to see a road sign, an address—maybe a landmark."

Jessie's face contorted as she fought to bring the scenes back. After a few seconds her head snapped to the side as though she were listening for something. "There is a hill, a big hill that looks something like a bridge. I think the people are screaming. Their faces show . . . fright I think." She hesitated again, then spoke. "That's it. That's all I can see; all I remember."

"What about the monkeys, Jessie? Are they in cages? Maybe at the zoo? Try to bring it into focus. See all that you can possibly see."

Again Jessie squeezed her eyes tightly shut, concentrating on the visions she had seen flashing by while she waited in the car.

"Slow them down, sweetie. Sometimes you have to slow them down."

"An umbrella! One of the monkeys has a blue umbrella. And one is riding in a little red wagon!"

"Good, Jessie. It has to be some sort of a show. The monkeys are part of an act. Do you want to try an experiment?"

"Sure. I'm up for anything that will help us find Amy."

"Okay, Jessie, I'm going to take your hands in mine. Then I want you to bring it all back. Relive that moment in the car when you heard Amy." Suzanne reached over and took Jessie's hands. She felt a slight tingling run up her arms and across her neck. Good. They were connecting.

She had only tried this once before, with a young mother whose baby had been snatched from her at the mall. The woman had been so upset, so crazed with grief, that her ability as a witness was affected. Suzanne had held her hands and relived that terrible moment with her. However, Suzanne, with her keen eye for detail and cool detachment, had noticed things the mother had missed. They were able to find the kidnapper with the information Suzanne provided. So often her own particular type of psychic ability was helpful only after a death. It had been thrilling to bring that baby back to his mother's arms alive.

"Now, Jessie. You are sitting in my car waiting for me. What happened? Remember it all."

Instantly, Suzanne heard the voice. "Jessie, please! Please come for me!"

Then other images began clicking through Suzanne's mind: monkeys, a man with a beard, people with their arms in the air. They flashed by in rapid succession, becoming almost a blur.

Suzanne took a long, deep breath. "Try to relax, Jessie. Breathe in as far as you can, then let it out slowly. Think of the images. Pretend they are a slide show, and you are slowing the pictures down so everyone can get a good look."

Jessie took a long, shuddering breath. The images continued to click by rapidly. She felt her head spinning as a wave of nausea overtook her. She released Suzanne's hands, then flung herself down on the couch.

"I'm sorry. I don't feel so good."

Suzanne grabbed on to Jessie's hands again. The vision came through clearly, and she watched as Amy dropped to the floor, then tried to get back on her feet. She could feel the dizziness as Amy's eyes looked around briefly, then closed as she slumped to the floor.

Instantly, Jessie sat back up. "It's gone. I was feeling so sick, but now I'm fine. Weird! Totally weird!"

"You were feeling Amy's sickness. I saw her. I felt it, too. Her head was spinning, then she must have blacked out. I'm almost certain that was all it was."

"Did you see the monkeys? Did you?" Jessie demanded.

"Yes. I saw all that you told me about. But I couldn't slow them down. I don't understand that. I can almost always control the scenes—slow them down or telescope out for a broader view—but this time I couldn't."

"Probably because *I* couldn't," Jessie said. "You were getting into *my* mind while I was getting into Amy's. That's the difference. You can only see what I see, right?"

Suzanne thought a few seconds before answering, surprised at Jessie's insight. "Yes. Yes, I guess that's so. I would be limited to what you saw when you were in my car."

"Could it be that Amy was dizzy and maybe blacking out, and that I saw the images flashing by real fast because that was what *she* was seeing and not what *I* was seeing at all? Could it?"

"Whoa! Slow down. Let me get this straight." Suzanne paused, contemplating Jessie's words. "You're saying that just before Amy passed out, she saw monkeys, a bearded man, and people with their arms in the air?"

Jessie looked down, picking absentmindedly at a frayed spot on the couch. "Pretty dumb, huh?"

"I don't think so, sweetie. There has to be a reason you are picking up these images. They all have to tie-in together somehow, with Amy. We have to trust what you are seeing and work from there."

Chapter
Nine

By late afternoon, the day that had started off as merely a hot May day had turned into a record-breaking scorcher, with the temperature soaring to nearly one hundred degrees. Even the few clouds which had begun drifting in, offering hope of rain, did nothing to squelch the oppressive heat. Inside the police station on Locust, tempers rose as steadily as the mercury.

"We have no choice, gentlemen," Chief Caswell all but shouted over the murmur of disgruntled voices. "Nordyke is already screaming. Seems somebody tipped him about the eyebrow and semen, so we can't claim this was a copycat killing."

"Did you tell him to keep his mouth shut about that?" Harry snapped. "We don't want the *Star* printing those two facts or some asshole will decide to off his wife and blame it on the butcher."

"I didn't put it quite so succinctly," Caswell answered, sounding annoyed. "I did inform him we were not releasing that info to the press."

"Why can't we hold him as a material witness, if nothing else?" Jim asked. "It seems to me, since body parts were found in his apartment he would at least be a witness we should protect."

Caswell rubbed the back of his neck in frustration. "Yeah, I thought of that, but Nordyke beat me to the punch. He said if Clark was wanted as a witness, he would personally see to it he returned whenever we wanted him, but since he had already spent almost two weeks behind bars for murders he did not commit, it would be a *gross infringement on his rights* for him to spend so much as another hour locked up!''

"Damn it, Chief! Clark is as guilty as hell,'' Harry interrupted. "You know it and we all know it. We can't let him be released.''

Caswell looked hard at his number one detective. "No. I don't *know* it, McDermott. We have another killing *identical* to all the other murders, only this one takes place when our star suspect is in jail. *He* didn't do it, so where the hell does that leave us? And remember, Davis couldn't account for the body parts found in Clark's apartment. They didn't come from any of the known victims. He has always said not to assume too much until we get the report back from the FBI. Sonofabitch, Harry. Did it ever occur to you that maybe you were wrong?''

Harry refused to concede. "Look, we don't even know for certain if this killing *was* done exactly the same as the others. We won't know that until Davis gets finished with the body and gets the DNA evidence back on the semen.''

"Did I hear my name being taken in vain?'' The door to Caswell's office pushed open to reveal Chief Medical Examiner Stanley Davis. "Thought you boys might want to know what I found.''

"Thanks, Stanley.'' Harry smiled at the little man. "I really appreciate you stopping by. And if you've brought us evidence that will keep Clark in jail, I'll kiss your shiny bald head.''

"Well, damn!'' Davis laughed. "Much as I hate having to miss out on that, I'm afraid this killing is, for the most part, similar to the others.''

"But not exactly?'' Harry asked.

Davis took a seat at the front of the room, spreading papers out on the edge of Caswell's desk. "Let me start with the similarities. First, the cuts were in the identical areas as all the others—except that these were a little rougher cut, more like the cuts found on the first two or three victims.''

"So what does that mean?" Caswell asked.

"I'm not sure. As the murders progressed—as more and more girls were killed—the killer learned a little about joints and bones. The last girls butchered were—if you will pardon the expression—carved *more professionally*. But this one again looked like the killer had a little rough time. Maybe he was in more of a hurry, I don't know. The face was made up with the identical makeup used on all the other girls. Same brand. Same colors. I personally ran the tests twice to be certain.''

"Shit!" Harry slammed his notebook down on his leg.

"And of course you know," Davis continued, "the right eyebrow was shaved, then penciled in, same as all the others. I'm sorry, gentlemen, but I don't think you'll be keeping Clark behind bars on my findings.''

"Well, that just about tears it then." Caswell heaved a long sigh. "We have the wrong sonofabitch in jail!"

"You mentioned differences," Jim said. "How exactly was this one different?"

"This girl was raped, for openers. *Really* raped, not just made to look like it. She was a virgin, too, just like most of the other victims. Also, she was killed by suffocation. She didn't bleed to death like the others.''

"Was she dead when the dismembering began, then?"

"Yes. She was raped first, then suffocated. After that, nicks were gouged on the body, the makeup was applied, the limbs cut off and the semen placed on her torso—not necessarily in that order. And we'll have to wait for the DNA report to know about the semen.''

"Are you saying this girl wasn't tortured? On all the rest of the victims, you were certain they were alive when the gouging was done and even for a short time when an arm or leg was being removed. As I recall, one girl was still alive when her neck was being cut." Harry looked at the diminutive ME for confirmation.

Davis nodded. "That's right. She may not have been

conscious, but she was damn sure still alive.''

''Any other differences?'' Harry asked.

Davis shook his head. ''No. Everything else pretty much matched all the other killings, except for one thing, which may or may not be helpful. I think the killer vomited as he was cutting up the body. He tried to clean it all up, but some had mingled with the victim's blood.''

''There were at least two others who vomited at the scene,'' Jim said, remembering the hallway. ''Could it have come from them?''

''No. This was right on the body and had been wiped up. I assume your men would know better than to pull a stunt like that?''

''Of course,'' Caswell stated flatly. ''So what do you think this means? Is our killer getting squeamish at this late date?''

''My bet is that it was a different killer,'' Harry said. ''And no, I can't explain how he happened to know all the details from the other murders which weren't released to the public. But I'll bet my sweet ass this was a copycat!''

''You don't have one shred of evidence to back up that theory,'' Caswell said. ''There were certainly more similarities than differences.''

''If it *was* a copycat,'' Jim said, ''then it looks to me like he would have to have some tie-in to us. And by *us* I mean the handful of detectives working this case. Either someone in our unit has been talking, or''—he looked at Davis—''someone at yours.''

Davis shook his head. ''It can't be coming from my office. I've worked alone on these murders, and as you know, my wife does all the transcribing of my notes.''

''I can't believe anyone from our offices has been talking,'' Harry said. ''If they were, the *Star* would have it by now.''

There was a light tap on the door and Officer Karnitz entered. She walked over to Chief Caswell. ''Sir, Andrew Nordyke is back. He's demanding we release Clark. What should I do?''

Caswell threw one arm in the air in exasperation. "Release him. We can't possibly hold him now."

"Just a minute, sir," Harry said. "Give me a few minutes to set up a tail. If he *is* the butcher, we don't want to give him the opportunity to start in again."

Chief Caswell rubbed at an ache in the back of his neck he couldn't quite find. "All right. But watch yourself. I don't want Nordyke on my ass!"

As Harry left the room, the full implication of the examiner's findings hit him. Either Clark was totally innocent, or someone close to the investigation had leaked detailed information and a copycat killer had struck. He wasn't happy accepting either of those premises.

"How about we clean up your apartment before we go for groceries? I think you'd feel a lot better if we got rid of at least part of this mess."

"What? No bulldozer?"

Jessie looked scornfully around the littered living room. "Well, since we don't have one, it looks like we'll have to do it."

"*We* don't have to do anything, young lady. I'm perfectly content with the way things are. *You're* the only one who can't seem to live with it."

"That's not true," Jessie stated confidently. "It's bugging you, too. You're just afraid to open up and admit it. You like *hiding out* in this jumble."

Suzanne made a low bow. "Yes, Doctor Freud. Geez, kid! Since when do fourteen-year-old girls care that much about what a place looks like?"

"Are you kidding? Our *barns* are cleaner than this apartment. The state board would condemn our dairy farm if it was kept like this. And besides that, you smoke too much. Don't you know those things will kill you?"

Suzanne threw up her arms in mock surrender. "Okay! okay! One vice at a time." She looked around in frustration, then nodded her head slowly. "Yeah, I know this place is a dump. I haven't really done much since I moved in here. I haven't even unpacked most of my boxes. They're still piled in a storage room off the kitchen.''

"Maybe that's why you don't have anything on the walls, huh?'' Jessie answered. "And why there isn't even anything sitting around to make it look like *home*.''

"Maybe that's because I never considered it home. I sold my *home* when I left Omaha.''

"Oh, pooh! Home is where you're at. My mom sets more things around when we stay at a motel, than you have here.''

Suzanne hated to admit it, but she knew Jessie was right. After Miss Emily's death, she had spent weeks redoing their house; making it hers, but still with a touch of Miss Emily. Furthermore, she had kept it clean—and done the washing, the ironing, the cooking. Here, she had turned into a vegetable who locked herself in her apartment and shut out the world. She made her mind up quickly.

"Okay, sweetie, you win. Let's see if we can put some order back in my life. God knows I could use it!''

Across town, Randal Clark took Nordyke's hand, pumping it up and down. "I can't thank you enough for getting me out of there,'' he said with a nod back at the building he had just exited. "I can't stand being penned in. Drives me nuts!''

Andrew Nordyke couldn't explain the slight ripple of goose bumps that traveled down his arms at Clark's touch. He hoped to God he hadn't made a mistake insisting on his client's release. No. Clark couldn't be the butcher. The murder last night had pretty much cinched that. Up until that point, though, he had thought Clark as guilty as hell.

"Good luck, Randal,'' Nordyke said. "And don't forget what I said about a tail. I have a hunch they may follow you around for a couple of days. If they make a nuisance of themselves, call me.''

Clark's weathered face broke into a wide grin. "I'll do that now. I surely will!'' He turned and walked up the street. He would sure as hell get rid of a tail. It had been

almost two weeks since he'd had any fun! He wondered
if there was any chance the girl was still alive. Amy. Amy
with the long, blond hair, the sea blue eyes; Amy, the
young girl he had followed as she went to church each
Sunday and to choir practice on Wednesday; Amy, with
her innocent, wide-eyed look, her gentle ways. He knew
what she was really like, the whore! She was just exactly
like all the others. Pretending to be so good—so pure!
Fooling everyone! Everyone but Randal Clark! He was on
to all of them. The bitches!

Give him an honest to God hooker every time. At least
they didn't pretend to be someone they weren't. You knew
where you were right up front. No phony sweetness and
goodness act.

Randal thought of all the things he was going to do to
Amy—if she was alive. A ripple of excitement traveled
down his spine.

But first he had a bone to pick with Floyd. That double-
crossing ass had almost cost him his freedom. *Don't rape
her* he had told him. Just *pretend* to rape her. He had laid
it out for him step by step. But no. Floyd couldn't keep
his pecker in his pants and had almost blown the whole
thing.

*Still, he did get me out of jail. And now it will be his
DNA on file, not mine. Maybe the bastard did me a bigger
favor than I thought!*

Suzanne stood at the entrance to the living room and sur-
veyed their handiwork. The floors were vacuumed, the furniture shining, and Jessie had even rummaged around in
boxes until she had located a few pictures for the walls.
The curtains were pulled back, letting sunshine filter
through sparkling windows. She looked at Jessie with gen-
uine admiration. "You're a whiz, kiddo! We did this entire
apartment in three hours."

Jessie looked around. "Hey, this place is really cute—
when you can see it."

"All right, all right. I admit it. The place looks better and I feel better. Are you satisfied?"

Jessie's eyes twinkled. "Not quite. We have to do the laundry and go shopping for groceries."

Suzanne flopped down on the couch. "You're a slave driver. Do you know that?" She looked up at Jessie expecting a flip answer. Instead, she saw Jessie sink to her knees and begin shaking violently.

Jessie's head snapped back and she felt a hard, gripping pressure around her chest. She emitted a loud, gut-wrenching moan. "No! Oh, nooooooo!"

Suzanne rushed to Jessie, kneeling beside her on the floor. "What is it, Jessie? What's happening?" But she knew without the girl telling her. "Take my hand, Jessie. Let me experience it, too."

Jessie extended a shaky hand and Suzanne clasped it firmly in her own. Suzanne tried to empty her mind, to enable Jessie's visions to become her own. Almost immediately the scenes began emerging. She saw Clark walking down a sidewalk and heard his thoughts about Amy. *Kill the whore! The bitch! Make her suffer!*

As the images became clearer, Jessie let out a high-pitched scream, then collapsed in Suzanne's arms. "He's horrible! He wants to cut her! Make her bleed!" The child buried her head in Suzanne's lap. "No! No! Oh, no!"

Suzanne could do nothing but hold Jessie as the wretched images slammed into her brain. She shuddered, knowing Jessie was living the nightmare—watching as Clark thought about torturing and taunting Amy.

Finally, as the scenes faded and stopped, Suzanne shook Jessie gently. "It's only what he *wants* to do, sweetie. That is what you are seeing. He's in jail. He can't hurt Amy."

Jessie's tear-stained face raised from the comfort of Suzanne's lap. "No. I saw him outdoors, on a sidewalk, with the sun shining on him." Her next words were spoken in a flat, dead voice which caused Suzanne to shiver. "He's free. I know it."

Gently, Suzanne placed her arms around Jessie, holding

her tight against her body. "I'll call, sweetie. I'll call the police station and find out for certain. Would you like that?"

Jessie nodded, pushing away from Suzanne. "Please. Do it now. I have to know."

Chapter
Ten

Harry couldn't believe he was back at square one. There wasn't a solid lead in his files, except those pointing to Randal Clark. It was Clark who the witnesses placed at the school from which the fifth victim had disappeared. It was Clark's Dumpster where Amy Matthews's purse had been found. And it was Clark's apartment that had yielded what appeared to be parts of perhaps eight different bodies. They wouldn't know for certain until the completed FBI report was back. And what *roommate*? There had been nothing in Clark's apartment to indicate it was occupied by two men.

He could still hear Andrew Nordyke's cold words ringing in his ears. "I'll tell you what happened, *Detective* McDermott. Your boys found two pimple-faced teenage hoods who swore they saw Clark hanging around the school, and the next thing you know, there is enough evidence to *hang* my client! Pretty damned convenient, I'd say!"

Harry hated attorneys. He hoped in another life he came back as a judge—just so he could hold them all in contempt and levy enormous fines at them. *And you, Mr. Nordyke, are fined fifty thousand dollars for assholery!* It was a nice thought.

This hadn't been his day. He had gotten chewed out by his boss, lost his prime suspect in a serial murder case, and his office couldn't even hold the hell on to a fake nun.

And God only knew what her angle was. To top it all off, Monica, from whom he had been divorced exactly thirteen years, had called and wanted to see about getting back together. Of course that wasn't anything new. Monica called every few years, in between her marriages, pledging everlasting love and fidelity to him, her "one and only." What husband was it she had just discarded? Harry had lost track after five. Thank God their brief union had not resulted in children. *But, Harry, darling, do you have any idea what children would do to my modeling career? I could just kiss it good-bye now, I really could!*

But Harry had to hand it to her. Monica had always known what she wanted and set out to get just that. Even now, at thirty-eight, he still ran across her picture now and then in some of the magazines. And her assortment of husbands read like a roster from *Who's Who*. Except for him, of course. He had the dubious distinction of being husband number one—prior to her breaking into the big time.

Before their two-year marriage had ended, Harry was lying awake nights agonizing over how to ask Monica for a divorce. He could hardly stand the sight of her in bed beside him, but he knew her fragile ego would have a hard time dealing with the idea that any man would reject her—especially a lowly cop. And Harry was too much of a gentleman to want to hurt her.

Then, wonder of wonders, he had come home from work one night and there she stood, bags packed. *Now, darling, don't be upset with me, but I have taken this absolutely wonderful modeling assignment in New York. It was just too good to pass up.* Then, almost offhandedly, *And please forgive me, Harry, but I want a divorce!*

Harry could have turned cartwheels across their living room, yelling yahoo at the top of his lungs. He could have smiled broadly and explained that he, too, badly wanted a divorce. He could have told his wife of two years that she had made him the happiest man on the face of the earth that day. Instead, he put his arms around her and asked her if she was certain that was what she wanted. He told her she was a fine woman, and wished her well with her life. Her last words to him, as she went out the front door, were, "You are such a good man, Harry! I suppose someday I'm going to regret this."

Harry had never regretted letting Monica leave with her pride intact. To this day, she still thought she had hurt him deeply by her going. And over the years, they had become friends—the kind of friends who could touch base once every few years, talk for hours, then go their separate ways until the next time.

Harry sat brooding, wondering why his reminiscing about his failed marriage kept forcing to his mind the fresh-scrubbed face of the young woman posing as a nun. He guessed it was those enormous brown eyes she had turned on him—haunting eyes, that seemed too wise for her years.

He pressed down on the intercom. "Jena, I'd like to listen to the tape you made of that woman talking to Clark. Could you bring it in? And do you have the transcription?"

Officer Karnitz entered Chief Caswell's office, smiling to herself at the manner in which Harry McDermott always seemed to take over the chief's room. Harry despised doing business at his allotted desk in the general room, so whenever possible, he made himself at home in Caswell's office. Caswell didn't seem to mind. He had been trying to get more offices for his detectives for years, but space was tight. Until then, he didn't mind sharing his quarters.

Jena wondered if Harry would say yes if she invited him out for drinks. Their shifts ended in thirty minutes, and so far, Harry had failed to respond to any of her signals. Maybe she should just try the direct approach. "There wasn't much to transcribe, Harry. The nun, or whoever she was, only said a couple of things. She said, 'Bless you, my child,' and later said, 'Will you receive the blessing, my son?' Then, later it sounds like maybe she whispered something to Clark, but the mike didn't pick it up."

Harry quickly read through the transcription. Most of what was said was coming from Clark.

Sister Mary Elizabeth: Bless you, my child.
Randal Clark: So, Sister. What do you want with me? (Clark laughs) Are you here to save my soul?
(Silence for about a minute and a half)
Randal Clark: Hey, what's the matter with you, Sister? You some kind of nut, or what?
Randal Clark: You trying to break my arm, Sister?
(Sister Mary Elizabeth stands and puts her thumb on Clark's forehead)
Sister Mary Elizabeth: Will you receive the blessing, my son?
(Sound of whispering)
Randal Clark: (Screaming) Get her away from me! What are you guys trying to pull on me, anyway?

Harry looked up. "That's it? That's all that was said?"
Jena nodded. "I tried to get Clark to tell me what he was talking about, but he clammed up. He seemed spooked, somehow, by her visit. And the nun, or whoever, was definitely shook up. Her face was white and she was trembling like she had just had a bad scare or something."

"Weren't you watching them? Did you see anything at all that the nun was doing to make Clark react like that?"

Jena shook her head. "All the nun did was put her hand on his arm, then later her thumb on his forehead. But whatever she whispered, it sure got a reaction out of Clark."

"All right. Let's listen to it, and I want you to tell me everything you can remember about what was happening. Okay?"

Officer Karnitz was only too happy to oblige. "Sure, Harry."

They ran through the short tape three times, without any further enlightenment as to what had really transpired between Clark and the woman.

"Damn, I wish we hadn't lost her," Harry said in frustration. "It's obvious she knows something about this case."

"I'm sorry, Harry. She really looked sick to me. And I had no reason to think she would run. After all, she didn't know we were going to hold her."

"I know, Jena. I'm not blaming you." Harry sat tapping a letter opener against the chief's desk. "Tell you what. Why don't you take this tape to the lab and see if the boys can enhance that whisper? If we even knew what she said to set Clark off, that would be a help."

"Do you want me to wait for the results? I don't mi—"

Harry interrupted. "No, no. You're off duty shortly. I'm going to be around here for another two or three hours, anyway."

Jena left quickly with the tape. If she hurried, she might still be able to catch Patrolman Taylor. She had seen him writing his day's report just before she went in to see Harry. With a little luck, he hadn't finished yet. She was *not* going to eat supper alone tonight!

By his own dictate, any questions coming into the station concerning Clark were to be referred to Harry or his partner, Jim. So it was no surprise to Harry when he was stopped on his way to the lab.

Officer Downing had spotted him and waved, motioning toward the phone. "It's someone with a question about Clark. They want to know if he has been released."

Harry picked up the extension phone. "Yes? This is Detective McDermott. How can I help you?"

He recognized the woman's voice instantly. "This is, uh, Beverly Smith from, uh, the *Kansas City Star*. I'm just doing an article on Randal Clark and I was wondering. He is still in jail, isn't he?"

Harry signaled to Officer Downing, mouthing, "Get a trace." Officer Downing jumped into action.

"You know, I'm not certain," Harry lied. "I just came on duty. Let me go see what I can find out. Can you hang on?"

Across town, Suzanne answered, "Certainly."

After what seemed an eternity to Suzanne, but was in reality only three minutes, she heard the rustle of the phone as it was being picked back up.

"Yeah. Are you still there, miss?" Harry tried to keep his voice casual.

"Yes."

"Randal Clark was dismissed about an hour ago." Harry couldn't miss the loud gasp from the other end of the line. "Is anything wrong, miss? Can I help you in any way?"

Suzanne was finally able to speak. "Why? For God's sake *why* was this madman released?"

"Chief Caswell has scheduled a press conference for seven o'clock this evening. Didn't the *Star* get notification?"

"I . . . uh . . . maybe. I don't know." Suzanne slammed the phone down, breaking the connection.

Harry looked at the name and address on the paper in front of him. Suzanne Richards. Yeah. That sounded better. The tall woman with the lovely brown eyes looked more like a Suzanne than a Sister Mary Elizabeth!

Sterling Heights, Michigan

The old nun sat in her wheelchair by the west window of the Holy Cross Retirement Home, warming her upturned face on late afternoon rays of sun which streamed through the window. Her gnarled hands constantly worked across the beads of her rosary, counting, as she whispered her prayers.

It was taking her longer to die than she had counted on. She had been ready now for over a year, as her sight failed and she could no longer stand without help. But God had not called her home. Once in a while she groused at Him a little for letting her stay here, suffering. She wanted it over. She was ready to meet the Maker she had devoted her life to serving.

Sometimes she worried that maybe God was forcing her to stay—sort of a penance for sins of the past. For she had surely sinned. There was no denying that. She had lied. She had falsified records. And she had taken it upon herself to personally orchestrate a little girl's life.

At the time it had seemed such a tiny sin—a sin which wouldn't hurt anyone, and would only bring happiness to two people she loved. But the lie kept escalating until she had found herself lying to the bishop himself.

No. That had happened years ago. Surely God had forgiven her by now. Still, it worried her that perhaps He wanted her to atone for her sins. Perhaps He felt the girl had a right to know about her past. Could that be what was holding up God's calling her home?

Sister Mary Elizabeth's sightless eyes closed as tears started forming rivulets down the deep furrows of her wrinkled cheeks. "Sweet Jesus, I never meant any harm," she whispered.

Chapter
Eleven

Slowly, Amy regained consciousness. She was aware of a hot, bitter taste in her mouth, and a tingling in her limbs. She had to have water soon. She tried to swallow but her swollen throat wouldn't cooperate. She sucked on her cheeks and ran her tongue around her mouth to try to generate enough saliva to swallow.

She wasn't going to make it. She was going to die in this cement prison, and no one would ever know what had happened to her. Not for years and years. Not until some farmer stumbled across this horrid room, or an earthquake broke it open, and her bones tumbled out.

"No!" Amy spoke aloud in a ragged whisper. "No. The man didn't come back like he said he was going to do. Maybe he was captured. Maybe the police will start checking on all of his properties and find me. Or maybe he will tell them where I am.

"Yes! That's it! They are probably searching for me now." She crawled over under the pipe. "Help! Help! I'm down here!" But the sound coming from her throat was only a hoarse whisper.

Her energy spent, Amy fell back to the floor. Oh, God, why had she ever talked with him that day? Her father had warned her about that very thing. *You know, Amy, people are different in a large city. You've led a pretty protected life. Don't go trusting everyone you meet in Kansas City, like you do here.* Why hadn't she listened to him?

He had sat down next to her at the lunch counter, then commented on the ivory cross she always wore around her neck. At the time she hadn't thought it odd that he had asked what church she went to, and had somehow elicited the fact that she attended services on Wednesday night. He just seemed like a nice man. She hadn't even questioned it when he asked if that was the Methodist church on Central. *Why had she been so stupid?* And why had she given him her first name when he left? He had stood and extended his hand, saying, "I'm Clarence. It has been nice talking to you . . ." He had left the sentence hanging, looking at her with raised eyebrows, and without a second thought she had answered, "Amy."

Amy felt her throat tighten as she remembered leaving the church that Wednesday evening. God, she had made it so easy for him! She had slipped out early, before the closing song, because Terry, a young man who worked in her department, had said he would call and she hadn't wanted to miss him. When the man called out her name, she assumed it was someone she knew, perhaps even Terry. She had walked over to the van without a care. Then, so quickly she hadn't had time to react, the side door had slid open and she was yanked inside, a foul smelling rag forced over her face, then oblivion.

She had come to in this death trap, with the man standing over her. There was tape covering her mouth, but her hands and feet were free. She had reached up to remove the tape, but he had stopped her. "No. You will leave the tape on until I go." He had leaned down, brushing her hair from her face. "And when I return, you and I are going to have a little fun." He had laughed, grabbing his crotch. "At least *I* will have fun!" He had then used the long knife he was carrying, running it down her arm, drawing blood. "And then, Amy, sweet Amy, I'm going to cut you into a thousand little pieces! Maybe you will die with the twentieth cut, or the fiftieth. But I can promise you this. You won't die with the first. You will be screaming in pain before I let you die, my *sweet* Amy." This time when he said the word *sweet,* it was dripping with venom.

He had then leaned down and pulled the tape from her mouth. Surprisingly, it hadn't hurt. "I covered the tape with Vaseline," he explained. "I want you picture perfect when I return!"

He had then reached up, grabbed the sides of the cement box, and hoisted himself out. She had sprung to her feet, but he had ordered her to lie back down. *Or I will do you now, sweet Amy!* She had obeyed and watched in horror as a wooden lid was placed over the opening. When she heard shovelfuls of dirt being scooped on top, she screamed in terror. Then his voice seemed to boom at her, and she noticed the small, round pipe which was inserted in the lid. "It will do you no good to scream, Amy. We are miles and miles from civilization." He had laughed again, a deep, chilling laugh, and Amy had held her hands over her mouth to keep from screaming again. "I'll be back in a day or so, Amy. Sweet Amy!"

It had seemed to Amy that she could hear the thuds of the dirt hitting the lid for a long, long time. Yet when she became aware that the noise had stopped, she was still too terrified to move.

Finally, Amy felt confident that he had left and she began moving around her prison. When she stood, her head just missed hitting the lid the man had put in place. At least that was one thing, she could walk about without hunching over. The room itself was about the size of a small walk-in closet, about four feet wide, and six feet long. It was made of cement, everything but the lid. For the first several days, she had pushed against the ceiling, trying to loosen it, to no avail. Then, as hunger and thirst caught up with her, she had stopped trying. She knew it was hopeless, anyway.

Her one source of comfort was the light. For some reason, the man had installed a small, dime-store lamp for her to see by. Amy often stared at the naked bulb for hours on end, willing it not to burn out. It was the only thing between her and insanity. The cord leading from the light disappeared into the cement wall, just inches below the top. She knew this meant there was a source for the electricity nearby. A farmhouse perhaps? The man had gone to a lot of trouble to provide her with electricity.

He had also "papered" her prison with posters. They were bolted into the walls, acting as a sponge to catch any moisture which might seep through the walls. They were stained and faded, suggesting they had been in place for some time. Amy had no idea what the original purpose of her prison had been.

The one thing she did know was that the man who left her here was the Kansas City Butcher. That much she had figured out. How many other young girls had been forced to await their destiny in this dungeon?

When things got really bad, as they were now, she almost wished he would return. At least then she would have a fighting chance. As soon as that thought would cross her mind, she would remember the knife trailing down her arm, breaking the skin, and his promise that her death would be painful. And how could she fight him if he did return? She was so weak by now, that she could no longer even stand for more than a few seconds. She had to have water, and soon.

"Oh, God," Amy whispered hoarsely, as she lay beneath the pipe. "Please, God. Let it rain. I'm so thirsty. So very, very thirsty."

The knock on her door startled Suzanne. She exchanged a questioning glance with Jessie, shrugging her shoulders. "Who is it?" she called through the door.

"Detective McDermott," Harry answered. "I need to talk to you about something."

Suzanne put her eye to the peep hole on the door. "Oh, no!" she whispered to Jessie. "It's that officer from the police station. What are we going to do?"

"How did he find us?"

"I don't know. No one followed us. I'm sure of it. And

anyway, he would have been here long before now if that's the case.''

There was another knock on the door. "Miss Richards, please. All I want to do is talk to you. That's all. Won't you open the door?"

"I think we should let him in," Jessie whispered. "Maybe he can tell us some more about Clark."

"Yeah, or maybe he'll haul me right off to jail!" Suzanne whispered back.

"If that's what he came for, it won't stop him just because you won't answer the door, will it?"

Suzanne's shoulders slumped as she recognized the wisdom of Jessie's remark. "You're right, of course. Just remember, that whole nun bit was *your* idea. Be sure to visit me in jail. Okay?"

She opened the door, trying to put an annoyed look on her face. "Yes? What is it?"

"Miss Richards? Suzanne Richards?"

"Yes. How can I help you, officer?"

Harry couldn't help the grin which spread across his face. "Well, for openers, you can tell me what you were doing at the police station this morning posing as a nun."

Suzanne tried to brazen it out. Her large brown eyes snapped as she lied. "I don't have any idea what you are talking about. Jessie and I have been right here all day." She turned to the girl. "Haven't we, Jessie?"

Jessie nodded her head up and down, vigorously. "Yes. All day!"

Harry looked at the younger girl. A sister, maybe, or a neighbor. He didn't think she could be Suzanne's daughter. "And who are you, young lady?"

"My name's Jessie Matthews. What's yours?"

"I'm Detective McDermott, Jessie." He held out his hand. "I'm happy to meet you."

"Officer, you've obviously made a mistake," Suzanne said. "And I'm going to have to ask you to leave."

Harry stepped into the apartment. "And I'm going to have to ask you what your connection is to Randal Clark.

And please don't insult me by saying you don't know who he is. I ran a trace on your phone call to the station inquiring about his whereabouts. I also have a tape of your voice asking Clark the whereabouts of Amy Matthews.''

Harry suddenly stopped talking and looked over at Jessie. ''What did you say your last name was?''

Jessie's face reddened until it visibly matched her hair. ''I . . . uh . . . Matthews, sir. I'm Amy's sister, and I'm here to find her. We didn't do anything wrong, honest we didn't.''

Suzanne's frustration suddenly boiled over. ''*How could you let Clark go?* That's what I can't understand. After what he did to those poor girls, how could you do that?''

''Wait a minute here,'' Harry interrupted. ''Just what is your connection to Clark? And why did he react like he did? We couldn't quite make out everything you said, but whatever it was, it certainly set him off.''

Before she could answer, Harry unhooked the two-way radio from his belt. ''Jim, come on around. They aren't going anywhere.''

Suzanne studied the tall, handsome detective as he spoke. She knew there was no use lying to him. He would know who she was as soon as he ran a background on her. She might just as well deal with it now, and get it over.

''Detective, do you remember the Baxter Underwood case in Omaha?''

Harry nodded, puzzled. ''You mean that serial killer who got off because of some psychic, and then promptly killed two more little girls?''

Suzanne felt the old familiar knot in her stomach at his words. Would it ever leave?

''I'm the psychic who was involved.''

''Oh, Christ!'' Harry exploded. ''Why, after all that happened in Omaha, would you see Clark? Didn't it occur to you that he might use the same defense as Underwood? That all of our hard work might go down the drain and he would be back on the streets?''

''He's back on the streets, anyway!'' Suzanne snapped.

"And we have reason to believe Amy Matthews is still alive, but we don't know where to begin looking."

Harry looked at the tall, attractive brunette with disdain. "Now let me guess. You looked into your little crystal ball and saw Amy Matthews, so you contacted her parents and offered your services. How much is it going to cost them?" He turned to Jessie. "Will your father still have a dairy farm when this fortune-teller gets done with him?"

Suzanne's face flushed with anger. She reached over, placing her hand on the detective's arm. She would show this jerk a thing or two!

Harry looked down. "What are you doing? Trying to impress me with your wonderful power? Please! Spare me!"

Suzanne dropped her hand. She had felt absolutely nothing. No images had flashed into her mind.

"Shake his hand, Suzanne," Jessie said, understanding what was transpiring. "He'll have to believe you then."

Harry snorted but extended his hand. Suzanne clenched it in her own. Again nothing happened. Sometimes, for reasons Suzanne had never determined, the bond just wasn't there, and she could not get a reading. It just happened. Infrequently, but it happened. It had been that way with her father, although Suzanne always figured the element working there was fear. Her own. At least the bond had nothing to do with how receptive the other party was to her abilities. She cursed her misfortune. For some reason, she wanted to prove her worth to the cocky detective.

There was a light rap at the door. Harry dropped Suzanne's hand and moved to open it. He introduced Suzanne and Jessie to his partner.

"There's nothing here, Jim. Miss Richards is a psychic of some sort, hired by the Matthews family to find their daughter, Amy."

"I was not *hired* by anyone, Detective McDermott," Suzanne responded angrily.

"It was me!" Jessie interrupted. "I came on the bus from Pueblo last night to find Suz—Miss Richards. My parents didn't know anything about it until we called them. And no one is paying Suzanne *anything!* And why haven't you found my sister?'' Jessie's face contorted as she tried to fight back a torrent of tears. ''She's been gone for almost two weeks! Why haven't you been able to find where Clark is keeping her? And why, oh *why*, did you let him go?'' Jessie dissolved into tears.

''Whoa, there, little darlin'.'' Jim walked over and hugged the girl to him. ''We're doing everything we possibly can to find your sister.''

Suzanne moved to the other side of Jessie, embracing her, also. ''I'm certain these detectives are doing everything they can. We'll find her, sweetie.''

''And we have a tail on Clark,'' Harry added. ''He can't go anywhere without our men knowing about it. If your sister is alive . . .'' his voice trailed off. ''I mean—''

''I *know* what you meant!'' Jessie said. ''But there isn't any *if* about it. I know Amy is still alive. She's somewhere where there are monkeys with umbrellas. And don't you dare tell me I'm crazy! I know it! I saw it!''

The look on Harry's face changed from concern to interest. ''What did you say? About the monkeys?''

Suzanne noticed the sudden change and glanced at the detective. She had expected derisiveness, not interest.

Jim's arm was still around Jessie's shoulders, and he turned her to face him. ''What about the monkeys, darlin'? Where did you see your sister with the monkeys?''

Jessie dropped her eyes. ''You won't believe me. That man''—she pointed to Harry—''that man made fun of Suzanne because she said she was a psychic. Well, he can just make fun of me, too, then, because *that's* how I saw Amy.''

''Just a minute,'' Suzanne interrupted. ''That part about the monkeys means something to you, doesn't it? There is some connection to Clark, isn't there?''

The two detectives exchanged glances, then Harry spoke. ''Randal Clark is an electrician. A pretty good one, we're told. He works for a carnival part of each year.

When we were doing background on him, we went to the carnival. One of their attractions is a group of trained monkeys who do a 'high-wire' act on sawhorses, using umbrellas to balance themselves. How could she know that?''

"She *told* you how, Detective!" Suzanne said. "She is a psychic, just like me! Well, not *just* like me. I usually have to touch the person before I can get a reading, Jessie doesn't.''

Harry looked at the gorgeous young woman. *Dammit, why did all the knockouts have to turn out to be kooks?*

Suzanne realized the detective still wasn't buying their story. She reached over and placed her hand on Detective Stahl's arm. Scenes started flashing into her mind immediately. Keeping her hand on his arm, she began speaking.

"Detective, your wife's name is Ruth. You have two sons, who have given you five grandchildren. Oh, and you have one more on the way. Let's see, you used to live in Chicago and you know a man named Willie. Willie Rodriquez. He is helping you on this case, somehow.'' Suzanne glanced at Detective McDermott and was pleased to see she now had his undivided attention.

"Your favorite food is chili, but the doctors have told you to quit eating it. Sometimes you sneak off to a restaurant called Manny's and eat it, anyway. Oh, and you have a dog named Carrot—a dachshund. You are worried about having to put him to sleep because he is almost seventeen years old.'' Suzanne held up her arms in question. "Well, do I need to go on?''

Jim stepped away from Suzanne. "No. You've made a believer out of me.''

"I don't understand,'' Harry said. "Do you mean to tell me that simply by touching a person, that person's life unfolds in your mind? Every aspect of his life?''

Suzanne shook her head. "No. Only those parts of the life which hold some meaning, or have been on a person's mind at some point.''

"Does this happen every time you touch someone?''

Jim asked. "Like at the grocery store or when you're on a date?"

Inexplicably, quick, hot tears filled Suzanne's eyes. She nodded in answer to the detective's question, not trusting herself to speak.

"But you couldn't read me, right?" Harry asked. "So it doesn't happen with everybody?"

Suzanne swallowed hard, trying to keep a tremble out of her voice when she answered. "*Almost* everyone, Detective. There have only been a few times in my life when the scenes didn't come, whether I wanted them to or not. I could never do a reading on my father. Of course the fact that I was terrified of him could account for that. Aside from him though, there have only been three or four times in my life when I have been unable to get a reading."

"Doesn't it drive you nuts?" Jim asked.

"Sort of. But I can control it by simply not touching anyone. Other psychics get bombarded by images when they are at home alone, or just walking down a street. At least I don't have that to contend with."

"Yeah," Jim said, understanding her problem perfectly, "but I doubt there are many psychics out there with your degree of talent."

"She was the psychic involved in the Underwood killings," Harry said. "You remember, those serial killings in Omaha where the guy got off because his lawyers said the psychic had made him testify against himself, or some such rot? Then the minute he was released he killed two more little girls."

Jessie, who had been standing silent, taking it all in, responded to Harry. "Yeah, and if Suzanne hadn't been there when they stopped the guy for running a red light, he might have killed a dozen more girls before he was stopped. Doesn't anyone ever think about *that?*"

Harry was beginning to feel like a world-class heel. "I'm sorry," he said to Suzanne. "I've just never believed in any of this psychic stuff. It's a little hard for me to realize I might have been wrong."

"I know. That's what the detectives in Omaha said until they saw me work, which, by the way, I don't do anymore. I only agreed to help the Matthews family because this young lady"—she nodded toward Jessie—"nagged me into it."

Harry knew he shouldn't ask his next question because of future court action, but he asked it anyway. "So what did you find out from Clark?"

Suzanne shrugged. "He's your man. No question about it. But I didn't get very far. All at once it was like a brick wall had been thrown up and I couldn't get beyond it. When I asked about Amy, I started to get a vision. I saw her lying down, with Clark standing over her, shoveling dirt. But then an extreme terror came over me and somehow it was me in the vision, me who Clark was standing over. Yet, strangely, I don't believe it was Clark who frightened me."

Harry's eyebrows shot up, as once again skepticism set in.

"You said there was no question he was our man. How were you able to determine that?" Jim asked.

"I saw the other girls. I saw their faces. I saw them being hacked apart, and Clark was the one doing it. There is not a doubt in my mind that he is the Kansas City Butcher. None!"

Jim and Harry exchanged glances, then Harry spoke. "That's what we think, too. By the way, there isn't any way Clark could know who you are, is there?"

Suzanne shook her head confidently. "No. Absolutely not. I certainly never gave him my name, and I have kept a pretty low profile since moving to Kansas City. I only know a handful of people, and none of them knows anything at all about my psychic work, thank God."

"Good," Jim said. "At least that's one thing we won't have to worry about."

The two men sat in a worn, plastic-covered booth far to the back of Rocky's Bar & Grill. "I don't have much time, you stupid bastard!'' Randal Clark said. ''I gave the police the slip about twenty minutes ago, but they'll find me before long. What the hell were you thinking of, raping that girl? You were supposed to stay with the game plan. The same MO, remember? You could have screwed the whole deal.''

''What are you so friggin' nervous about? You're here, ain't you?'' Floyd answered. ''I must have done somethin' right.''

''Well, never mind. We have more trouble than that to deal with. Some woman came to visit me in jail. She was dressed up like a nun, but she was definitely no nun. I think she was one of those *seers* or something. You know—a mind reader, or psychic. She kept putting her hands on me, then she'd sort of go into a damned trance or something. Scared the shit out of me, I'll tell you.''

Floyd felt the blood drain from his face as he set his glass of beer down on the table to keep from spilling it. ''A psychic? How old? What did she look like?''

''You're thinking . . . ?''

''Maybe. I don't know. Last I knew, she was in Omaha, helping the police.''

''Well, we have to find out, man! She asked me specifically about Amy Matthews. And you know where she is. Don't forget the property is in your name. If anybody finds her, it leads right back to you, my friend.''

''I should have killed that bitch when I had the chance!'' Floyd said.

Randal Clark managed a grin as he stared across the table, speaking to Floyd with forced friendliness. ''But just think how much more enjoyable it will be now, man! Hell, we might even do a *butcher* number on her if she gives us too much trouble!''

Chapter
Twelve

Randal Clark sat puzzling over his best plan long after Floyd had left. He had picked up his tail again, spotting the cop almost as soon as the man had entered the bar. He'd wait awhile, then go up and offer to buy him a drink. Lousy cops. Most of them couldn't find their ass with their hands, but they sure as hell pranced around like they owned the sun and the moon. He hadn't even made it difficult for them to find him. He had parked his car right out front. They sure couldn't say he was trying to elude them. He decided to stay right where he was while he contemplated what to do about Floyd. That was his number one problem right now.

The biggest worry with Floyd was that he simply wasn't the brightest guy on the block. If the chips were down, would Floyd just cut a deal and throw him to the wolves? Of course he would. In a friggin' New York minute. Even though Floyd had an alibi for some of the murders that he, himself, committed, would he be able to withstand cross-examination while they were confirming this? Doubtful. Floyd, when you got right down to it, was a coward. Sure he killed once in a while, but never where there was much chance at detection. Hell, he probably shit his drawers over doing that little favor for Randal!

He had to admit, though, that it had been a lucky day for him when he teamed up with Floyd, ten years ago. They had made a pact. If either one of them ever really got in trouble, the other would commit a crime, using his MO. Randal had known when they shook hands on it that he would be the only one to ever need that insurance. His killings were signature killings. There were plenty of little details that were only his handiwork. It would be easy for someone to copy his killings, given the information.

Floyd was another story altogether. He killed at random, whenever it profited him to do so. And his deaths were almost always people that society would never miss. If he killed a widow for her money, you could bet your sweet ass she wasn't the cream of the crop. Floyd would kill for a thousand dollars. Hell, once he had killed some guy whose car had broken down on the interstate for fifteen dollars in cash and six lottery tickets. So how he thought he was getting a good bargain in their little deal, Randal never knew. There was no way in hell Randal could duplicate one of Floyd's murders. There wasn't anything similar about them. But then Floyd wasn't exactly the brainy type. Not like him. Except perhaps on one score. He didn't know Floyd's real name. The guy had used at least a dozen different ones since he had known him.

Maybe he should just get rid of the bastard. Perhaps set him up to take the fall for a butcher killing, but then make certain he didn't leave alive. Hell, maybe he could even set the scene to make it look like Floyd took his own life. But then what would happen if it turned out that Floyd was in jail or something on one of the nights the butcher killed? No. He needed to take it easy, not go off half-cocked. Good planning was essential. Not that he was any too worried about the police figuring out jack!

Randal eyed the cop at the bar in disgust. If it weren't for the pressure he knew would be put on, he would let the butcher start wasting some of the city's finest—those men in blue who were supposed to watch out for the weak and defenseless! Shit. They couldn't even protect a little seven-year-old kid—and didn't have enough brains to know when they were being had!

*   *   *

When he awoke, the pain was almost more than he could bear. His jaw was wired, and his eyes mere slits in his head. His father! Oh, God, what had happened to his father?

He saw her hand sliding across the white blanket toward him, and shrank back, trying to make himself invisible.

"Don't be frightened, dear. I'm right here. You are going to be fine. Your father won't be beating you anymore. May God forgive me, but I shot him—to protect you. You don't have anything to worry about anymore.

Randal squeezed his swollen eyes shut to hold the tears back. His mother didn't like tears—said they were a sign of weakness, and she would not have that in a son of hers.

"Oh, my poor, poor baby. Go ahead and cry if you want to. I'm so sorry you had to go through all of this. So sorry. I should have protected you better. I should have known what was going on."

Slowly, through the haze of pain and medication, Randal realized there had to be someone else in the room. That was his mother's public voice—the one she always let the world hear. He turned his head toward the police officer standing on the other side of his bed. He remembered the moment his dad had come home early from work and saw what his wife was doing. He remembered the shock on his face when the shotgun blew him back against the wall. He had to tell—for his dad and for his little brother. He looked up at the officer and spoke through clenched teeth quickly, before his nerve left him. "My mother. She did it!" The officer looked down at him, then patted the bedcovers near his arm. "Now don't you worry, son. We aren't going to press charges against your sweet momma. She was just doing what she needed to do to protect you and your brother. You can rest easy, now. You'll be going home with your momma just as soon as you are well."

Randal could feel hard pressure on his wrist, as his mother lay across the bed, her blond hair spilling across *his chest and her body covering the death grip she had on him. The sound of her loud sobbing drowned out the words he was whispering. He looked up at the officer who was now gently patting his mother's back, consoling her. At that moment, Randal hated him, almost as much as he hated his mother.*

Randal's hand tightened around the shot glass as he remembered the cruelty he had had to endure for eight more years. Leonard, his frail, sickly younger brother could not tolerate their mother's deadly blows, so Randal quickly learned to divert all of her anger onto himself to spare the boy. When he was nine, his mother's punishment for "touching himself" had been swift and savage. He could still remember the look on her face as she ripped the lamp cord from the socket, then cut the cord and plugged it back in. Had he known what would happen, he would have fought her, would have run. But he figured she was only going to beat him with the cord. Right up to the minute she touched the hot cord to his penis, he hadn't realized what was happening.

Later, when he was older and starting to get interested in girls, he discovered his body wouldn't respond in the way it should. His first attempt had been with a bright-eyed girl from the church who laughed at him, then ended up taunting him for his inaction. "Look at you, Randal. You're all shriveled up. What's the matter with you anyhow? Don't keep pushing yourself on me like that. Jesus, you're a weirdo!"

He had gone home and killed his mother. The bitch. He had waited for her to return home from Mass, then held her hair tight as he forced her to put on layer upon layer of makeup. He had slammed her face into the mirror. "There, you whore. Now you look the part. Don't go trying to make everyone believe what a good saint of a person you are." She had begged for her life then, telling him how much she loved him and his brother. He had laughed the entire time it took him to hack her body into pieces.

It had taken him almost a week to dispose of her body.

When he completed his task, his mother was scattered over the state of Idaho. Her head was buried at Horseshoe Bend, her legs near Mountain Home and Twin Falls. The arms, which had caused him so much grief, he buried together on Snake River Plain, figuring the name said it all.

He washed the kitchen down with a solution of water and bleach. Then, not satisfied that he had removed all traces of his mother's blood, he tore up the tile covering the floor and replaced it himself, using his mother's credit card to pay for the flooring.

He told the neighbors his mother had remarried and moved to Alaska, leaving him to care for the sickly Leonard who would not fare well in the cold, harsh, Alaskan climate. No one questioned her disappearance. By the time the credit card payment was due, he had found work at Wally's Electric and had a weekly check coming in. He opened a bank account, found out how much he would need to save for real estate taxes on the house, and figured he was going to become a solid citizen. He thought so right up until the time he killed Mary Beth Williams.

Chapter
Thirteen

And this just in from Doppler weather. Sit back. Fasten your seat belts, K.C. This unseasonable hot spell we have been experiencing is going to be broken with another humdinger of a spring storm. Look for torrential rains, severe lightning, and possible flooding. Should be moving into the area by tomorrow night, so stay tuned, folks. It looks like we have a rough one coming!

Jim Stahl leaned over and flipped the air conditioner button in Harry's Crown Victoria to high, wiping sweat from his bald head with a McDonald's paper napkin. "Sure couldn't tell by this heat that we have a cold front moving in," he grumbled. "If it's this hot in May, what the hell are we going to do in August?"

"What do you mean *we*, asshole?" Harry said. "In August you'll be lying around in your underwear in air conditioned comfort watching reruns of John Wayne movies."

Jim stretched out his arms, then locked his fingers behind his head lazily. "I know. Ain't it wonderful! Ain't it just purely wonderful?"

"Well," Harry answered the question with one of his own. "What did you think?"

"About what?"

"About our little defrocked nun? Was that a great parlor trick or what?"

Jim heaved a long sigh. "Yeah, Harry. She and I

worked that up just before she let you in. Pretty good, huh?''

"You're turning into a sarcastic SOB in your old age, aren't you?'' Harry asked. "It's going to be nice to break in a new partner who has a little respect."

"I have as little as most.'' Jim chuckled, thinking that both he and Harry were going to miss each other more than either one could possibly know. "As to Miss Richards, she has to be the real McCoy. I've worked with a few psychics over the years, even a couple who actually were on the level, but I've never run across any that could do what she did.''

"I've requested a background check on her, which I sort of regret doing. I would hate for Clark to be released on the same line of reasoning that set Underwood free.''

"Well, it's too late. If we called off an investigation now, sure as hell if we ever *do* get Clark in court, her name would surface and his lawyers would scream 'cover-up.' ''

"Which is exactly what we would be doing.''

"Right.''

"Speaking of Clark, what time were we supposed to meet Caswell for the press release?''

Jim glanced down at his twenty-dollar Timex—a Christmas gift from his six-year-old grandson. "About five minutes ago, I'm afraid.''

"Shit.''

"Right.''

Tears once again welled in Jessie's eyes. "But what if the police lose track of him? What if he gets away and goes wherever he has Amy?''

Suzanne didn't have a good answer to the young girl's question. The light bantering that had been taking place all day between the twenty-seven-year-old and the fourteen-year-old, had vanished. The sense of urgency had magnified with the release of Clark, and the visions of his thoughts, which had been picked up by Jessie and transferred to Suzanne. Both were painfully aware that time was running out.

"We just can't afford to worry about what *might* happen," Suzanne said. "Right now all we can do is trust that the police will keep him under surveillance, and give us time to do *our* job."

"Which is?"

"To find Amy. And maybe to find Amy, I need to try and touch Clark again. I don't know what happened at the police station. Something interfered. Some block was thrown up in my mind. I couldn't get beyond it. But maybe if I try again, I can force myself past the fear."

Jessie shook her head, bewildered. "But how are you going to be able to do that? We don't have any idea where Clark is, and besides, he knows your face now."

"Maybe not. When I'm out of the nun disguise, maybe he wouldn't pay any attention to me. Also, I have another plan. That detective said Harry worked at a carnival. If we could find out which one, maybe we would get lucky and pick up some sort of reading. We know you saw the monkeys in your vision. Amy either was looking at the monkeys, or possibly looking at pictures of them. In either case, we might learn something by visiting the carnival."

"That's a great idea." Jessie jumped to her feet. "How do we find out which carnival it was and where it is now?"

"Newspapers maybe?" Suzanne asked it as a question. "Perhaps at the library? It also probably wouldn't hurt to read everything the *Star* has to say about Clark. We might pick up an idea there."

"I was at our library reading about Clark when I got the idea to contact you," Jessie said. "Somehow I just knew you would be the one to help me."

"You never did say how you managed to find me."

"I called the newspaper in Omaha. I told them I worked for Marilyn Mars—the lady who wrote that book, *Amazing Psychics*. I said she was looking for you and wanted to know if they had a phone number or address. Some reporter came on and questioned me a little, but luckily, I remembered her book pretty well and just spouted enough about it to make me believable.'' Jessie gave a little giggle. ''Actually, I told him Ms. Mars would mention his name in her new book—thank him for his cooperation, that sort of thing.''

''And he had this address? In Kansas City?''

''Oh, yeah. He said he wrote to you every once in a while, but kept getting his letters back. He wanted me to put in a good word for him, if I ever got to meet you.''

''That's weird. The *Omaha Herald* practically hung me out to dry. I figured the only reason they would be contacting me was to rub my face in all of it again.''

Jessie shrugged. ''I dunno. This guy sounded nice and like he really was interested in you. But maybe it was all an act. Anyway, he gave me your address and said for me to tell you he was sorry for everything you went through. He said he had some clippings he wanted to show you, but you always refused the letters.''

''Yeah. Probably some group wasn't satisfied with merely running me out of town—they wanted me tarred and feathered to boot!''

''Maybe you just needed someone on your side. In *our* family we call it *circling the wagons* when someone gets in trouble. My mom has five sisters, and they have families, and my dad has six brothers and three sisters. When we all get together it is a madhouse. If anyone picked on *me* in the newspaper, my whole family would probably stage a sit-in or something!''

''It sounds absolutely wonderful, Jessie. Now that Miss Emily has died, except for Sister Mary Elizabeth, I don't have any family at all.'' Long-forgotten memories flitted across Suzanne's mind. She had a family, once. Had it been her fault they were now all dead? Had she in some way caused their deaths?

Caswell sat at a long table littered with microphones and looked over the sea of reporters in front of him. He knew all hell was going to break loose when he told them Clark had been released. He recognized most of the faces, but there were a few new ones—most likely national news agencies had sent in their own people. McDermott and Stahl were late as usual, but he was not going to do this release without them. They were his lead detectives on the case, and he'd be damned if he was going to have to field all the questions himself. He glanced at his watch. Shit. He'd *have* to start in a few minutes. Sonofabitch!

As if on cue, Harry McDermott suddenly entered the room, followed by Jim Stahl. Both men picked their way through the swarm of reporters, brushing off questions as they made their way to the front.

Chief Caswell closed his hand over the nearest microphone, whispering harshly, "Damn nice of you to make it, boys!"

Harry leaned over and spoke quietly. "Chief, don't go too far out on a limb saying Clark can't be the killer. We just got information that points pretty strongly to him."

Caswell's face reddened. "What the shit are you talking about?" he whispered furiously. "I've already written my press release saying that since he was in jail at the time of this new killing, that pretty much clears him."

The older detective leaned down close to Caswell's face. "Harry's right, Chief. If there is some way to explain his release without actually saying he is innocent, it will save your face on down the line."

Caswell looked at the front row of reporters, who were all straining to hear the exchange among the three men. He smiled lazily, reassuring them he was just exchanging pleasantries with his two lead detectives. His smile stayed in place as he looked at Harry. "What new information are we talking about here?"

Before Harry could answer, a small woman with enormous black-framed glasses and a harried, no-nonsense look on her face, approached the table. "Chief Caswell, our station left a slot for this on the seven o'clock news. We're late already. How much longer before we can go live?"

Caswell took his large hand from the microphone he was holding, pulling it toward him. He nodded for Jim and Harry to each grab a mike, then mouthed okay to the woman, giving her enough time to start the cameras. "I have a short announcement to make concerning Randal Clark. At four o'clock this afternoon, Mr. Clark was released from custody. We no longer believe..." He glanced over at his two detectives. "Uh . . . we no longer were able to hold Mr. Clark on murder charges."

As Caswell expected, the room erupted. Shocked, angry voices yelled questions. "*Released* him? How could you have released him? Are you nuts? Do you have another suspect?" Finally the room quieted down. Caswell looked at Arnie from the *Star,* who was holding a yellow pencil in the air, waiting to be heard.

"Yeah, Arnie?"

"Does this have anything to do with the death of Sandra Murphy? Was she another butcher killing? We heard rumors both ways."

Caswell looked over at Harry, who took over, smoothly. "Now, Arnie, you know we can't give you that kind of information. In the first place, we are still checking all the evidence, and in the—"

"Come on, Harry," Arnie interrupted. "Was Sandra Murphy chopped up like the other girls, or not? *My* informants tell me Sandra's body was found exactly as all the other girls. And now you're telling us Clark has been released? It looks to me like you jumped in too fast accusing Clark of being the butcher."

"Yeah," another voice from the back of the room yelled. "And what about the body parts that were supposedly found at Clark's apartment? His lawyer has always said they were planted. Could it be he was right? You sure as hell wouldn't release someone who had body parts strung all over, would you?"

Caswell grabbed his microphone angrily. "We, the police, have never claimed we found body parts at Clark's apartment. That was leaked to the press two weeks ago, before any analysis of the evidence had been done.''

"What analysis do you need, Chief?" a voice yelled.
"A finger is a finger; a toe, a toe. Heck, I bet I could tell
you what they were without any *analysis*.''

"You didn't deny it, Chief!" another voice yelled. "In
two full weeks you didn't deny it!"

Harry spoke up. "And we aren't denying it now. Chief
Caswell said we had to release Clark. He did not say we
felt he was innocent. There's a big difference, my friends.
We have Clark under surveillance at this very minute. If
he so much as spits on the sidewalk, he'll be back in
here.''

"That tears it!" Caswell swore under his breath. "Are
you nuts, McDermott? Are you fucking nuts?"

Harry leaned over and spoke in Caswell's ear. "We
have to leave it like this. We have to keep the city alerted
to Clark. If enough reporters and policemen are watching
him, then maybe we can get the evidence we need before
he kills again. We *have* to play it like this, sir. We *have*
to!''

Caswell angrily pushed away from the table and stood
up. "That's it, folks. We'll keep you informed of any new
developments, but right now we have to get back to
work.'' He turned abruptly and walked rapidly from the
room. The group of reporters exchanged looks of astonishment.

"Aw, hell!" Jim said to Harry. "I knew it was too good
to be true. Only two months till retirement and you've
probably just gotten my ass fired!"

Harry raised his eyebrows at his partner. "If you think
he's mad now, wait until he discovers our new information
came from a psychic!"

Jim groaned. "I'll flip you to see who tells him."

"I found it!" Jessie yelled over to Suzanne, then remembering where she was, she clamped her hand over her
mouth. No one in the library paid any attention to her.
Suzanne left her screen and crossed over to Jessie's.

"There it is!" Jessie whispered excitedly. "The Fife and Drum Carnival." They had scanned twelve back issues of the *Star* before finding an article which mentioned the name of the carnival where Clark had worked. Then it was a matter of scanning through the ads, hoping to find the carnival playing in the area.

"It's in Bonner Springs this week." Suzanne couldn't believe their luck. "We can be there in less than an hour."

Jessie was silent for a few miles as they drove west.

"Something on your mind, sweetie?" Suzanne asked.

"Yes. I was just thinking about you. How come you have to touch people before you can pick up anything? Was it always that way for you?"

"Yes. Pretty much."

"Do you know what caused you to be psychic? My mom told me sometimes it runs in families and that she had a niece once who might have been 'that way.' Mom said she never really believed it, though, until *I* came along."

"I don't know if others in my family had the sight as well, which sometimes happens. My only way of knowing anything about when I was a child is from my own memory, or what my father told me. But he died when I was eight years old, and actually, he didn't talk to me much. So I really know very little about my early background."

"You don't remember your mother?"

Suzanne tried to bring forward in her mind a picture of her mother, but she could not do it. Only a feeling emerged, a feeling of warmth and safety. "No," she said to Jessie. "I was five or six when my mother was killed in an automobile accident. I should be able to remember her, but I don't. I just know that she was beautiful, but that's all I really know."

"Don't you have any pictures of her?"

"No. When my dad loaded up the truck and left the farm, he left everything behind—pictures, my toys, most of my clothing, even most of his. I probably wouldn't even remember that, except over the months after we left, he kept griping about how much it cost to buy new clothes and furniture." *Do you have any idea how much you are costing me, young lady? I oughta just drop you off along-side the road, that's what I oughta do.*

"That wasn't very nice of him to threaten to leave you by the road. That would be pretty scary for a little kid!"

Suzanne glanced over at her young companion. "Have you noticed how you seem to be able to read my mind just about any time you choose?"

Jessie nodded. "Yeah. It's weird. I've never been able to do it this much with other people. But I can hear you loud and clear, especially if it is a powerful thought."

"I guess that's because I'm psychic, too. The lines are open both ways. It isn't so easy when only one of the people involved has the gift. It comes, but just not as rap-idly or clearly."

A look of despair played across the young girl's fea-tures. "Do you think we will reach Amy in time? I haven't picked up anything for hours now. You don't suppose— you don't think—"

Suzanne closed her eyes, feeling queasy for just a mo-ment. She opened them as she felt the car pulling toward the side of the road. Her right hand reached out in the darkness of the car to find Jessie's. "Sweetie, don't you go getting negative on me at this late date. You've con-vinced me we have at least a shot of finding Amy alive. Let's hold on to that. Okay?"

Jessie took Suzanne's hand and held on to it tightly. Something bad was coming. She had felt it now for the last several moments. Something evil and horrible. And they were driving right into the middle of it.

As the circuit made the connection, Suzanne looked over, her eyes locking fast to Jessie's. *Do we continue?* She didn't say the words aloud, yet wasn't surprised as she watched Jessie slowly nod her head in answer.

Chapter

Fourteen

A vein in Chief Caswell's neck was pulsing as though
it had a life of its own. It reminded Harry of some
movie about aliens he had once seen. He opted not to tell
Caswell this observation, deciding instead to keep his
mouth shut until he found out if he were still on the force,
let alone heading up the butcher investigation.

When Caswell spoke, his voice cracked under the strain
of trying to keep from yelling. "Are you telling me that I
just went on live television and made an absolute jackass
of myself on the information furnished you by a *psychic?*
Have you two lost your minds?"

"Chief," Jim began, "remember the psychic in Omaha
who broke the Underwood case? The one who was actually on the police payroll? That's who this young woman
is."

Caswell sat down on the edge of his desk and pulled a
rumpled package of Camel cigarettes from his shirt pocket.
He carefully straightened out the last bent cigarette and
stuck it in his mouth. His hands shook slightly as he
brought his lighter to his mouth. "So," he said as he lit
the Camel and inhaled deeply, "what you are saying is
that the same person who got Underwood's case thrown
out of court, waltzed in here and took a crack at Clark,
which means if he *is* our killer, then there is a better than
even chance he'll walk. Do I have the facts about right?"
His eyes narrowed as he looked at Harry for confirmation.

"Chief, we would have never let her near Clark if we'd known who she was," Harry answered. "We didn't find that out until a couple of hours ago."

Detective Stahl, who had more police work under his belt than the other two men, spoke swiftly. There was one advantage to being the "Old Pro" of the precinct. Most times you were listened to. "Chief, the point is, this woman sees things the rest of us don't. I can absolutely swear to you she is for real, because she told me things she could not have possibly known from any source. She spent about two minutes with Clark and saw the faces of many of the young girls Clark had murdered. She told us he is definitely the butcher. Now that, along with all the other evidence we have against him, is enough for me. We have to bring him in again. We simply can't run the risk of our men losing him."

Caswell shook his head. "And what about this latest murder? Are you forgetting that almost all of the small details which weren't released to the public were found at this crime scene? This was a butcher killing. If Clark had still been on the streets when this killing transpired, you wouldn't question that it was the same killer. Right? Even Stanley Davis said his findings were consistent with the other murders. When the medical examiner makes a statement like that, are we supposed to ignore it? We still have laws in this country, you know."

"What about the DNA evidence?" Jim asked. "Is it back yet on this latest girl? Do we know whether or not she was smeared with semen from several different men like the others?"

Caswell shook his head. "No. It isn't back yet. I asked for a rush on the sample taken from inside the girl. That's the only part of this latest killing that doesn't follow the pattern. Davis insists the other girls were not really raped, only made to look like it. But this latest victim was raped—and sodomized. So we should be able to get an accurate DNA profile."

"Unless, of course, other semen samples were smeared

around like on all the other victims, and compromise the integrity of the sample," Harry said. This was the area that had been puzzling them for months. Where was the killer coming up with all the different semen samples? Each body they found had semen from four or five different sources smeared on the torso. At last count, they had thirty-two different DNA profiles as evidence. But the public had not gotten wind of this particular quirk of the man the newspapers had dubbed the Kansas City Butcher. And Harry was almost positive the body of this latest victim was covered with several different samples. He had investigated enough of the deaths to recognize the similarities. On all the victims, the torso area was wiped clean, then right above the pubic area were evenly spaced dried splotches of a clear liquid. This latest young girl had looked to him just like all the other victims in that respect.

"You realize what we are saying, don't you?" Jim asked. "We are saying that contrary to all of our evidence, there are *two* men operating as the butcher. And if that's the case, don't you think it would be prudent to at least bring one of them back in while we try to find the other one?"

Caswell rubbed the back of his neck in frustration. He had a lot of respect for Jim Stahl, who, like him, was one of the old-timers on the force. There was only one problem. Most of the old-timers had not yet learned that there was a new age in police work. The public was scrutinizing the actions of their police departments as never before in history. And he supposed rightly so. Maybe in the old days, all that was needed to hold a suspect was a gut feeling by a detective, but that time had long gone. If he tried to hold Clark after another identical killing had taken place during his incarceration, Clark's attorney, the *Star,* and every reporter in town would howl for his head on a platter! No. He had to follow the book on this one. He had already heard the rumblings of a move to oust him as chief and bring in a younger man. He had no intention of handing them the ammunition they needed to fire him. "I can't bring Clark back in, Jim. But I will assign two more units to help keep track of him. That's the best I can do.''

Across town, Randal Clark looked out his living room window at the unmarked police car waiting in front of his apartment. He went into the bathroom and looked down at the alley. There was another car with two men sitting, smoking. That was all right. He needed a little time to put his apartment back in order, anyway. Kansas City's finest had left it a mess when they tossed his place. The furniture and walls were covered with a light film of white powder, and every item in his home was out of place. It looked like a tremor had hit, spilling everything askew. Damned cops. He hated the thought of them going through all of his personal items. Touching everything. Leaving a mess. He would clean things up first, then leave by the window in the boiler room. The Fife and Drum was set up in Bonner Springs for a few days, and he needed to retrieve his box from the cook's freezer. He knew Sam hadn't given it to the police. If he had, Clark knew he would certainly still be behind bars. He had been acquainted with Sam for about twenty years. He was actually the only person Clark had ever considered a friend. He hated the fact that he would have to kill him, but who knew for sure whether or not he had ever looked in Clark's box? No. He couldn't take the chance.

When he had first been called on to do the locks at the Addison-Jones Sperm Bank, he had known he had hit pay dirt. There, he had virtually an endless supply of semen to use at his carefully staged murder scenes. He had even swiped the containers from the bank. They still had the firm's logo imprinted on them, as well as the contents. Sam might have gotten suspicious to find a box containing twenty-five or so samples of semen in his freezer!

Suzanne could feel Jessie's apprehension as the child clutched her hand. Was she doing the right thing? Was she exposing Jessie to danger, bringing her to the carnival where Clark had worked? No. What could that hurt? Clark was under surveillance by the police. He wouldn't be in Bonner Springs at the carnival. There was no reason to be fearful. Yet she was. There was no denying it.

Suzanne took the Bonner Springs exit, and as she came off the ramp, almost immediately saw the sign. She dropped Jessie's hand and pointed out the passenger window as she pulled quickly off the road, hitting the brakes hard. "Jessie! Look! Look at that sign!"

There they were; pictures advertising the carnival. One picture was of monkeys, one of a bearded lady, and one of people riding a roller coaster. "I can't believe it!" Jessie said in awe. "It's just like in my vision. Only they were moving too fast for me to really see what they were. Look!" She pointed to the picture of the roller coaster. "The people have their arms in the air. And it wasn't a hill I saw, but the curving of the ride."

"These are all just advertisements for the carnival! That's what you saw. And we know Clark worked for them. We must be getting closer."

"Come on, let's go." Jessie's voice had lost any sign of the fear Suzanne had detected earlier. "He must have hidden Amy somewhere at the carnival. That has to be it!"

Floyd made himself a pot of coffee, pacing around his small kitchen as he waited for it to finish dripping. Something was eating at Clark. That much he knew. He hadn't spent thirty years of his life hustling people not to know when someone was jiving him.

Outside his tiny apartment on the Kansas side of the Missouri River, he heard a siren blaring and jumped. Damn. His nerves were getting the better of him. He wasn't afraid of many things in this life, but he was afraid of Randal Clark and the hold he now had over him.

Why had he raped that girl? He hadn't planned on doing it, but then she had looked so pretty, so frightened, it had turned him on, and he figured what the hell. He was supposed to make it look like a rape, so why not actually do it? Stupid. Clark was right. It was a stupid thing to have done. He wasn't worried so much about the police unless Clark decided to hand him over to them. And what about the psychic? That worried him as much as Clark. Could she possibly be the same one? If so, then he was in a world of shit! He would have to get to her, before she got to him. There was no phone listed, that much he had found out. At least not under the name he knew her by. And the newspapers knew nothing about her living here. Maybe the nun's habit? Perhaps she had rented it locally. How many costume stores could there be in Kansas City? And what story could he use to get the information?

Harry sat atop Caswell's desk, slapping a red file against his knee, impatiently. He had called the five detectives assigned to him back to the precinct after getting the call from the FBI.

"Okay, okay." Harry held up his hand to silence the small group. "We need to go over everything Mr. Jamieson from the FBI gave us. Let's hit just the highlights of what he had to say when he was here three months ago." He read down the list.

"First, he told us that our killer probably had an injury of some sort that prohibited him from sexual activity. And as you know, Clark has a shriveled penis from an attack on him by his father.

"Second, he told us that our killer was intelligent, but an underachiever, probably not finishing high school, certainly not college, but that he was self-taught in some area where he got along well when he wanted to, and when it was on his own terms. And we know Clark only went to the eleventh grade, but he worked for an electrician and became expert in that field.

"Mr. Jamieson also told us our killer probably drove a later model, dark-colored car which he kept in good running condition, polished, and clean. And Clark, in fact, drove a 1996 navy Ford Taurus, which was in perfect condition. We don't know if this is the vehicle he used to grab any of the girls or not. We have no reports of a car fitting this description at any of the sites where they were abducted.

"And Jamieson also said our killer would have a neat apartment, live alone, not be well known by his neighbors, and would quite possibly have either clothing or some body part from the women he killed. There again, a clean match to Clark."

"If you ask me, we had the right guy all along," Gordon Connors said. "That FBI guy came so close to Clark, it's spooky!"

Harry held up his hand. "But not totally. He said our killer had a deep rage against his mother, not his father. And we have medical records indicating it was the father who abused Clark, not the mother. So Mr. Jamieson was wrong on that score. He also said our killer had had some bad run-ins with the police, and harbored resentment, but Clark has absolutely no police record—not even a parking ticket."

"What does he have to say now that we've released Clark?" Connors asked.

"He thinks we've fucking lost our minds, thank you very much," Harry answered him. "He says Clark fits the personality profile so closely, that this latest murder almost assuredly has to be a copycat."

"So where do we go from here?"

"Back to the beginning. Gordie, I want you to sift through every piece of information we have on Clark, plus, I want all the background information verified. Go back and talk to his teachers, relatives, and neighbors. If he so much as broke a window with a baseball in the third grade, I want to know about it."

Connors nodded.

"And, Howard, I want you to go back through all of our other suspects in this case. We know that at any one time, there are anywhere from forty to fifty serial killers doing their handiwork across the country. They all have their own little idiosyncrasies, their own signature. So review everything we have on the butcher, including the full FBI report, then start looking at the other suspects we had. I want you to look not only at whether you think they might be the butcher, but whether or not they might be a copycat, or connected with Clark some way.''

Detective Kane grinned, scratching his head as if perplexed. ''I see. Our assumption being that we may have two serial killers at work, plus a copycat. Right?''

Harry raised his eyebrows and managed a weak smile. ''Don't be a wiseass, Kane.''

Bruce Langston, the third member of the special unit, spoke up. ''And me?''

''You,'' Harry answered him, ''are going to review every word we have spoken to the press, and go over every officer's record who has had any connection whatsoever to this case, and everyone else who is involved, no matter how little.''

The intake of breath in the small room was audible. He knew what he was suggesting was going to come as a shock to his crew, but something in his gut told him it was necessary. He held his hands up. ''I know. I know. But there are just certain things about this case that don't add up. Why was Clark so confident there wouldn't be a DNA match to him? And why was he so outraged when he heard about the body parts found in his apartment? If there is the slightest chance they were planted, I want to know about it. And don't look so horrified. Clark wouldn't be the first guilty person to be convicted on trumped-up evidence, and you know it. No one screams any louder than a guilty man convicted on evidence he knows he didn't leave at the crime scene!''

Chapter
Fifteen

A man with a lighted baton waved them into the parking grounds. Behind him, Suzanne and Jessie could see an enormous Ferris wheel, with bright lights flashing against a dark sky. To the left, farther down, cars that were filled with screaming people sped over the rails of the roller coaster. A shiver of excitement, mingled with fear, ran down Suzanne's spine, as she listened to the calliope music filling the air. Whatever was in store for them, it was too late to turn back now. The determined look on Jessie's face told her that.

As soon as they exited the car, Jessie began trotting toward the midway. It was all Suzanne could do to keep up with the young girl. "Hey! Don't get too far ahead, Jessie," she called.

Jessie slowed, turning around and walking backward as she talked to Suzanne. "Come on, come on! Amy's here. I just know it!"

Suzanne threw away the cigarette she had just lit and started jogging after Jessie. She caught up to her at the ticket booth, where Jessie had already paid their five dollars and was being issued two tickets. "Jessie! Stay with me when we get inside. We must not take the chance of getting separated!" She firmly clasped Jessie's hand with her own. "This way, if you start picking up anything, I will be able to feel it, also," she explained.

The Fife and Drum Carnival was the largest traveling

carnival Suzanne had ever been to. Its midway was crammed with row after row of games of chance, each with a man or woman yelling out to the people the virtues of their game. Suzanne leaned down to Jessie. "Just follow my lead and don't say anything. Okay?"

A man of about fifty, with a short beard and a scar traveling across the bridge of his nose, finished placing a two-dollar teddy bear in the arms of a little girl whose father had just spent nearly twenty dollars pitching baseballs at stacked milk bottles. He turned to Suzanne and Jessie as they strolled up. "Only fifty cents a try, young ladies. And it doesn't take strength, just hitting the bottles in the right spot." He effortlessly tossed a tennis ball toward the bottles, and they fell away.

"I don't know. What do you say, Jessie?" Suzanne laughed and turned toward the girl. "Randal said he would meet us somewhere around here. We might as well have fun while we're waiting."

"Got yourself a boyfriend, huh?" the man said, winking at Suzanne. "Well, if he don't show up I'd be right happy to escort you two around—if you don't mind waiting about an hour."

"Why, how nice of you." Suzanne smiled. "But Randal works here, so I imagine he'll be along. Maybe you know him? His name is Randal Clark."

The man's demeanor changed rapidly. "You a cop or a reporter?" he asked bluntly. "We been overrun with both these last two weeks."

Suzanne turned innocent eyes on the man. "I'm just a friend. And if you mean all that business about the butcher, well, you can rest easy. They dismissed all charges against Randal today. Didn't you hear? He's out of jail."

"You mean Clark ain't the butcher?" The man seemed genuinely surprised. "Well, I'll be damned. We all figured he must have done it. Not that we ever said as much to the police you understand, but Clark always did seem like a queer duck to the rest of us."

"Huh!" Suzanne said, tossing her head. "I think he's

nice. What do you mean by saying he's a queer duck? In what way?''

The man shrugged. "Oh, I don't know. Most people who work the carnival are a little off the beaten path, if you know what I mean. Carnies are thrown with people when they work the midway, and even their off hours are spent with other carnies. Most of us are pretty, well, *sociable*.'' He spoke the word, as if being proud he knew its meaning.

"And Clark wasn't sociable?" Suzanne prodded.

"Oh, hell no! He kept to himself. And he *painted!* You know—like *pictures!* Pretty damned weird thing for a carnie worker to do, you ask me. But he done pretty good with it, I guess. The boss used three of his paintings to advertise the carnival. Had several hundred posters made up from Clark's paintings, the way I remember it.''

Suzanne and Jessie exchanged knowing looks, then Jessie asked, "Do you suppose I could have some for my poster collection? Where would I go to find them?''

"Hell, I don't know, little lady! He painted them up maybe six, seven years ago. Then he made off with a carload full of them, or so I heard. If you're here to meet Clark, why don't you just ask him for one?''

Suzanne stuck her hands in the back pockets of her jeans and leaned forward. "You wouldn't have any idea where Randal might be, would you? I can't wait around all night, you know. Where would he most likely be hanging out?''

The man tilted his head toward the east, enjoying Suzanne's teasing manner. "Down by the big rides, most likely. If he has his old job back, he'll be doing the juice for the big ones.''

Suzanne grabbed Jessie's hand and started walking away. "Hey," the man yelled as they disappeared in the crowded midway. "You be careful, now!''

Randal Clark pushed the elevator button to the basement, watching in satisfaction as the doors swished shut, protecting him briefly from the outside world. Hardly anyone ever used this old service elevator—only maintenance men. And unless the owners had already replaced him, *he* was maintenance—or at least had been until the cops started swarming all over his place. He wondered if they had searched the basement as well.

The boiler room was located at the end of a maze of small rooms crisscrossed with pipes and wiring. There, almost to the ceiling, was a solitary small window, probably added after the original building was erected, to comply with local codes. Clark had already checked it out thoroughly. It opened right behind two large Dumpsters, into an alley littered with trash. Even if he was unlucky enough to run into some of the homeless who frequented the area, they would only think he had been sleeping behind the Dumpsters.

A shiver of excitement coursed through Clark's body as he crossed over to a large steel vat and felt in behind it. His hand closed over the hair of the beard and he smirked in satisfaction. Stupid damn cops. Right under their noses, and they had missed it. He loosened the duct tape holding it in place.

In only minutes, he was out the window. Even though the window well hid the basement light from the alley, he had still turned the lights out before making his exit. He pulled himself out of the well and waited for any sound which would indicate another presence in the alley. Nothing.

Silently, he lifted the lid to the Dumpster and drew out two large trash bags. He threw them over his shoulder and started down the alley, stopping here and there to pick up debris, depositing items in the bags.

At the end of the alley he came within ten feet of one of the police cars. He paid no attention to it as he spotted an empty can and pounced on it. He stopped and opened one of the bags, placing the can carefully inside. He then started looking around for other treasures. He could see both officers watching him without the slightest change of expression. He hoisted both bags back over his shoulder and shuffled on down the street.

Suzanne and Jessie stood in front of the enormous roller coaster, a short rope fence separating them from a series of gears and wiring. Suddenly, Jessie stepped over the rope, motioning Suzanne to follow her. The boy taking tickets did not notice them as they disappeared back under the big ride. Jessie began running her hands back and forth over the cables.

"Let it come naturally, Jessie," Suzanne spoke softly. "Empty your mind. Make it a blank screen, like at the movies. There is nothing there. Nothing to clutter. It is a void, waiting to be filled." She grabbed Jessie's hand, holding it tight.

Jessie's head tilted to the left. Almost immediately, little mewing sounds began coming from her lips. "No. Please, no." She could see a single-edged razor coming toward the face of a girl whose features were frozen in terror. But then instead of slashing at the girl, the razor began making strokes over her right eye.

The girl's hair was golden, dressed in two long braids which hung to her shoulders. Suzanne and Jessie could see that her hair looked wet, as she fought against her attacker, scratching him.

Clark brought his hand to his face, and they could see blood when he brought it down and looked at it. She had at least struck a blow, but it cost her. Clark slapped her hard, back and forth, across the face.

"Jessie!" Suzanne spoke with authority, drawing the child from the scene. "You must get a wider view. Make your mind like a video camera. Pretend you are hitting the zoom lens for a larger picture. You can do it. Pan back to see who is holding the knife, and then wider to see if you can tell where they might be located."

Jessie nodded. She had read about this technique used by many psychics but had never had enough control to do it herself. She tried to clear her mind, but the frightened face of the girl was consuming her thoughts.

"No, Jessie." Suzanne's mind was filled with the terrified face of the girl in Jessie's vision. "Let it go! Move to the man. It's Clark, isn't it? See the hand holding the razor? Look at the man."

Suddenly, the scene cleared in Jessie's mind, as she followed Suzanne's directions. She gasped in wonder as she ordered her mind to obey and it actually did her bidding. It was as though she had taken several steps backwards—like moving from near the stage of a movie theater to the last row. Whereas before her mind could only take in small areas, now she was seeing the entire scene.

"That's it, Jessie!" Suzanne gave the girl's hand a tight squeeze. "You're doing it!"

"He's shaving her eyebrow off!" Jessie gasped. "Can you see it?"

"Yes. I'm seeing what you are seeing." They both watched as Clark began applying makeup to the girl's face.

The girl started to scream, and Clark hit her again. "Silence, you whore!" they heard him yell at her, then they watched in horror as he swung some type of cleaver down at the girl.

Jessie dropped Suzanne's hand and covered her mouth to stifle a scream. She began shaking her head violently from side to side to make the vision go away.

Suzanne grabbed Jessie's hands. "No, Jessie! You can't quit now. You're too close. Bring it back."

Jessie shoved, trying to remove her hands from Suzanne's death grip. "No. No more. It's too horrible, I don't want to see any more!"

Suzanne's tone was determined as she refused to release Jessie. "You have to get past this. I know it's hard. I've had to do it hundreds of times when I've been helping the police. If I could do this for you, I would, but I get nothing when I touch the cable. It has to be you, Jessie. Just reach deep down inside you and find the strength to face it. You have to, Jessie. For Amy."

At the mention of her sister's name, Jessie stopped pushing against Suzanne. Her knees started to buckle, but Suzanne held her up. "You can do it, Jessie. Take a few deep breaths. Concentrate. Take hold of the cable again. Clark has been here. He has worked with this cable. It is your lifeline to him."

Jessie reached down and caught the cable again with her hand. When she saw the fright on the girl's face and heard her screams, she sucked in her breath and went by it.

"Good, Jessie! Keep going. What else do you see?"

The scene unfolded for the two psychics, and they could see Clark as he lined small bottles up along beside the body of the girl they had just watched him kill. He began opening bottles and smearing a liquid on the victim's torso.

"What is he doing?" Jessie whispered.

"I don't know. See if you can get a better picture of the bottles."

Jessie concentrated hard, panning around the bottles every way she could. "It's no use," she said to Suzanne. "The bottles have some kind of a white sticker on them, with typing, but I can't see what it says."

"Okay, Jessie. Now go wider than just Clark. Look at the room. Pull your mind around the room, then out the door. Look for anything that will tell you where they are. A street sign. A number on the house. Anything." Suzanne was aware the young psychic had gone farther, faster, than she had any right to hope for. Learning to control the visions was not something a psychic picked up overnight.

Suzanne could feel the tension as Jessie forced her mind deeper into the scene. "You don't care about Clark now, Jessie," Suzanne coaxed. "The room. Empty your thoughts of Clark and the girl. It's the room you care about. You are there in the room. Look around. Make a circle with your head, because you are going to see it all."

Jessie swayed as she tried to concentrate on the room. She forced her mind away from Clark and the girl and onto their surroundings. Suddenly, she saw another person. A little girl with long dark hair was standing across the room, watching. "Oh, no!" Jessie gagged as she spoke.

"There is a little girl in the room! He's got a little girl!"

Suzanne's mind picked up the image of the child as Jessie saw her. She appeared to be about four or five years of age, with matted, long brown hair, and a tear-streaked face.

"Oh, God, Jessie. Why is she standing there like that? What has he done to her?"

The minute Suzanne spoke, the image vanished. At once, they were back at the carnival, the connection broken.

"Try again, Jessie!" Suzanne ordered. "We need to go back."

Jessie picked up the cable once again, but nothing happened. Whatever she had tuned in to was gone. She knew the end had come, at least for the moment. Suzanne, holding her hand, knew it, too. "All right. Don't worry, Jessie. We'll walk around, talk with some of the other workers, and see if maybe there is a trailer Clark used when he was working here. It will come back. Your mind just got overloaded with the horror of it all, and shut down."

Jessie looked at Suzanne in a new light. "How could you keep on doing it? It's horrible! When all those little girls were killed in Omaha, how could you keep putting yourself back into the scene? Didn't it make you nuts?"

Suzanne put an arm around Jessie's shoulders. "Sweetie, it does make me a little crazy. I can't deny that. But think how I would feel if I knew I could stop a killer and did nothing because putting myself into the scene would leave me sick and shaken for days. *That* would make me crazier—to know other little girls had died because I refused to act." As she said the words, for the first time in many months, Suzanne realized the truth of her statement. She had done what she had to do in Omaha. She had done what the police asked her to do. It was time she quit beating herself up over the outcome.

Randal Clark obeyed the man with the lighted baton and drove into the carnival parking area with the Toyota Camry he had hot-wired. Only instead of parking with the license plate out toward the road, he backed into his allotted slot, inching the Camry backward until it almost touched the front of the car in the space behind him. No sense in making it easy for them.

He had gotten rid of the trash bags but had kept on the fake beard. He didn't want any of the carnies to recognize him. After all, he had at least two police cars full of officers providing his alibi back at his apartment. He checked his wristwatch. It was a little after ten. Perfect. In all likelihood, Sam would be smashed by now.

Clark bought his ticket and entered the midway. They had obviously found someone to take over his job. The big rides were up and going. It didn't concern him. He knew he was the best juice man in three states. Any electrician could get the rides going. It was knowing what to do in a crisis, when the rides broke down, that earned him the big bucks. Let the roller coaster stall out with cars of people stranded high in the air and see how fast they wanted him!

Clark stopped at one of the booths and purchased a corn dog and a large Coke. He had finished both by the time he reached Sam's trailer. It took him exactly one minute to drive one of Sam's own filet knives into his heart, retrieve his box from the freezer, and slip out the door into the night. Sam, who had been passed out on the kitchen table, never knew what hit him. Clark, who waited to inspect his package when he was away from the trailer, realized that it was exactly as he had left it. Sam had neither opened the package nor informed the police of its existence. For just an instant, Clark felt a twinge of guilt for killing him.

At the exact moment that Clark plunged the knife into the old man, Jessie went cold inside, fear numbing her senses. All she knew was that at that very second, Clark was killing. It wasn't a flashback, or the recreating of a scene as before. The white-hot energy exploding from the periphery of her vision told her the event was happening right then. She grabbed Suzanne's hand. "He did it! I think he just stabbed Amy!"

"Oh, no, Jessie." Suzanne pulled the girl into her arms, aware that people had stopped to stare at hearing her strange words. "Are you certain?"

Jessie's voice rose as Suzanne half carried, half dragged, the child out of the stream of traffic to the back of a booth. She shook the hysterical girl. "Stop it, Jessie. Get out of the scene."

"He's here! Clark is here! At the carnival!" Jessie turned wild eyes on Suzanne. "We didn't find Amy in time! He came back for her, just like I said he would. And he killed her! He killed her!"

"Wait a minute," Suzanne spoke quickly. "You first said you *thought* he had stabbed Amy. That indicates you weren't sure. Did you actually *see* her? Please, Jessie, don't freak out on me now. Try to calm down."

Jessie's hands shook as she held tightly to Suzanne, forcing her mind back into the other realm. Suzanne could feel what the girl was trying to do. "Jessie, please. You are too upset to go back. Let it go," she whispered. "Let it go."

Jessie felt as though her heart were going to explode from her body, but she kept pushing her mind toward Clark. Then she saw a small, silver trailer and a bearded man leaving it with a small box under his arm.

Suzanne saw it, too, and conceded that perhaps this was something Jessie needed to know. "The trailer, Jessie. Open the door and go into the trailer. You can do it. Your powers are strong. You have to know this! *Open the door, Jessie.*"

Jessie steadied herself. In her mind's eye, she pictured the door to the trailer opening and herself floating in. Almost immediately, she saw the old man slumped over the table, the knife still sticking out of his back.

Jessie turned dead eyes toward Suzanne. "It wasn't Amy," she said, and fainted.

Chapter
Sixteen

Suzanne checked her watch, then settled down on her couch to wait for the *Noontime with Nora* show. Jessie was still sleeping, for which Suzanne was thankful. It had been nearly one o'clock before they had gotten home the night before. At Suzanne's insistence, Harry and Jim had arrived at the carnival and conducted a trailer-to-trailer search for the man Jessie had seen in her vision. She would never forget the look on Harry's face when they emerged from the right trailer. It had seemed to Suzanne that he somehow held her responsible for the old man's death. "What were you doing here?" he had yelled at her. "Are you nuts? Are you trying to arrange for the Matthewses to lose *both* their daughters?"

"No, no," Suzanne had stammered, baffled by his anger. "We were always together. I wouldn't have let anything happen to Jessie."

He had ordered another officer to return with them to the precinct for their statement. "Get their story, and then get them home," he had spoken bluntly to the officer. Suzanne had not heard him add, "And have someone watch her apartment until I get this sorted out. We don't know what really happened here yet, or what the killer saw."

It was at the precinct that Suzanne and Jessie heard for the first time that Randal Clark had not left his apartment all night.

"But that's not true," Jessie had tried to explain. "It

was Clark I was searching for in my mind. It *had* to be him, sir. Beard or no beard.''

Suzanne was used to the look which passed between the officers. She and Jessie exchanged knowing glances and gave up trying to explain.

Suzanne sat straight up on the couch, arching her tired back to try to relax tight muscles. It had been quite a night. She picked up the remote control, hitting the button for sound as she saw Nora Myerson walk onto the set. Nora was soon introducing two mothers who pleaded with the public to help in locating their daughters. One girl was seventeen, the other twenty. Both were home and family oriented, both active in their churches, and when their pictures appeared on the screen, it was obvious to Suzanne that they were both attractive blondes, but in a natural, home-spun way.

Nora Myerson's face filled the screen. Ordinarily, Suzanne didn't watch this show. Nora had always seemed too much like a watered down version of Tammy Faye, for her liking. Tears flowed down her cheeks as she pleaded with the good citizens of Kansas City to be on the lookout for the bodies of the missing girls. She closed with an appeal to the public to call the police with any information, no matter how trivial, that might aid in the capture of the butcher, now that the main suspect had been released.

"Oh, brother!" Suzanne said the words aloud. She had worked with the police enough over the years to know the nightmare this kind of announcement would cause. When hundreds and hundreds of tips flooded the police, it was impossible to keep on top of them. Sometimes important leads got lost in the shuffle. It was almost always a disaster.

"Get me four more phone lines in here," Caswell barked as he snapped off the television. "And see if you can free up eight rookies to man the phones and handle people coming in. It's going to be a zoo around here."

* * *

Patrick rushed from the back room to pick up the ringing phone. It never failed. Let him leave the front for a minute, and the dang phone always rang. "McFadden Costume Shop," he spoke pleasantly into the phone, nevertheless. "And how can I be helping you, now?"

"Yeah. Do you rent nuns' costumes?" the voice on the line asked.

"Yes," Patrick answered. "That we do, now. How many would you like, and for when?"

"No, no. I'll tell you why I'm calling. I'm trying to locate a young woman who rented a nun's costume yesterday morning. One of my men happened to see her, and thought she would be perfect for a new play I'm putting on. Her name is Richards. Suzanne Richards. But we can't find a listing for her in the telephone book. All we know is that she rented a costume from somewhere. She's real good looking and tall. I'd say about five feet eight or nine inches. You rent a costume to anyone who looked like that?"

"Well, sure and if I didn't." Patrick smiled. "And I agree with you, I surely do. She's pretty as a picture and has a smile that would light up Ireland. That she does."

"So you have her phone number and address?"

"Sure, sure. Just hold on a minute, and I'll get it for you." Patrick punched hold, replaced the phone in its cradle, then went to his customer file.

"What was that all about?" Nellie asked as she popped her head around the curtain.

"Well, you won't believe it," Patrick answered her. "Do you remember the pretty colleen you loaned the rosary to yesterday? Suzanne Richards? Seems she caught some director's eye and they are trying to get in touch with her."

"Oh, Patrick, you didn't give out her address, now did you?" She had honored the girl's wishes, and not told anyone, not even her husband, about Suzanne's real purpose in renting the costume.

Patrick stopped thumbing through his file and looked at

his wife's white face. "What is it, Nellie? What's the matter?"

"Did you, Patrick? It's important, now!"

Patrick pointed to the phone. "Not yet. I put the man on hold while I looked it up. I don't understand. What's going on?"

Nellie walked briskly over to the phone, punched the hold button, and spoke into the receiver. "I'm sorry. My husband was mistaken. There was a young woman named Suzanne *Rivers* who rented a nun's habit from us, but that was at least two months ago. She needed it for a play. You'll have to forgive my husband," she said, winking at Patrick. "Sometimes he gets a little addle-headed."

Floyd slammed the phone down and sat staring at it. That brat had done nothing but cause him trouble since the day he had first laid eyes on her. In fact, his whole life had turned out wrong because of her. They could have made a fortune in blackmail, the two of them, but oh, no. Miss Priss would have none of that! Her and her voodoo, her witchcraft! Well, he would show her what the grown-up world was all about! Either that, or he would run for his life. He hadn't quite made up his mind which was the smarter thing to do.

After sixteen years in the Detective Division, Harry McDermott didn't think there was much that would surprise him. However, as he sat reading the report on Suzanne Richards, he was more than surprised, he was dumbfounded. If what he had before him was true, and he had no reason to think it was not, then Suzanne Richards had put away just about as many criminals as he, himself, had.

San Diego, Phoenix, Omaha, Long Island—the list went on and on. Serial killers, rapists, pedophiles—she had helped nail them all. Furthermore, she was held in high regard by all of the police departments from which he had received reports—including Omaha. That in itself was astonishing, given the skepticism of most police officers toward anything of that kind.

He picked up the manila envelope from Child Services, the agency he had contacted for earlier background information, scanning through the contents quickly. There was a letter addressed to him from a Ms. Savage.

Dear Mr. McDermott:

I'm sorry, but I was unable to trace the history of Suzanne Richards back any further than the third grade. She attended school in Omaha that year, but her father never sent any reports from other schools, even though the records were requested many times. Her name at that time was Suzanne Webb. Her father's name was Carl Webb. He committed suicide, and his daughter was placed at a local convent, the Doors of the Blessed Sacrament, where she was later adopted by a spinster lady, Miss Emily Richards, who has since passed away.

School records in Omaha show that Suzanne's mother was killed in a car wreck when Suzanne was five or six. But this was just a notation made by the principal upon enrollment, and they have no prior address to check further. I talked with the principal of Langston Elementary where Suzanne attended school, and he remembered her as being quiet, withdrawn, and a loner. After she discovered her father's body, the school scheduled her for counseling, but she was moved to the convent before it was started.

Emily Richards, the woman who adopted Suzanne, is a sister to the nun who was in charge of the Doors of the Blessed Sacrament, Sister Mary Elizabeth. Sister Mary now resides in the Holy Cross Retirement Home which is located in Sterling Heights, Michigan. If you need any more information, you could probably get it from her. I'm certain she would have better background information than I was able to find.

As you are probably aware, Miss Richards went on to become quite a noted psychic and has helped police in many states in the capturing of criminals. She is a real celebrity around Omaha.

If I can help you further in any way, don't hesitate to ask.

Sincerely,
Helen Savage

Harry hit his intercom button. "Jim, would you please see what you can find me on a Carl Webb, last known address, Omaha, Nebraska? He committed suicide there about twenty years ago. See what the Omaha police have on that, and see if you can find a previous address."

"Will do," Jim answered. "Who is he?"

"The father of Suzanne Richards. All I'm really looking for is where she came from, originally, whether she has any relatives around, that sort of thing."

"Gotcha. I'll have it back for you in just a few minutes."

It was probably nothing, but the thing that sounded strange to Harry, was the part about no records. In this day and age, it was just about impossible to so much as take a short walk in the park without some sort of permit. School systems were notorious for their paperwork. If they couldn't get the information from the father, why hadn't they contacted previous schools themselves? And how horrible for Suzanne to lose her mother at such a young age, then find the body of her father who had taken his own life! It seemed to Harry that Miss Richards had been surrounded by death since a very early age.

He picked up the report from Omaha again. It was clear that the police department had been solidly behind Miss Richards in the Underwood disaster. They found no fault with anything she had done to help in the capture of Nebraska's infamous serial killer.

One investigator from Omaha, a Charles Botello, had

faxed a personal note saying how much they all missed Suzanne, and how the newspapers had done a complete flip-flop, and were now saying the intervention of Suzanne probably saved many lives.

So that was it. Suzanne had run from Omaha when the heat was turned on over the Underwood case. That was probably why she had done no psychic work in the months she had been in Kansas City.

Harry looked up as Jim entered his office. "I don't know what to think, Harry," he said as he pushed a piece of paper toward his partner. "According to what I found out with just a couple of phone calls, Carl Webb has been dead for thirty-five years. He died at the age of eleven from an allergic reaction to aspirin."

Harry looked up, puzzled. "Well, you must have the wrong one. My information is that Carl Webb committed suicide in Omaha. I'm pretty certain of that."

"Right." Jim nodded. "I took the Social Security number that the Omaha police gave me for a Carl Webb who committed suicide and ran it through Social Security to get a full background report. But the birth certificate belonged to this kid, Carl Webb, who was dead. His family lives in Pawhuska, Oklahoma, and I could find no record of your Carl Webb, before he showed up in Omaha."

"So what are we talking about here? A graveyard pluck?"

Jim raised his eyebrows knowingly. "Sure looks like it to me. The guy comes to town and pulls the scam to get a new Social Security number. It used to be pretty easy. And of course if that's really the case, we do know one more thing about our man. At least at one point, he was in Pawhuska, Oklahoma, checking out grave markers."

"Why would he go to all that trouble, and then kill himself a few months later?"

Jim shook his head. "Beats me. But maybe Suzanne will remember her real last name. She had to be, what, five or six years old? Perhaps old enough to remember if she had another name before Webb."

Harry motioned for Jim to sit down as he picked up the telephone. "Operator, would you please get me a number for the Holy Cross Retirement Home in Sterling Heights, Michigan? And then I want to make a person-to-person call to a Sister Mary Elizabeth there." He placed his hand over the receiver and spoke to Jim. "We have one other place to check before we talk to Miss Richards."

The phone felt cold when the young nurse placed it in the hand of the old nun. Sister Mary Elizabeth felt for the cord to make certain she was putting the right end of the receiver to her ear. "Hello! Hello! This is Sister Mary. Is that you, Suzanne?"

"No, Sister Mary," Harry spoke loudly into the phone. "My name is Detective Harry McDermott. I'm with the Kansas City Police."

There was an audible gasp on the other end of the line. "Suzanne? Oh, please! Don't tell me something has happened to Suzanne!"

"No, no!" Harry practically yelled into the phone. "Nothing like that. Suzanne is fine. I am just calling for some information."

"Well, land sakes, you didn't need to scare a body to death!" Sister Mary snapped. "And why are you yelling at me? I'm not deaf, young man!"

Harry lowered his voice. "I'm sorry, Sister. And I didn't mean to frighten you. I'm just looking for some information about Suzanne's birth parents. I understand Suzanne was adopted by your sister, Emily Richards. Isn't that so?"

So it was going to come out. After almost twenty years, the whole thing would come out. Would they arrest her for kidnapping or some such thing? No. Of course not. She was too old, too frail. But it would bring shame on the church. It was certain to do that.

The silence on the other end of the line was beginning to make Harry uncomfortable. "Sister? Are you there?"

The old nun's voice trembled as she spoke. "Yes, sir. I'm right here. I take full responsibility for my actions.

And I want you to know, I acted alone. No one else at the Doors of the Blessed Sacrament knew what I did." There. It was over. She had admitted her sin. Now maybe God would bring her home to be with Him.

"Ma'am?" Harry said, puzzled by her outburst. "You've lost me. Just what is it that you are taking responsibility for?"

The nun's eyes closed, wearily, as she bowed her head. "For letting my sister, Emily, adopt the child. She was too old and she was not married. But she loved Suzanne with all her heart, and the child loved her, also. It didn't seem like such a bad thing to do."

"No, no, Sister Mary. I don't care about that. I'm certain you did what was right for Suzanne. All I care about is the name of her birth parents, if you know it. I'm not trying to cause any trouble for you about your adoption records. Truly I am not!"

Sister Mary could feel blood leaving her face, as her trembling hands clung to the receiver. It was time. She liked the sound of the detective's voice. She would tell him her story, and be done with it. "The man, he said, Carl, Carl Webb . . . took . . . but . . . but . . ." Sister Mary felt strange, as an overwhelming tiredness entered her body. She couldn't see the blood clot which had lodged in a small artery in her brain, but she knew exactly what was happening to her. "Not yet, Lord!" she tried to utter the words, but only a garbled sound escaped her lips. Tears formed in her sightless eyes as the phone dropped onto the floor. With her left hand, she felt for her rosary. "No, God, not yet. Please. I have to make this right." She could tell no words were leaving her lips, but she also knew her God would hear her.

Chapter
Seventeen

"Oh, hi, sweetie," Suzanne said, looking up as Jessie came into the living room. "Did you have a good sleep? Do you feel better now?"

Jessie nodded yes to the last two questions, then sat down next to Suzanne on the couch. "I had a weird dream, though. At least I think it was a dream, and not, you know, the other."

Suzanne put her arm around Jessie's shoulders and drew her close. "What was it? Can you remember?"

"It was the little girl we saw. You know, the one with Clark. She kept trying to get close to me, to warn me about some danger, but just as she would start to speak, a man's hand would come down and clamp over her mouth and drag her backward. Each time the little girl would get away from the man, but each time he came after her. Then once he threw her from the car, and she tumbled down a long hill, where no one could see her. No one but me, that is. It was so awful, because I knew if I couldn't find the place, the little girl would be lost forever."

"I'm sure it was just a dream, sweetie."

"Yeah, I suppose. I know seeing the little girl in that vision last night really spooked me. Have you heard anything yet?"

Suzanne nodded her head. "A little. The news had a short account of the murder. If there is any tie-in to Clark, they don't have it as yet. I've tried to get through to Harry or Jim, but either they aren't taking my calls, or they haven't received their messages."

"I don't think I like Harry anymore," Jessie said. "He was mean last night! Cranky and mean! I like Jim a whole lot more. I like the way he calls me *little darlin'* and tells me everything will turn out all right."

"Yeah, I like Jim, too."

"And not Harry?"

"I don't know. Last night I thought I hated him, but maybe he just had your best interests at heart."

"Or maybe he's a jerk!"

"Maybe."

"Not to change the subject, but what are we going to do today?"

"Absolutely nothing!" Suzanne said. "I was afraid when you collapsed like that last night. I think we had better slow down."

"I only fainted," Jessie answered haughtily. "Don't make a big deal of it. And we can't slow down. Not when we're getting closer."

Both flinched at the loud clap of thunder that reverberated through Suzanne's little apartment. Jessie jumped up and ran to the window, just as the first large drops of rain hit the pane. As she stood at the window, holding the curtains back with one hand, she stared at two drops of rain which raced each other to be first to the sill. All of her thoughts and energies were focused on the drops of water, and it was as though time were suspended for the young girl. At last she turned slowly from the window. "We have to find Amy today. She will die if we don't."

Suzanne breathed deeply. "Are you certain?"

Jessie nodded. "Yes. There—there is something about water, but I couldn't make it out. And sunflowers. Hundreds of sunflowers, beside a river of blood."

A voice in Suzanne's head grew loud, and a warning bell started clanging. She felt an enormous pressure in her chest, as all around, fingers of darkness grabbed at her from the light. She felt trapped, frightened, and alone. The warning was clear to her. If she went on, she would die. Unless she turned back now, she was lost. She watched in horror as the dark fingers began clutching at her throat, trying to cut off her air as she collapsed on the floor.

"Suzanne!" Jessie's scream cut through the nightmare, bringing her back to the present.

Suzanne picked herself up slowly, feeling her sore neck. "I have to get some air," she gasped to Jessie as she staggered toward the window.

Quickly, Jessie was around her, cranking open the window. Wind forced a light mist of rain through the screen and onto Suzanne's face. She welcomed the cool moisture.

"What is it, Suzanne? What's happening?" Jessie put an arm around Suzanne's waist.

"It's all right, Jessie. Whatever it was, it's gone now." *But it will be back,* Suzanne thought. *And whatever it is, it's going to try to kill me!* She knew with absolute certainty that she had never been so frightened in her entire life. She also knew Jessie was right. Time was running out.

"Let's get you fed, then let's drive by Clark's apartment building. We can get his address from the *Star.* They'll have it on file, I'm sure."

Jessie looked strangely at Suzanne. "Who is after you? Why are you so afraid?"

"I've been thinking about that," Suzanne answered slowly. "Ever since I went to see Clark at the jail, something has been going on, but I don't know what. It's like I'm afraid to go forward, but equally frightened of staying back. I can't explain what is happening to me. Sometimes my mind just goes numb with fear." She gave Jessie a quick hug. "But I don't want you worrying about that. I'll figure it out. Now, do we go by Clark's place or not?"

"I don't want anything to happen to you," Jessie said, stubbornly refusing to drop the issue. "Promise me you won't let it!"

"Sweetie, if I could promise you that, I would. But even with all my psychic ability, I have rarely been able to tell the future. But I will be very careful, you can bet on that!"

Chapter
Eighteen

The *plink, plink, plink* of water drops hitting the bottom of her plastic jug, awakened Amy Matthews. At first she thought she must be dreaming, but then she heard it again. *Plink, plink, plink.* She crawled over to the jug she had placed under the pipe and stared. Water! Maybe not enough to quench her thirst, but at least enough to keep her alive! With one hand she pulled the jug to her lips, tilting it up and letting the few drops roll into her mouth. She held her other hand under the pipe in order not to miss any of the moisture. "Thank you, God!" she whispered as the cool rainwater bathed her swollen throat. Quickly, she brought her hand to her mouth, lapping up the drops of water she had caught, and replacing the jug under the pipe.

Amy could hear the thunder now, and it seemed like music to her ears. Maybe she would make it, after all. Maybe she wasn't doomed to die in this cement prison.

Outside, the rain intensified, softening the ground and forming gullies in the hillside. The creek which meandered across the hillside began to swell, threatening to spill over its banks.

Amy didn't notice the tiny pieces of dirt spilling from the crack in her prison. Her eyes were only on the jug, as she waited for it to gather enough water for her to have another drink.

*   *   *

Justin Nelson glanced over at Sara, his wife of forty-two years. "They are saying for everyone to help check abandoned or little-used buildings in the hopes of finding the bodies of the missing three girls. How long has it been since you've checked our shop?"

"Now, Justin." Sara shook a finger at her husband. "When you broke your leg, you agreed we would just close up the store until you were better, but you try to invent a reason for me going clear across town every chance you get. Honestly! There are businesses all around our shop. If anything was wrong, we would have heard about it."

Justin Nelson was not one to give in without an argument, not on any point, not in forty-two years. "You can't know that, Sara. How long has it been? A month? How would you feel if some poor young girl was in there, cut up all over the place like they say that butcher leaves them?"

"Oh, God, Justin! Don't be gross! Who in their right mind would murder and cut up a body in a flower shop—especially one stuck right between a jewelry store and a bakery?"

"Now, you know there aren't any flowers in there right now, except for artificial ones. And what difference does that make anyway? You think some killer would smell the roses and decide not to do his deed that night? Huh? Is that what you think?"

Sara's eyes narrowed as she glared at her husband, who had been driving her out of her mind for the seven weeks since he had been housebound with a broken leg. They had decided to close up their flower shop since they had been discussing retirement, anyway. This was to be a test case, a little dry run, to see how retirement would feel. And having found out, Sara was dead certain retirement was not the answer. Not for a few years yet. Maybe, never. It was one thing to spend the day together at their shop. There they were busy with customers, creating arrangements, and making deliveries. But to be together all day at home, with Justin on her back constantly, wanting this, demanding that, was another story completely. It was a wonder she had not pushed his wheelchair into the swimming pool out back.

"Well, are you going to check or not? Otherwise, I'll need to call someone else to do it."

"Oh, for heaven's sake, Justin! Yes! Yes, if it will make you shut up, I'll go out in the rain and drive through noon-hour traffic to check!"

Clark's apartment was located only minutes from the Plaza, the one area in Kansas City with which Suzanne had some acquaintance. She found the address easily, drove by, then circled the block to look for a parking place.

"Are you getting anything, Jessie?" Suzanne asked. "Any vibes at all?"

Jessie shook her head. "Nothing. No one knows me, though. Not even Clark. Why don't you let me go into the building, even up to his door? Maybe I could get a better reading there."

"No. That's one thing we won't do. But I'll park and maybe we can come up with another idea."

Suzanne maneuvered her Cutlass into a parking place where they had a clear view of the entrance to the apartment building. She spotted the unmarked police car immediately. She had sat with too many units on too many stakeouts to be mistaken. "Stay here, Jessie. Let's see if I can learn anything from the police there." She tilted her head toward the Caprice.

Suzanne walked down to the end of the street and crossed at the light, wishing she had brought an umbrella as her blouse quickly became soaked. She trotted up to the passenger side of the car, motioning for the officers to roll down the window.

Quickly, she reached in, touching the arm of the young man closest to her. "Hello. Do you know where Randal Clark is?" she said without preamble.

For one awful minute, Suzanne thought the shocked officer was going to go for his gun. Instead, he turned in the seat enough to get a good look at her and smiled.

"Who wants to know?"

"My name's Suzanne," she said. "What's yours?"

Suzanne knew the officer's name was Mark before he told her. She also knew Randal Clark was still in his apartment and had not come out since Mark came on duty at seven o'clock that morning. There was nothing else she could learn about Clark from the policeman. She took her hand from his arm. "You know," she said, "that you would be made in a minute by anyone who really cared." She nodded to the litter of take-out packages across the dash of the car. "Most people don't eat breakfast and lunch in their cars. And you also are glancing at the top of the building too much. My bet is that Randal Clark is on the third floor, right?" This time she didn't bother going to the end of the block and crossing correctly. She merely dashed across the street to her car.

Once back, Suzanne repeated what she had learned to Jessie.

"So what now?" Jessie asked. "Are we going to just sit here and wait for him to come out?"

Suzanne shook her head. "As I understand it, after the police found Amy's purse in the Dumpster by Clark's apartment, they retraced her steps and found out the last place anyone had seen her was at Wednesday night church services. Isn't that right?"

Jessie nodded. "They found her car at the church, so they were pretty certain."

"That was on Wednesday night and Clark was arrested the next day?"

"Yes."

"So somewhere between the church and her car, Clark got to her. He had to have taken her someplace where she couldn't get away, and left her there so she would be available when he was ready to kill her. We know that because you heard Amy call to you yesterday. Right?"

"Right. Was that only yesterday?" Jessie asked in

astonishment. "It seems a hundred years ago!"

Suzanne nodded in agreement. "I wonder what would happen if we went back to the church and tried to follow Amy's trail, using our psychic ability. And when I say *we* I really mean *you* because your talents lie more in that direction than mine."

"That's a good idea. It's the Methodist church on Central."

"Okay. Let's go." Suzanne glanced up as lightning lit up the sky, followed almost immediately by a loud crash of thunder. She turned to Jessie. "Why don't you see if you can tune in a local radio station? We had better keep tabs on this weather. It's really starting to come down."

Neither of them noticed the Ford Taurus which pulled out of the parking garage across the street. The car let one vehicle in between it and the Cutlass, then eased into traffic.

Sara finished turning the key in the lock and pushed open the large, wooden back door of the Nelson Flower and Gift Shop. "No sign of forced entry," she spoke aloud, still miffed with her husband. Stepping inside she removed her raincoat and cap and laid them over a chair. As long as she had made the trip, she might just as well spruce things up a bit.

To satisfy Justin, she walked from room to room, glancing around to make certain things were in order. They were. Everything seemed exactly as she had left it.

She went into the back where their work area was located. It could stand a little straightening up, she decided. When she had cleared out the shop that day, she had been exhausted by the time she had finished taking flowers around and donating them to the local churches. She hadn't really cleaned up her mess very well.

Sara went over to the broom closet to get the Shop Vac. That was when she heard it. It had been there all along, but just had not penetrated her brain. The cooler was running! Surely she had not forgotten to unplug the large refrigerated storage unit for the fresh flowers. Justin would really carp at her if that were the case! She walked over and pulled back the heavy plastic she had placed over the glass of the cooler to protect it. On one shelf, exactly at eye level, was the severed head of a young girl. As Sara's weak knees gave out and she slumped to the floor, she saw that the rest of the shelves which normally contained arrangements of flowers, were now each holding a body part. Her scream brought people running from both the jewelry store and the bakery.

Ten miles away, Stan Cooper used his key to open the lockbox of a slightly run-down Victorian house on Bluff Drive. The Jeffersons were his best shot in a long time to unload the enormous eyesore. They had said they were looking for an old, large fixer-upper. Hopefully, this property was just what they were looking for. It had been on the market for almost three years and was a running joke among the city's realtors. He wondered if there was still a pool on how long it would take to make the sale. He had entered it once, but the time he had guessed as a selling date had come and gone months ago.

Stan removed the key from the box and opened the front door. He didn't need to enter the house to know something was wrong. The stench nearly knocked him over.

Chapter
Nineteen

" ...**A**nd now for today's late-breaking news." The radio broadcaster interrupted Patty Loveless in the middle of *Hurt Me Bad*. "The bodies of seventeen-year-old Tiffany Blake and twenty-year-old April Merker have been located. The mutilated bodies of the two girls leave no doubt that they were victims of the infamous Kansas City Butcher. In an interview with KJST's reporter, Wanda Goldbloom, the families of the two slain girls credit Nora Myerson of the *Noontime with Nora* television show, with stirring the public to action and locating their daughters. That leaves only one missing girl, Amy Matthews, unaccounted for.

"And this just in from the weather bureau. Since nine o'clock this morning Kansas City has received two inches of rain, with no hint of relief in the forecast. Some of the lower-lying areas have already begun flooding, and the weather bureau is predicting up to three more inches before the night is over. Severe lightning is accompanying the rain, and folks—if you don't have to go out, please stay inside where it's safe. We will keep you updated on the storm and any breaking news."

Jessie's eyes went to Suzanne's strained face. "Those poor girls. What a horrible way to die."

Suzanne reached over and turned her windshield wipers a notch faster to keep pace with the rain. "I know that serial killers are supposed to get some sort of sick thrill by inflicting pain on others because of some enormous pain they themselves suffered through.'' She shook her head in anger. ''But this guy is the worst I have ever seen.''

''There it is!'' Jessie pointed out the window. ''That sign says Central Methodist Church.''

Suzanne switched over to the right-hand lane and pulled up in front of the church. She didn't notice the dark car in back of her as it parked only half a block away.

She turned in the car seat, facing Jessie, taking her hands. ''Listen to me, Jessie. Before we go any further, I have to warn you that sometimes the psychic power takes on a life of its own. Once you open yourself to your full potential, there will be no turning back. You will have to deal with it every minute of your waking life.'' She stopped the young girl before she could speak. ''No. Hear me out. Your powers are going to be strong—maybe even stronger than mine. They will consume you. It may already be too late for you to make a conscious choice not to continue, but once you finish going down this path we started last night, the choice will no longer be there.''

For once Jessie was not ready with a flip answer. She held on tightly to Suzanne's hands and spoke in a soft, but determined voice. ''I choose Amy. That is my choice. If I have visions jumping out of the darkness at me for the rest of my life, I will consider it a good bargain. And I know what you mean, Suzanne. I have noticed my powers increasing almost hour by hour. The more I do, the further I go with it. That is what you are trying to tell me, right?''

Suzanne slowly nodded her head. ''Yes. There is some connection that is pulling you. I don't know what it is, yet. I hope there is no danger, but I can't tell.''

Jessie's eyes did not waver. ''I'm ready. Help me feel what I need to feel in order to find Amy.''

Suzanne squeezed Jessie's hands. ''Okay, sweetie, here we go. The first thing I want you to do is close your eyes. Picture your sister as she was the last time you were together. Plant her memory in your mind. Remember her face, her scent, her goodness. Wrap yourself in your sister's soul."

Jessie thought of Amy as they had said good-bye the day she left for Kansas City. Her long, blond hair was silky against Jessie's face as she hugged her. Her skin smelled faintly of peaches.

"You are with her now, Jessie. You have been to church. You are by her side coming down the steps. Open your eyes, Jessie. Look out the window and picture yourself coming down the steps with Amy. What does she see? What does she hear? You are there, Jessie. You know."

Jessie stared at the church steps. Nothing happened for a few moments, but as she watched, a mist began gathering at the front of the church, then she saw her. It was so real, that for just an instant Jessie thought it was actually Amy coming toward her.

"No, Jessie," Suzanne said. "Don't come out of the vision. I see her, also, but only through your eyes. What is she doing now? Does she hear anything? See anything?"

Jessie forced her mind back into the other dimension. She heard the man's voice—warm, cordial. "Amy! Come here!" Then she watched as Amy walked toward a maroon van and was pulled in. Instantly, Jessie began gagging, trying to catch her breath.

"No, Jessie. You don't need to experience what Amy is going through. You are an observer only. Move back and see what is happening." As she spoke the words, Jessie quit coughing and took several deep breaths.

"I'm all right now," Jessie said. "He put something over Amy's face. She . . . she couldn't breathe. Now she is lying on the floor of the van, unconscious."

"This is only the beginning, Jessie. We have to know where he is taking her. Follow the van. Keep it in sight."

Jessie pointed up the road. "That way. He took her that way."

Suzanne dropped Jessie's hands, put the car into gear, and began driving in the direction the girl was pointing.

She then reached her right hand over and clasped Jessie's hand again.

"That's it, Jessie! Don't lose them. Concentrate on Amy. You are going to follow your sister. There is an invisible cord between the two of you."

Jessie was barely aware of Suzanne's words as she sank deeper into the scene. She could see Amy lying helpless on the floor of the van.

"Go wider, Jessie. Hang back just a little so you can see the street signs, a business, anything to tell us where we are."

Jessie's eyes closed tight as she willed a distance between the van and Suzanne's car. "I see a Wendy's. They are passing a Wendy's, and a McDonald's!"

Suzanne looked out the car window as she first drove by a Wendy's, then a few moments later, a McDonald's. There was no doubt. Jessie was following her sister's trail.

A block in back of them, the occupant of the Ford Taurus knew it, too.

"Has there been any further word on Sam Nickels, the carnie who was killed last night?" Chief Caswell asked Harry. "Have our boys been able to tie him to Clark in any way?"

"They knew each other. That's about all we know."

"Any speculation as to why Clark would want him dead?"

"None. Apparently he was just an old man who never caused any trouble, never had many friends, and who liked to drink after he finished with the evening meal. He didn't bother anyone, and no one bothered him. That is until last night."

"Our boys say Clark never left his apartment last night. We have a unit in front, a unit in back, and one in the parking garage. Surely someone would have seen him if he tried to leave."

"Do we know if the Taurus is his only vehicle?" Harry asked.

Jim answered. "It is the only one registered to him, at any rate."

"He couldn't have left," Caswell stated firmly. "Every exit at his apartment is covered. I think you gentlemen need to start concentrating on facts, and not psychic voodoo! What else have you found out about this Richards woman? Anything except what you showed me?"

"No," Harry answered. "I had a feeling the nun was going to give me a little information, but she had a stroke before she said much. We really don't know anything about Miss Richards before the age of eight, but I don't suppose it makes any difference to our investigation, anyway. We have pretty well established that she is who she says she is, and that was all that concerned me."

The light on Caswell's phone lit up. He punched the line. "Yes? What is it?"

"Chief, this is Stanley Davis. I just got a few preliminary reports back from the FBI and also from Genericode. You aren't going to believe what they say. Do you want me to give you a quick overview before I deliver it?"

"Just a minute," Caswell said. "Let me put you on the speaker. Jim and Harry are here. They need to hear it, too."

Caswell punched a line and replaced the phone in its cradle. "Okay, Stanley, go ahead."

"None of the DNA recovered from the scene matches Clark. It isn't even close."

"Shit," Harry exploded. "Not even the skin that was trapped under the fingernails of one of the first victims?"

"Not even that," Stanley answered. "None of the semen, none of the skin, nothing, period. But here's the really weird part. You know those body parts found at Clark's apartment? They were removed from different bodies because of gangrene and were preserved in formaldehyde probably—get this—thirty to thirty-five years ago. Clark would have been in diapers!"

Caswell put his head in his hands. "I don't believe this. Do you realize what this means? It means either the butcher is still out there, and we don't have a clue as to his identity, or it's Clark, and we don't have a snowball's chance in hell of convicting him! His attorneys would have a field day with this!"

"Is there any chance there was a mixup of some kind?" Jim asked. "Switched tubes, that sort of thing?"

Stanley's voice came over the speaker. "None. As you know we used both labs, the FBI, and Genericode. Their findings were consistent."

"What about the Murphy girl? Any results back yet? You said you believed there would be a clear DNA profile from her," Harry asked.

"Come on, Harry!" Stanley said. "That was just yesterday. You know better than to expect a profile that fast."

"Well, keep on them. We need a break in this case. I'm tired of finding the cut-up bodies of young girls all over K.C. I'm developing nightmares!"

Stanley's voice sounded weary. "Yeah. Me, too."

As he punched the button disconnecting the ME, Chief Caswell's thoughts were black. How could the investigation have taken such a wrong turn? He knew the rumblings about replacing him were now going to turn into a loud roar. "We have nothing left to tie Clark to any of the murders. Not one thing except those teenage boys who said he was hanging around the school shortly before the disappearance of Tiffany Blake. Pull in the surveillance. I can't justify keeping a tail on Clark, now."

Harry and Jim exchanged worried glances, but knew better than to open their mouths.

Suzanne's mind drifted as she followed Jessie's instructions. She had had to release the girl's hand when the wind and rain became so fierce she was in danger of losing control of the car. Now she could only trust in Jessie's directions. She marveled at the way the young psychic was able to hold on to the scene. She had taken to all of Suzanne's directives instantly, seeming to sense almost before Suzanne spoke, what was needed of her. She was an

amazing child, truly gifted. Her ability to focus was un-
canny, and, Suzanne suspected, much of her strength came
from a firm grounding in her family and knowing who she
was. Her parents had done a marvelous job of raising their
child. Her spirit had been allowed to fly free.

Unlike hers. No wonder she had fled Omaha when
things got a little rough. She had spent many years of her
early life running from real and imagined ghosts and fears.
She had been almost Jessie's age now by the time Miss
Emily had finally persuaded her that she was safe and se-
cure. The three years she had spent crisscrossing the country with her father had been hellish. She lived in constant
fear she would do something to displease him and have to
endure his wrath. Then something had happened that
changed him. For a few weeks before his death, he had
treated her a little nicer. The verbal lashings stopped, and
he seemed to at least try to get along with her. Still, Suzanne knew that when she saw his body in the kitchen that
day, there was relief, mixed with the horror of it all. Perhaps that was one of the reasons she had gone through so
much agony after his death. She was ashamed that she felt
relief at the death of her father. After all, he had cared for
her after her mother died. He had not left her by the side
of the road as he had threatened.

Suzanne was jarred back to the present as Jessie spoke.
"Turn east here. Where the sign says Interstate Twenty-
nine. They took this road, I'm sure of it."

Suzanne had to quickly maneuver her Cutlass into the
right-hand lane, following the arrows to Interstate 29. She
didn't notice the car in back of her do the same.

Randal Clark's mind was working rapidly. He didn't know
why, but the police car had turned off, and another unit
had not replaced it. He had known he was being followed
from the minute he had left his garage. Stupid cops. But
why would they have called off the surveillance? He gave
a little chuckle. Probably it was the charmed life he led!
At any rate, it certainly made his plans a whole lot easier.

If the occupants of the Cutlass made it all the way to the farm, he would have them. He reached under his coat and touched the handle of his Ruger Bearcat for reassurance. A little shiver of anticipation coursed through his body. He thought of what he would do to the two of them, once he had them secured.

Clark's thoughts slammed into Jessie's head, forcing out the picture of Amy in the van. She let out a loud scream, causing Suzanne to career wildly across several lanes of traffic. "What is it, Jessie? What's happening? Give me your hand so I can see it, too." She brought the Cutlass under control, returned to the correct lane, and reached for the girl's hand.

Jessie brushed aside Suzanne's hand as she seemed to be warding off an unseen attacker with her arms. Her screams continued.

Suzanne noticed an exit immediately in front of them and swung her car hard to the right, barely making it. Ahead she could see a King's X supermarket and drove quickly into its parking lot. She slammed on the brakes and grabbed Jessie. As soon as she touched the girl, she felt herself slipping into another dimension. Icy fingers of fear grabbed at her as she saw what Jessie was seeing. Randal Clark had them both. He was jabbing at them with a knife, making them scream in terror. On the floor beside him was the emaciated body of Amy, a kitchen knife through her heart. Suzanne gasped at the image.

Jessie stopped screaming and began chanting. "Oh no, oh no, oh no, oh no . . ."

Randal Clark swore as he fishtailed his Taurus, making the exit. He was grateful the heavy rain was keeping traffic light. Ahead he could see the Cutlass pull into the parking lot, coming to an abrupt stop. This was it. He was going to finish them off. He would just walk over to the car and empty his .22 into them.

*　　*　　*

Jessie pushed against Suzanne. "Let's get out of here. I want to go home. NOW!" she yelled. "Get out of here, now!"

Suzanne didn't question the girl. She could feel it, too. Evil was coming. She yanked her car into gear and spun out of the parking lot.

Chapter
Twenty

The usually docile creek had been rising steadily since morning. Soon, the downward meandering had turned into a churning, boiling mass as rushing water ate away at already water-soaked banks. The saturated ground would hold no more and began forming small offshoots, each sprinting rapidly down the hill, carving out chunks of the landscape, flooding the lower levels.

Amy was having the most delightful dream. She was sitting by a lake surrounded with lush, fruit-filled trees. To eat, she had only to reach up and pluck a banana or apple from a tree. The water was fresh and cold as she scooped it up with her hands, splashing it across her face and body. As she sat by the lake she noticed the water getting higher, until it was soon lapping at her legs.

With a start, Amy jerked awake. Her eyes quickly checked the plastic water jug. Thank goodness. It had not turned over. She pulled herself into a sitting position, and felt her leg. It really was damp! Her head snapped around to the crack in the cement wall. Black mud was oozing in, and with it, a steady stream of water.

For a few moments Amy sat, mesmerized, watching the advancing water. After two weeks of sameness, it was at the least a diversion. She scooted over closer to the water, then slammed her hands down into it as a toddler would do in a wading pool. She delighted in the wetness which splashed up onto her. Soon she was sitting in the puddle, soaking her parched skin, and taking small sips of the dirty water.

It was several minutes before the danger penetrated Amy's brain. It wasn't until she noticed the water had risen until it now covered most of the floor, that she began assessing her new predicament. "Get the light, dummy," she spoke aloud. "You don't want to electrocute yourself!" She rose to her feet, pleased that she was able to stand. On shaky legs she walked to the little lamp, bent over and picked it up. The electrical cord entered her prison from the top, so all she had to worry about was keeping the lamp, itself, out of the water.

Surely, Amy reasoned, she didn't need to worry about too much water coming in. Sometimes their basement at home flooded, but it was usually just a few inches. Nothing to be apprehensive about.

Still, maybe she should see how rapidly the water was rising. She reached over and marked a line on the wall with her fingernail, approximately one inch from the water line. Then she checked the time on her watch. It was fifteen minutes past three.

Outside, the rain continued coming down as the sky blazed with electricity. The small gully which had formed, causing water to pour into the opening around the cement box, widened, creating a pool. On top, the wooden ceiling groaned and creaked against the extra weight of the wet dirt and the debris spilling down the hillside.

Floyd heard the slam of a car door and quickly moved to the window, drawing sun-streaked chintz curtains slightly back. Clark! Muscles tightened in his stomach as he felt the front pouch of his sweatsuit, making certain his Colt was in place. The bastard wasn't going to catch him unprepared.

Floyd swung the front door open before Clark had a chance to knock. "Are you crazy coming here? I thought you had a tail!" he whispered harshly, deciding to go on the offensive.

Randal brushed past him before answering, grabbing the door and slamming it shut behind him. It angered him to be spoken to in that tone, but he never let it show. The smile he turned on Floyd just missed reaching his eyes. "I've got it. The nun's address."

"No shit? How?" Floyd quickly lost his uneasiness. "Did you find the right costume place?"

"No. She came by and parked right across the street from my apartment. Hell, man, she even went over and talked to the cops parked out front. I'd sort of been keeping an eye on them, when I noticed this dame walking up to their car. Looked a little strange to me, in the rain and all, so I got my binoculars, and bingo! It was her!"

"So how did you get her address?"

"I just went to the garage and got my car and waited for her to leave, then I followed. Simple as that."

"And the cops just let you drive away?"

"No. They stayed on me, but—"

"Damnation! I suppose you led them right here? To me? You crazy bastard, what's the matter with you, anyway?"

Clark's arm swung fast and hard at Floyd's head, spinning him backward. "Don't ever call me crazy again," he said coldly. "Of course I didn't lead the cops here. You go down, *I* go down, right? They called off the tail. I knew the minute they dropped me. Then when I got back to the apartment, the units there were gone, also. I called Nordyke, my lawyer, and he said the lab work had cleared me."

Floyd rubbed the side of his face, trying to decide what to say. The lab work might have cleared *Clark,* but it sure as hell hadn't written *him* off. "If you're in the clear, then what are we hanging around for? Ain't no reason we should be takin' chances like this. Let's get out of town."

"Aren't you even the least little bit curious about the nun?"

"Is she the one?"

Clark smiled slowly. "Suzanne Richards ring a bell?"

Floyd paled. Even though his gut instinct had told him all along that it had to be her, having it confirmed sent a shiver down his back. He guessed he was wrong when he thought Clark was about the only person he feared. He feared a little brown-haired girl named Susie, who was now all grown up. "You're certain of that?"

Randal Clark grinned, relishing Floyd's discomfort. "Pretty sure. I didn't want to go in the apartment building and risk the chance of her seeing me so I waited until I got back to my apartment. I called the manager of the complex I saw them go into, and asked if Suzanne Richards lived there. She said yes, apartment twelve, on the first floor. That satisfy you?"

Floyd suddenly realized how much Clark was enjoying his anxiety, and it irritated him. "I wouldn't be so damned sure *you're* out of the woods," he said, pulling his billfold from the back pocket of his sweatpants. He slid out several worn newspaper clippings and handed them to Clark. "She's brought in worse guys than you, buddy!"

Randal scanned down the articles, then looked at Floyd. "You know what we have to do, don't you? We can't take a chance on her doing a number on us like she did on these others."

"Somehow I always knew it would come down to this. Just her and me. I knew someday she would come after me. When I figured out who she was a few years back, I should have done her right then. She knows too much. She may not *know* she knows, but she damn sure could put me away for the rest of my friggin' life!"

"From what it says in these newspapers, she already knows *my* history, too. It says here she only has to touch a person to know just about everything they have ever done. And her hands were all over me yesterday."

"Yeah, man, you're made!" Floyd chuckled. "Looks like you'll have to help me kill her."

Clark looked at Floyd with contempt, hating that he was forced into any kind of dealings with such an ignorant man. He knew what he was going to do. Just as soon as

all this business with the psychic was over, he was going
to kill the scummy weasel!

The pandemonium at the station house was just exactly
what Suzanne knew it would be after Nora Myerson's announcement on her television show. Everyone seemed to
be in a perpetual state of panic, as they clamored for attention and demanded that they be listened to.

Suzanne managed to catch the eye of an officer she recognized. Jena Karnitz ushered Suzanne and Jessie past the
assemblage of people into the coffee room. "Now, you
won't slip away out the window, will you?" She laughed.

Suzanne had the grace to look embarrassed. "No. And
I'm sorry about that."

"How did you know we were going to hold you?" Jena
asked. "Was it really by psychic means, or were the guys
trying to rattle my cage with that choice bit?"

"No. I am a psychic," Suzanne said, "as is Jessie
here." She nodded toward her young companion. "When
I touch a person, their life just sort of unfolds in my
mind—things from long ago, as well as current thoughts."
She smiled. "So, has someone named Harry asked you out
yet?" As soon as she spoke the name, it occurred to Suzanne who Harry was. Her cheeks reddened.

Officer Karnitz laughed. "You read that in my mind
yesterday? Boy, you're dangerous to have around."

"I'm sorry. I shouldn't have said anything about it. That
is your own private business. Forgive me."

"Honey, I've been working around cops for the last
twelve years. I don't believe there is a thing on this earth
you could say that would embarrass me. Nothing. And as
for Harry, well, there's lots of other fish in the sea. I'm
about to give up on him."

"He's a jerk!" Jessie said. "He was mean to us last
night. Well, to Suzanne, anyway. He yelled at her, and
almost made her cry! And he doesn't believe in psychics.
Even after we told him things that should make him believe."

Jena nodded her head. "Yeah. He can be a real jerk, and that's a fact. But I'll bet he was only concerned about you and Miss Richards. Sometimes, when guys get really worried, they snap at the people they like the most. I'll bet that he just really, really likes fiery redheads and didn't mean to crab at you at all."

"Sweetie, it's me he is sore at, not you," Suzanne said. "He must still think I'm trying to take advantage of you and your family some way." Suzanne pushed long hair back from her face, arching her back to relieve sore muscles. It had been an exhausting day. They had only been back at Suzanne's apartment a few minutes when Jessie insisted on going back to the church and starting over. But nothing they had tried had worked. The connection was broken. Over and over Jessie had tried to force her mind into the other dimension, but it was no use. She could not pick up her sister's route. When Suzanne finally mentioned her other idea, Jessie had jumped at it.

Suzanne sensed, more than saw, Harry McDermott silently enter the room and come up behind her. Nevertheless, she jumped slightly as he spoke.

"I understand you wanted to see me?"

Suzanne turned. *Please,* she pleaded silently. *Don't give me a hard time tonight. Not tonight. I've had about all I can take.* "Detective McDermott," Suzanne said the officer's name tentatively, "we need your help."

Harry looked at the tall, lovely woman in front of him, who seemed to have no concept of her beauty or the effect she was having on him. Her hair was damp from the rain and smelled faintly of strawberries. There were tiny lines around her mouth, and a slight darkness under her eyes, suggesting she was tired and in need of rest. Harry felt an overwhelming urge to pull her to his chest and comfort her. Instead he spoke gruffly. "For what?"

"I thought maybe you would let us go into Clark's cell and see if we can do a reading."

"Mr. McDermott," Jessie interrupted before Harry could speak, "unless we find her, Amy is going to die tonight. I saw it. And I saw how Clark got her into his van. He called to her as she left the church, and she went over to see who it was. He grabbed her and put something over her nose. She couldn't breathe. I felt it.''

Suzanne spoke up. ''Furthermore, Jessie was able to track her sister from the church to a few miles down Interstate Twenty-nine. Then we lost the trail, but we might be able to pick it up again if we connect with a place he's spent some time in. Please, you must let us try.''

Harry took Suzanne by the elbow and guided her toward the couch, motioning to Jessie. ''Come sit over here, Jessie, with us. I need to tell you both a few things. First of all, Clark has been cleared. None of the DNA was a match to his, and the body parts found in his apartment turned out to be older than he was. So even if they were his, which he insisted all along they were not, they have ceased to be pertinent to this investigation.'' Harry reached over and took Jessie's hand in his own, enveloping it. ''I'm sorry, honey. Truly sorry.''

''Detective McDermott, that can't be right,'' Suzanne said, warmed by his tenderness toward Jessie. ''Last night we—Jessie—actually saw one of the murders. I saw it, too, by holding her hand. That's how I work, remember? I can do a reading by touching a person. In this case, I tuned in to what Jessie was tuned in to. And we saw Clark murder a girl!''

''Which one? Could you be a little more specific?'' Harry asked, slipping back into the role of adversary.

''Why won't you believe us?'' Suzanne suddenly demanded, angry. ''Last night we told you an old man had been murdered. Weren't we right? Why do you have to be so pigheaded!''

Harry squirmed, uncomfortably.

''Jessie, would you mind waiting for me outside? I'll tell the detective about the murder, but you don't need to relive it all. Just wait for me.''

Jessie's jaw locked stubbornly. ''It's my sister who is

missing. I think I should stay. You might miss something. Like the bottles.''

Harry looked at the girl. ''Bottles? What bottles?''

Suzanne answered him. ''We couldn't tell what was in them, but after he finished killing the girl, he opened several little bottles and smeared the contents around the bottom of the girl's torso.''

The semen! Harry thought. *He was putting the splotches of semen on the body!*

''Tell me what else you saw.'' Harry was suddenly interested in everything the two had to say.

''We think we saw him shave off one of the girl's eyebrows,'' Suzanne said. ''The right one I believe. Then he put makeup on her—really thick. She was alive through all of this, and terrified.''

''She scratched him once,'' Jessie added, ''across the face. He was really mad about that. He put his hand to his face, and it came back bloody, then he slapped her real hard for it.''

Harry remembered the scrapings of skin they had found under the fingernails of one of the earlier victims. ''What did this girl look like? Do you remember anything at all about her?''

''She was pretty,'' Suzanne said, ''with long, blond braids. And her hair was wet, like maybe she had been swimming or working out.''

It was the little Hunter girl. No doubt about it. She had disappeared coming home from the gym. It had been a gruesome murder, and her severed head, with its made-up face and long, beautiful braids had invaded his dreams for months.

''There was a little girl about five or six years old, standing to the side, watching,'' Suzanne said. ''She seemed almost in a daze or something. But we lost the vision after she appeared, so that's all we know.''

''A child? That's strange. We have had no evidence that Clark went after anyone but young women.''

Suzanne jumped on the detective's statement. ''I

thought you said Clark was no longer a suspect."

"He isn't!" Harry spoke more vehemently than he intended. "At least not officially. Actually, not even unofficially, truth be known. My team that worked this investigation are about the only ones who think he could still be the butcher. And of course you told me yesterday you *knew* Clark had committed those murders, and your background checks out pretty impressive."

Suzanne couldn't have been more surprised if Harry had admitted to being the butcher himself. "You mean you actually believed me?"

"Well." Harry backpedaled. "I think I believed *you* believed it."

"Why have you been so mean, then?" Jessie demanded, with the bluntness of a teenager.

"Because you keep jumping into the middle of my investigation and placing yourselves in danger! Like last night. You had no business going out to that carnival all alone. *You* might have been killed, as well as the old man. If you are right, and Clark *is* the killer, then you have to remember that he knows Suzanne's face. You both have got to be more careful!"

"How much of what we have told you is accurate?" Suzanne asked.

Harry rubbed the back of his neck in frustration, hearing little cracking sounds as his hand kneaded out the soreness. He looked at the woman and the girl who had disrupted his life for two days. "All right. Maybe you need to know.

"Jessie"—he turned to the girl—"we have found traces of chloroform on the faces of a few of the girls. That could sure be what you were experiencing when you 'relived' your sister's abduction. But we have no knowledge of a van. Clark drives a 1996 Ford Taurus. However, we do have a report of one witness who swears she saw a maroon van hanging around a different church where one girl was abducted. And the details in the murder you saw are consistent with the evidence." He glanced at Jessie, unsure if he should continue.

"I need to know everything," Jessie answered his unspoken question. "Something you tell me might be the thing that lets me find Amy."

Harry nodded. "Okay. Each of the girls had small patches of semen smeared on their bodies. Semen from five or six different men. The psychologist told us the killer picked clean-cut, pure-looking girls, then made them up to look like whores. I suspect what you saw him doing was removing semen from those bottles. By smearing semen from several different men, he was branding them in some sick way—showing the world they were not what they seemed."

"A deep hatred of his mother, right?" Suzanne asked.

Harry shrugged. "No, actually if the killer is Clark, it was his father who abused him, not his mother—or at least that we know about. But you're right. Our psychologist said the killer's hatred of women probably stemmed from a hatred of his mother. That has been one area that has puzzled us."

"Maybe he hated his mother for not protecting him," Suzanne suggested. "That sometimes happens."

"Maybe. I don't know."

"So *can* we try doing a reading from Clark's cell?" Suzanne changed the subject. "You can stay right with us if you wish. It won't bother us."

"Okay, ladies, let's do it."

Chapter
Twenty-one

O f all the manners in which Amy had visualized meeting her death over the last twelve days, she had to
admit that drowning was not one of them, not even when
she had clocked the rising of the water and saw it was
climbing at an alarming rate of an inch every five or six
minutes. After all, how much could it rain, she had reasoned. But now she was standing in water almost to her
hips, and it seemed to be pouring in from everywhere. The
opening for the electrical cord had water coming out of it
at a steady rate; there was water dripping from several
places across the wooden ceiling; and the crack in the cement had widened.

Amy held tight to the lamp, holding it and the cord up
out of the water. She knew she should shut off the light,
but could not make herself do it. Better to go in one blind-
ing flash of electrical shock, than die a thousand deaths in
a dark, watery grave.

She pictured her mother, father, and Jessie at home on
the farm, perhaps huddled together on the couch, or pacing
back and forth, waiting for news of her. They would be
near panic by now. Tears burned at Amy's eyes as she
clamped a trembling hand over her mouth and listened to
the silence of her tomb.

Suzanne and Jessie stood facing each other, their hands
locked. The older psychic could feel the tension in the

younger one. "Relax, Jessie," she said softly. "Clear your mind." To Harry she tried to explain. "Sometimes with a psychic it's like sitting in a room listening to three or four televisions, a stereo, and a radio or two. Everything just comes at you at once so that you understand nothing. The information is coming from too many sources. What you have to do is learn to concentrate on only one of the voices. Then you can understand what is trying to get through."

"It doesn't bother you that I am here or that you are talking to me?"

"No. If it is going to come, it will come. If it does, and you want to ask us anything, go ahead."

As if on cue, Jessie's head tilted to the left and her eyes closed tight. She could see Randal Clark sitting on the chair by the small table in the cell.

Suzanne saw him also but did not feel the enormous fear she had felt when she had touched him.

Many images began bombarding Jessie's mind. Bodies, and knives, and blood. Razors, bottles, and sunflowers. All going around and around in her head.

"Pick one, Jessie," Suzanne said. "Concentrate on one thing. Perhaps the sunflowers. Remember that I, too, saw sunflowers. They must have some meaning."

Jessie forced the other images from her mind. Suzanne could see them fading and the sunflowers becoming stronger. They seemed to be lining a pathway of some kind.

Suzanne began speaking in a low, hypnotic voice to Harry. "We are on a road, the same road I saw yesterday when I visited Clark here at the police station. It is a gravel path, with sunflowers thick on both sides. It seems to be a hill. We are going up the path of a hill, but—oh, God— there is blood washing down the road. We can't stand up. It is all over us!" The image began fading. Suzanne pressed Jessie's hand. "No, sweetie. This time we must go on. Stand up. Get out of the blood. Look around for another marker. Try to see the name of a nearby road, anything!''

Jessie's head tilted back. ''The blood is all over me! Oh, please! Don't let it be Amy's blood!''

''Look, Jessie.''

''I can't!''

''You can. You can do this.''

''No! No! I can't! The blood is almost up to my knees!''

''Jessie, open your eyes and look at the hill. Look for something that will tell us where to go.''

Jessie's head began going from side to side as if she were looking. ''There's a fence. It has little—it's an electric fence. Like we have at home. Wait. Wait! There's a board nailed to one of the posts. The printing is faded, but I can almost read it . . . uh . . . Let Freedom Ring! That's what it says. Let Freedom Ring.''

So much of her energy had been consumed in finding a marker that Jessie's knees gave out and she would have sunk to the floor had Harry not caught her. He set her down on the cell bed.

''Does the sign mean anything to you, Detective?'' Suzanne asked.

''Harry,'' Harry answered. ''You can't seem to decide what to call me so how about just plain Harry, and no, I'm afraid the sign means nothing to me.'' If there had been any doubt about the young girl's talent, it was dispelled with the scene he had just witnessed. A scene that had slightly unnerved him.

''At least I didn't see Amy on the floor with a knife sticking out of her, like earlier,'' Jessie said. ''I guess that's something.''

Suzanne sat down on the small bed next to Jessie, gathering her close. ''Sweetie, it's like I told you. I think you were into Clark's mind again, that's all. You were picking up what he was *hoping* to do, or *imagining* doing. Remember, in that vision he had the two of us, and we know for sure he doesn't have *us,* right?''

They all looked up as Jim Stahl entered the cell. ''Harry,

Connors wants to see you. He was able to dig up some background on Clark that he thought you'd want to see.''

"Right. Would you see these two ladies back to their car?'' Harry walked over, touching Suzanne on the arm. "Would you mind if I came by later to see how you both are doing? And promise me you won't strike out after Clark on your own.''

Jessie answered before Suzanne had a chance. "We aren't promising anything. We have to find Amy tonight.''

"Just let us know what you are doing, darlin'.'' Jim smiled. "We're here to help you, not keep you from finding your sister.''

Suzanne's eyes had not left Harry's face. It was a strong face, full of warmth and compassion. It was also an incredibly handsome face, in a rugged man's man sort of way. Thick, long lashes framed cerulean eyes which were alive with energy.

"Oh, by the way,'' Harry said. "You wouldn't happen to remember your birth parents' name, would you? We've run into a little snag on your background.''

Suzanne tore her eyes from Harry's face as she gave a small gasp. "My background? Why are you still worried about my background?'' Harry's smile seemed circumspect to Suzanne now.

"It's probably nothing, but we ran a check on your father, Carl Webb, and the birth certificate that was used to get a Social Security number belonged to a boy in Oklahoma who died when he was eleven.''

"That's impossible. I have my father's death certificate at home. He died in Omaha by his own hand.''

"Yes,'' Harry answered. "We aren't questioning that he died, but we think he was using an alias when he killed himself.''

"Why? Why would he do that?''

Harry shrugged, realizing for the first time that Suzanne was starting to get agitated by his questions. "I'm sorry. I . . . we . . .''—he looked to Jim for support—"thought you might remember another name. You would have been about five years old when he applied for that number. Do you remember ever having another name? Besides Webb?" It was only a loose end. As Harry looked at Suzanne's stricken face, he was sorry he had brought up the matter.

Unexpected tears filled Suzanne's eyes. "I don't really remember much about my childhood. Just bits and pieces. I can remember my mother being killed in a car wreck, then several years of moving from place to place with my father." As she spoke, memories of small, dirty apartments, and food eaten directly from cans flitted across her mind. It was a horrible time for her. No wonder she had blocked it all from her memory. "But you know, maybe my father had another name he went by—like a middle name. I seem to remember my mother calling him Roy."

"How about a city or state?" Jim asked. "Do you remember where you were living when your mother was killed?"

"No." Suzanne shook her head. "I've often tried to remember because I've thought of trying to look up my mother's grave. It was a farm, I'm pretty sure of that, but where, I have no idea."

"And the only name you remember is Roy?" Harry asked.

"No. I used to think my mother's name was Jean. However, Miss Emily, the lady who adopted me, tried to trace a Jean Webb for me, so I would have some idea of my background, but she never had any success. We figured I must be wrong in remembering the name." Suzanne looked at Harry, her face trying to hide a mixture of emotions. "Why do you need to know this? Am I a suspect of some kind?"

"No, no." Harry spoke quickly. "Don't think that. We just came up against this puzzle of your father by chance. It's just something you, for your own sake, might want to check into."

Suzanne's eyes darted back and forth between the two detectives. She had worked for enough police departments to know things rarely happened "by chance" in their investigations. Harry McDermott had launched a full-scale background check on her. There wasn't any doubt about that.

"Hey!" Jessie interrupted. "Let's get going."

Harry pulled his eyes from Suzanne's face. "Yes. I've got to meet one of my detectives." At the door of the cell he turned once again to Suzanne. "I'll see you later?" He asked it as a question, but all he received in answer was a shrug, as Suzanne deliberately turned her attention to Jessie.

"Well, sweetie, at least we got something from this visit. We know there is some sort of sign saying Let Freedom Ring that is important to us."

Jim Stahl interrupted. "What did you say? About the sign?"

Suzanne explained the hand-printed sign Jessie had seen in her vision. "Detective McDermott didn't know what it was. Have you ever heard of it?"

Jim nodded. "Yes. I think so. It sounds familiar, but I can't quite place it. Let me do some checking, and I'll see what I can find out."

As they walked from the tiny cell, Suzanne took hold of the arm Jim held out to her. For a man of sixty-three, it was surprisingly strong. But Suzanne detected something more as she held on to the detective's arm, and it frightened her.

"What do you have, Gordie?" Harry asked.

"Well, I don't know. Take a look at this." Gordon handed him several faxes of medical records. "According to what I can make out, Randal Clark sustained numerous injuries, including the one to his penis, *after* the death of his father."

"What? That doesn't make sense. The report we received from the police in Boise said the father was responsible, and the mother had killed him defending her sons."

"I don't think so. Look. This is the hospital report when he was seven. The one where his mother killed his father. See? There is no indication of any injury to his private parts. Then two years later, he was admitted to a hospital in Twin Falls, having supposedly injured himself accidentally with an electrical cord. Actually, I have reports from seven different hospitals showing severe injuries over a period of about eight years after his father's death."

"How could that be? Surely old injuries would have shown up."

"Not necessarily. When you look at the injuries, a chilling pattern develops. I see electrical shock, small burns, fingernails and toenails missing, heavy bruising around the stomach area—where no bones will break—just hurt like hell. Shit like that. And there were a number of old scars from cuts, but according to the hospital notes, his mother explained them away with a variety of stories."

"Good God! What kind of a monster was she?"

"I don't know. Everyone who ever had any dealing with her said she was an angel—including the hospital employees. It's right there in their notes."

"What about the brother? Did he suffer the same injuries?"

"Not that I could find. He was sick a lot, that's what the neighbors I talked with said. There were still a few around who remembered the family. The brother died not long after the mother left town. Clark stayed around for a few years, then he took off."

"Did the neighbors seem to think the mother was an angel, too?"

"Oh, yeah. A dear, sweet, God-fearing angel. I heard it at least a dozen times."

"Still no info on where the mother is now, or what her married name is?"

"No. A few people remembered that she had moved to Alaska when she left Idaho. No one seemed too surprised she had remarried. She was a real looker with—get this— long, blond hair."

"Why am I not surprised?"

* * *

"Isn't it ever going to quit raining?" Jessie said as she dashed across the parking lot with Suzanne. "It's almost dark now, and it's still coming down. It was hard enough seeing the road in the daylight. It will really be yukky now!"

They both reached the car at the same time and tumbled in, shaking water from their hair.

"I think we should go home for a little while," Suzanne said, fatigue overcoming her. "And before you start objecting, hear me out. We both could use some dry clothing and a bite to eat, and since we never made it to the grocery store today, I suggest we order pizza. That will give us a little time to dry out and regroup. I know you are not going to want to quit. I understand that. But we won't do Amy any good if we're too tired to think."

"I guess you're right," Jessie said, feeling Suzanne's weariness and knowing she needed a break. "And it *is* about three hours past my suppertime. I am sort of hungry, now that I think about it." Jessie turned solemn. "Why were you frightened when you took Jim's arm back at the station?"

"Boy, nothing gets by you, does it?"

"Well, let's just say we had better not ever try to keep secrets from each other," Jessie said.

Suzanne nodded. "I don't know what it was when I took Jim's arm. All at once I experienced a feeling of dread—of doom. I hope nothing is going to happen to him."

"Me, too." Jessie sat back in the car seat, pulling her seat belt a little tighter. She also hoped nothing was going to happen to her friend. For the last several minutes, she had been seeing flashes of Suzanne in her mind's eye—and the image was growing darker, just as it had done with her aunt Vera. Jessie wasn't certain if Suzanne could sense the danger when they touched, and was equally uncertain whether there was anything she could do about it, even if she did see it.

Chapter
Twenty-two

$\mathbf{F}$ loyd's eyes darted back and forth between the parking lot and the old brownstone. He had been watching the place for almost an hour, coming to the conclusion that some of the tenants used the front entrance, and some the west side. He assumed it had to do with which part of the building their apartment was located.

He had driven through the parking area earlier, checking for the vehicle Clark had told him about—an old gray Cutlass, license number R2R 576. It was nowhere around.

Getting into the building was not going to be a problem. As near as he could tell, there was no security of any kind, not even a locked outer door.

He felt in the deep pocket of his raincoat for his gun. His hand wrapped comfortably around the 9 mm Colt that had set him back a pretty penny, but which was rapidly becoming his best friend. It was far and away the greatest confidence builder he had ever owned. He snapped the nine-round clip into place, feeling in his other pocket for the metal piece that made the Colt worth every cent he had paid for it. He smiled as he screwed the silencer into place.

Clark had told him he would be here—as backup if nothing else. Probably a good idea, since there might be two of them in the apartment. If it was going to be messy, he wanted no part of it. He didn't mind killing, as long as it was fast and easy, with no surprises. If it was going to get complicated, he would let Clark handle the whole damned thing.

He hadn't really realized what a nutcase Clark was until he had killed the Murphy girl for him. Shit, he was still having nightmares over that little piece of work! A friggin' nut, that's what Clark was. A friggin' nut! Cutting those girls up like that, taking time to slather on all that makeup. Floyd felt a little shiver of anxiety race down his arms. Yeah. Just as soon as they had finished their little project tonight, he was going to hightail it out of town and never look back.

As he limped along in the rain, Willie Rodriquez deeply regretted never learning to drive a car. He was wet clear through to his boxers, despite the small black umbrella he was carrying. He had tried to reach Jim at the station, but had been cut off three times by a harried-sounding operator who informed him each time that Jim was on another line. Finally, he had decided just to walk the fourteen blocks. Served him right for getting suckered in and giving Jim a bum steer.

Willie took his white handkerchief from the pocket of his jeans and wiped moisture from his face as he trudged along. It had been a long time since he had fallen for a street plant. Who would have guessed the slimy-looking man shooting pool at Charley's wasn't on the level? It had taken him two days to trace back the rumors, but Willie was certain now they had been a plant, arising initially from the dark-haired sleazeball who had shaken him down in a friendly little game of pool.

Willie didn't like someone trying to make a fool out of him, especially not when it involved his good friend, Jim Stahl. He hadn't yet come up with the jerk's right name, but he would get it. He would damned sure get it! All he knew for positive was that the name wasn't Floyd Webster, as he had been told.

Willie was fairly certain he had not been singled out because the man knew about his link to the police. The guy calling himself Floyd had been in and out of a hundred different places, slyly dropping small innuendos about the butcher here and there—almost always asked as a question. "Say, what's this about some guy living with Clark? I heard it was some pro with his fingerprints burned off. You hear anything like that?" It hadn't taken long until the matter was a regular buzz on the streets.

It was an old trick, sometimes started by attorneys looking for a little ammo in court, sometimes started by relatives trying to get their family member off. It was extremely hard to trace back to a source. If the man had not personally used Willie to help start the rumor, Willie would probably never have been able to track the story.

Fire flashed from Willie's eyes as he walked along, dragging his bum leg. He would report in to his friend, then he had some more checking to do. Before the night was out, he was going to have the asshole's real name. He hadn't worked the streets of Kansas City over twenty years for nothing!

The uneasiness had been growing in Suzanne since leaving the precinct. It was just an overall feeling of apprehension. It seemed to her that she was missing something. Something important. What? She took her right hand from the steering wheel and began massaging her temple. *Think! What is it! What have you overlooked?* A hard knot began forming in her stomach.

The chaos at the precinct had only abated somewhat as Jim made his way to Caswell's office where Harry was waiting. The nasty weather had at least slowed the number of people who were actually coming to the precinct to offer suggestions about the investigation, but the phone lines had been going nuts. With the knowledge that the butcher was still on the streets, citizens were calling by the hundreds with their own suspicions. It always amazed Jim how many people were willing to go on an anonymous tip line with accusations against people they had known all their lives. Even after two of the bodies of the missing girls had been found, over a thousand calls had been logged with suggestions from the public as to where they might be found. It was insane.

The door to Caswell's office was closed. Jim tapped out a short beat and stuck his head in. "Anything new I need to know about before I go home?" He had been at the station for twelve hours. It was now after eight o'clock and Ruth had been waiting dinner since six. He was tired and feeling every one of his sixty-three years.

Harry motioned him on in with a wave of his hand, explaining quickly the new information Connors had brought.

"Huh!" Jim grunted. "That makes Clark almost a perfect match to the FBI profile, then. Have you informed Caswell?"

"Hell, no," Harry answered. "The last thing he said to me before leaving tonight was that he wanted a new list of suspects on his desk come morning. I'm not mentioning any more on Clark until we can nail it down."

Jim gave a long sigh and sat down. "Harry, we have no DNA match, and the body parts found in Clark's apartment have no bearing on this case. Just how, exactly, do you plan on nailing it down?"

"Damn it, Jim—something isn't right! So those fingers and toes we found floating around in formaldehyde were old and gangrenous. What the hell were they doing in Clark's apartment? Where would you even come up with something like that? What could he possibly be doing with them?"

Jim shrugged. "I suppose there is a chance Nordyke was right. I don't suppose there is a cop anywhere who doesn't know that serial killers have a custom of saving little mementoes, like body parts, from their victims. Maybe one of our boys was certain Clark was the killer, so he decided to—"

"You don't believe that, Jim, and neither do I," Harry interrupted. "Besides, where the hell would one of our boys come up with that stuff? They're not exactly something you have lying around!"

"You're right about that!" Jim stood and started for the door. "But I'm fried. I'm going home and sleep on it—just as soon as I run something through the computer."

"What's that?"

"Let Freedom Ring. I sort of vaguely remember that slogan from somewhere."

"Good. I was going to do that next. I can't say that it means anything to me, though, except as the end of some song like the *Star Spangled Banner* or something."

Jim gave him a wry smile. "I thought it came from *God Bless America.*"

Willie Rodriquez walked into the room, leaving a trail of water dripping behind him. "You are both wrong, señores. It is the last line of *My Country 'Tis of Thee,* one of my favorite songs!"

"Willie!" Jim said in astonishment. "You look like a drowned rat! What are you doing out on a night like this?"

"I come to apologize, Jim," Willie said. "I told you wrong about the butcher. He got me on an old trick—one I have never fallen for before."

"He? Who are you talking about?"

"I don't know the man's real name. He said it was Floyd Webster, but I'm certain that isn't right. For two weeks he has been planting stories on the street about Clark having a roommate, someone with his fingerprints burned off, that sort of thing."

"So your info was wrong?" Harry asked.

Willie nodded. "You both seemed so certain about Clark I decided to dig a little deeper. I learned this Floyd Webster had started the stories." He looked at Jim. "I'm sorry, man! I should have thought of a plant right away, but this guy seemed like such a worthless character, I never thought he'd feed me no line of bull."

"That's okay, Willie," Jim said. "Don't worry about it. This investigation has been screwy right from the beginning. You aren't the only one who has problems."

Neither Willie nor Jim could understand the look that crossed Harry's face.

Suzanne drove into the small parking area on the west side of her apartment building. By now the knot in her stomach was a burning cauldron of acid. Something was wrong. Her fingers trembled as she removed the keys from the ignition and turned to Jessie. "Can you think of anything we didn't tell Harry? I just can't shake the feeling that we have overlooked something important."

Jessie shook her head. "No. But, Suzanne, I keep seeing you in my mind, and your image just gets darker and darker. I'm afraid for you. It's just like with Aunt Vera." There. She had told her.

Suzanne reached over, taking Jessie's hand. The instant she touched the younger psychic, she saw it, also. It was an unnerving vision. "It's probably nothing," she said, shaking it off for Jessie's sake. "We've been placing ourselves in danger. I'm sure that's all that it is."

As they dashed from the car into the apartment building, both psychics felt an overwhelming flush of fear, but neither saw the cold eyes following their every move.

Sister Mary Elizabeth motioned for her young nurse to come close. The doctor had given her a shot to dissolve the clot which had caused her trouble. Since it had been given within minutes of her stroke, she knew her chances for recovery were greatly enhanced. The nurse leaned down to her. "Don't try to talk, Sister Mary," she instructed. "Your left side is partially paralyzed. You have had a mild stroke."

Does she think me daft? Mary Elizabeth thought. *Of course I have had a stroke.* To her God she gave specific instructions: *You will give me the strength to finish this job, my Lord!* The silent prayer would brook no room for disagreement.

With her right hand, the old nun grabbed on to the arm of the nurse who had been watching over her for many months, pulling her down within earshot. "I need to make a phone call," she said, her voice weak but clear. "You have the number. I heard the man leave it with you before the doctor came."

"Sister Mary, you are not at the home any longer," her nurse said. "I came to be with you while you're here in the hospital, but I know they are not going to let you make any phone calls." She looked down fondly at the old nun who had rapidly become her favorite patient when she began her rotation at the Holy Cross Retirement Home.

The nun kept a strong hold on the arm of her nurse as she looked at her with sightless eyes. "Please. Help me. I have to make this phone call. I cannot die with this sin on my soul. Please."

For just a moment, the young nurse thought perhaps the old woman was merely rambling incoherently because of the stroke and medication. But the clarity of her words belied this.

"Sharon! You must do me this last favor! Please! Hand me the telephone!" The urgency in Sister Mary Elizabeth's voice caused her nurse to obey. She picked up the telephone on the stand by the bedside and placed it next to her patient.

Tears of gratitude welled up in the nun's blank eyes. "Thank you, dear. Now place a call to Detective McDermott at the number he left with you. You'll probably have to call collect. I don't think the operator will put through a long-distance call from the room."

Harry picked up the telephone in Caswell's office. "McDermott here."

"Detective McDermott? This is the operator. I have a collect call for you from a Sister Mary Elizabeth in Sterling Heights, Michigan. Will you accept the charges?"

"Yes, operator! Put her through."

"Detective, this is Nurse Sharon Willis. Sister Mary wants to finish her conversation with you. In fact, she's quite adamant about it."

"How is she? Didn't you tell me she was having a stroke? Can she even speak?" A dozen questions leaped to Harry's mind.

"Yes, sir. She had a stroke and we've got her in the hospital. But Sister Mary is able to speak. I'm not positive just *how*, since by all rights she shouldn't be able to talk at all, but I've learned never to question what Sister Mary can and cannot do." She squeezed the old nun's hand, then handed the telephone to her.

"Detective," Sister Mary started in immediately, "I'm not going to waste time on small talk, because I may not have that much time left. But I wanted to tell you what I did. It may mean something to Suzanne someday."

"Certainly, go ahead," Harry said, wondering what could be so important.

"My sister Emily adopted Suzanne when she was eight years old. I had to falsify a few documents in order for her to do so. I lied about Emily's age and marital status, in order for the adoption to go through."

"As I told you on the phone, I'm not really concerned about that, Sister," Harry said.

"Wait. I'm not finished. There is much, much more." She could feel her throat tightening, and instructed her Lord to give her more time. "Her father came for her a couple of years later. Her real father. He showed me the birth certificate. He said a man named Carl Webb had kidnapped Suzanne, and he had spent all those months trying to track her down."

"What?" Harry said. "Are you certain of this?"

"Yes. Quite certain. When Emily adopted Suzanne I placed her footprint on the adoption certificate. It was on file at the convent. I took his paper into another room and compared the two. They were identical."

"So what did you do then? After you knew this was her real father?"

The nun's voice was barely audible. "I sinned. Greatly. I told him that the little girl named Suzanne had run away right after she was brought to the convent. I told him we had no knowledge of her.''

Harry let out a long breath. ''Oh, my, Sister. That really *was* wrong.''

The nun's voice broke. ''I know. I know. And the man, he even went over my head to the bishop, and I still stuck to my story. Such a sin! I lied to my bishop!''

''And you've never told the girl? Suzanne?''

''No. I have never told anyone. Not even Emily.''

''Do you remember the man's name? The one claiming to be Suzanne's father?''

''Yes. It is burned forever into my memory. His name was Cole. Roy Cole. The mother's name was Jean, and Suzanne was born in Bartlesville, Oklahoma.''

''Did this Roy say what had happened to Suzanne's mother?''

''Yes. That was one of the reasons I lied. He said her mother had died in a car wreck, which was what Suzanne had always claimed, so I knew she would be going back to only this man. He seemed like such a dirty, uncouth, sinful man, that I decided Suzanne was better off with my Emily. But of course I had no right to make that decision. No right at all.''

''Sister Mary, I can't thank you enough for getting this information to me. I don't know what it all means just yet, but as soon as I know, I'll get back to you. You hang in there now!''

''Yes. Yes, maybe for just a little while yet. Maybe until I see Suzanne, and make it right with her. Even her name is wrong, you know. It is really Susie. Susie Cole. The other man, that Carl Webb, he is the one who started calling her Suzanne, I suppose to make the child forget who she really was. I should have told her. I should have told her father. I had no right! God forgive me, I had no right!''

Chapter
Twenty-three

Suzanne walked around the apartment double-checking locks at the windows and doors, her apprehension growing. She was certain now that her uneasiness was not just over something she had failed to tell the detectives. It was more than that. She was frightened. She was unreasonably, ridiculously, frightened. After all they had gone through in the last two days, why was she now, in the safety of her own home, so terrified?

Jessie looked at her watch. "The pizza should be here. What's taking it so long?"

"This is Kansas City, sweetie. It takes a little longer. Relax. It will be here shortly."

"*You* should talk! You're as nervous as a cat! I think you've checked those windows about a hundred times!"

"I know. I know." Suzanne rubbed her hands over her arms as though trying to get warm. "I can't imagine what's wrong with me."

Jessie looked at Suzanne and once again saw her growing dim in her mind's eye—her *psychic* eye. She couldn't shake the feeling that she should be doing something. She remembered Jo-Jo, their dog. She had seen the same darkness descend around Jo-Jo, though, and the dog had not died. *Only because you interceded, Jessie! If you hadn't gone to find him, he would be dead.*

Jessie made her mind up quickly. She would not sit by

until it was too late, as it had been for her aunt Vera. She would call Harry and Jim. They would know what to do.

Floyd sat watching the building, trying to form a plan where there would be no risk to himself. Unlike Clark, he was perfectly content to play it safe. With two involved, it doubled the chances that something could go wrong. As he watched, he saw a figure in a dark raincoat stop beside the side entrance to light a cigarette. That's odd, he thought. Why would anyone stay outside to smoke a cigarette on a night like this? As Floyd watched, he saw the man look toward him and give a little salute. Clark! He had made it! Good. A little backup never hurt. He raised his hand to his forehead in acknowledgment.

Timothy Simons drove through the parking area looking for a slot to park in long enough to deliver his last pizza. He was wet, and cold, and tired of people griping about the pizza being soggy. What did they expect, for crying out loud? It was raining cats and dogs!

The only parking spot he could find was in the farthest corner of the lot. He would be drenched by the time he got to the door. He decided to double park and hope some irate tenant didn't decide to leave, and report him for blocking their car. Plato's Pizza and the phone number were emblazoned right on the side of the van, making it a little hard to deny it was him.

Floyd entered the apartment house through the front door and walked down the long hallway, looking for 12 A. At exactly that moment Timothy Simons entered by the side door, carrying a large pizza. The two met at precisely the spot where the two hallways joined. Floyd could see ahead that there were only two doors that could possibly be the one the boy was looking for. On a hunch he said, "That for Suzanne Richards in twelve A?"

"Yeah. Is that where you're going?"

"Sure am. Here, I'll take it." He thrust a fifty into Timothy's hand. "Don't bother. You can keep the change for having to get out on such a night!"

"Thanks, mister!" Timothy smiled. Maybe it wasn't going to be such a bad night after all.

Jessie ran to the door when she heard the knock.

"Don't open it, Jessie," Suzanne warned. "Find out who it is first."

"Who's there?" Jessie called.

"Delivery. Plato's Pizza," Floyd answered.

Jessie unbolted the locks, then swung the door wide. "What took you so long? I'm starving!"

Floyd stepped in to the apartment, handing Jessie the pizza and closing the door all in one smooth motion. Suzanne stood a few feet away, staring at him. He recognized her from the photos he had seen in the newspaper. Other than the brown hair and eyes, she bore no resemblance at all to the little girl he had left in Omaha.

"That will be fourteen dollars and fifty cents, ma'am," Floyd said to Suzanne.

Suzanne still stood, unmoving. When she heard his voice, she knew. Fear gripped her, making it hard to breathe. "Uh . . . my purse. Jessie, would you get me my purse from the kitchen?"

Jessie started to remind Suzanne that they had already laid the money out, but at the last second she realized something was wrong as she picked up a tumbling whirlwind of thoughts. "Sure. I'll get it, Suzanne," she spoke as she started walking away.

Floyd's hand went into the pocket of his raincoat just as Suzanne screamed, "Run, Jessie! Out the back door!"

Jessie dropped the pizza and raced across the tiny kitchen to the back door. Her fingers felt like they were leaden as she fumbled with the lock, expecting the man to be after her any minute.

Floyd paid no attention to the young girl. Instead, he held the gun on Suzanne, smiling slowly. "Well, aren't you going to give your old daddy a kiss?"

*   *   *

Harry looked down at the information the police department in Bartlesville, Oklahoma, had faxed him. Roy Cole and his five-year-old daughter, Susie Cole, had both perished in an explosion at Roy Cole's farm twenty-two years ago. They had no record of a Jean Cole being killed in a car wreck. Jean Cole, Roy Cole's widow, was alive and well, still living in Bartlesville.

What the hell? Harry thought. Could this be a different family? He didn't think so. Sister Mary Elizabeth seemed pretty sure of her facts, and the names were all the same except for the child. Suzanne—Susie—could be. If so, who was Carl Webb, the man who had supposedly kidnapped Suzanne? And who had shown up at the convent claiming to be Suzanne's father? And if it wasn't Suzanne and her father who had died in that fire, who did? He, obviously, had a hell of lot more digging to do!

Suzanne started backing up slowly. She was not even aware that she was moving, as she stared at the specter in front of her. "No. You're dead. It can't be."

Roy Cole threw back his head and laughed, Suzanne's fright making him bold. "Well, now see? You ain't so much of a psychic, after all! Didn't even know that wasn't your old pa with his face blasted away by that shotgun!"

Suzanne remembered that horrible day. Coming home from school. Going in the bathroom. Blood and flesh covering everything—the floor, the walls, the mirror. It had been the most dreadful time of her life. Slowly what he was saying began to penetrate her brain. "It . . . it wasn't you? Then who? I don't understand. Where did you go?"

"I got out of town—split—hit the road, little Susie! You had started asking questions about the fire, and I couldn't let you open up that whole can of worms, now could I?"

Suzanne stared hard at her father, not understanding a word he was saying. What fire? What questions? She could hardly remember speaking to her father, let alone discussing a fire. "I don't have any idea what you are talking about. I remember nothing about a fire."

Roy's lips curled in derision. "Oh, Susie, Susie. We could have conquered the world if you would have just used your little *voodoo* in the way I wanted! Just think of it. Every hotshot politician, every head of the world's biggest companies—all of the kingmakers. You could have brought them all to their knees with only a touch! We would have made a fortune!"

Suzanne's eyes glinted. "What are you talking about? Blackmail? You wanted me to learn all of their dirty secrets so you could blackmail them?"

"You've got it, sweet Sue! But nothin' I ever did to you made you obey me." Roy ran his free hand over the stubble of beard on his face, relishing the fear in Suzanne's eyes. "Not even when I tried being nice. That's when it happened. You touched me one day and I saw the revulsion when you drew your hand back. You asked me about the fire, and then I knew I had to leave. I brought in one of them homeless men, dressed him up in my clothes, and blew him away with my shotgun!"

"Oh, God, how could you have left your own child to walk in on that?" Suzanne felt sick to her stomach, remembering the horror. It seemed impossible that her own father had set up that gruesome scene; had planned for her to go through the nightmare of finding that shattered body. "And you did it all for nothing. I was always so terrified of you that my psychic ability shut down in your presence. I don't know what you think I saw, but was it so bad that you had to set up your own daughter like that? My God, it was years before I stopped having nightmares!"

"Well, little Susie, that's just it. I didn't do nothin' to my own daughter, 'cause I ain't your pa!" Roy's pleasure at the look which passed over Suzanne's face was evident.

"What?"

"Oh, now I'll admit my name is on your birth certificate, but I was never your pa. Not in any sense of the word."

"What are you talking about?"

"Kind of a surprise, ain't it, Miss High and Mighty? Your real dad, why he didn't want nothin' to do with you. Not with you or that rotten mother of yours. She came crying to me, 'fraid her precious reputation would be ruined, and I took her in. I gave her a home, then when you came along, as far as people knew, why you was my kid. Susie Anne Cole. The Anne even came from my dead ma."

Suzanne's head was reeling. Could any of this be true? She stammered, trying to make sense of it all. "I don't believe you! My name is Suzanne. I used to be Suzanne Webb before Miss Emily adopted me. My name isn't Susie Cole and you're not Roy Cole." Yet even as she denied the name, a long-forgotten memory flitted across her mind. A woman singing to her, *Susie, Susie, my sweet Susie.*

Roy Cole sat down on the arm of the couch, motioning with the gun toward Suzanne. "Sit. Sit. We don't have to be so formal. Why we're practically family." He laughed at his own wit.

Suzanne slowly lowered herself into a wing-backed chair that had been a favorite of Miss Emily's. *And now I'm going to die in it.*

All hell had been breaking loose at the precinct. Phone lines were jammed not only with tips of the butcher, but with real dangers because of the rain. Emergency crews were being lined up to help in the flooded areas, and there had been some reports of looting on streets that had been closed due to excessive water flow. All available personnel had been called in to help.

Harry made his way through a sea of blue to the front desk. The reports from the officers who had been tailing Clark earlier in the day had not been handed to him as yet. Even though the surveillance had been terminated, he was supposed to have received their logs. He had called the desk fifteen minutes ago, and they had assured him the logs would be sent right back. Now he pushed through the throng, and saw why there had been a holdup. He couldn't even see the officer who thrust the notebooks at him. He simply yelled a thank you, grabbed the books, and headed back to Caswell's office.

In another room, Jim Stahl waited for the computer to come up with information on the sign Jessie had seen in her vision. He had printed in Let Freedom Ring and asked for a general search. He looked up as Jena Karnitz stuck her head in the door. "Did you get your phone message a little while ago?" she asked.

Jim shook his head. "No. My wife?"

"No. I think I heard them say it was from that little girl—you know, the one that was here? Jessie."

Jim slammed his hand down on the table. "Damn! How long ago? Who took the call?"

Jena threw her hands into the air. "I don't know, Jim. Maybe fifteen minutes ago? I was just walking by and heard one of the guys say some kid named Jessie wanted to speak to you. That's all I know."

Harry had just finished scanning the surveillance log when Jim walked through the door. "I think something might be wrong, Harry. I had a phone call from Jessie about fifteen minutes ago, asking that one of us come over. She was afraid something was going to happen to Suzanne. Apparently she told the officer she was a psychic, so he thought she was a nutcase, and didn't get it through to me. Anyhow, I just tried to call and didn't get a ring. Either the line is out because of the rain, or it's been cut."

Harry grabbed his jacket. "Let's get rolling. I just read the surveillance logs on Clark for today, and one unit said they tailed Clark for a number of miles and that he appeared to be following a gray Cutlass. One of the stops was the Methodist church on Central, then our boys followed him out on Interstate Twenty-nine, the exact route Suzanne and Jessie told me they took today. And wouldn't you know, right then the surveillance was cancelled. How much do you want to bet Clark followed them back to Suzanne's apartment?''

"Oh, and one more thing," Jim said as they ran for their car. "Willie called back in with something else. He said he had discovered the real name of the guy calling himself Floyd Webster. He has several aliases he uses, but his real name is Roy Cole.''

"You're wrong, little Susie,'' Roy Cole said, laughing. "When we left Oklahoma I didn't want people knowing who we were—after all, we were supposed to be dead and all. So I found me a name off a grave in some little town near Bartlesville, and presto. You became Suzanne Webb, and I became Carl Webb.'' Roy wiped a hand over his mouth. "You were only five years old. It didn't take me long to train you to the new name.''

So much was being thrown at her that Suzanne was having a hard time comprehending it all. If what this man was saying was true, there was at least one thing to be thankful for. He was not her father. "I don't understand. Why did you think we needed to change our name? And what do you mean, we were supposed to be dead?'' It occurred to Suzanne that the longer she could keep him talking, the longer Jessie had to bring help. "I think you're making all of this up. Nothing you have said makes any sense to me.''

Roy's face darkened. "Look, missy, you had better just mind your manners. And it ain't so all-fired hard to figure out. I married your ma when she was pregnant with you— pregnant by that hotsy-totsy, *married* college professor. And I loved her, too! She was the prettiest thing in Oklahoma, and that's a fact. But it wasn't long until I wasn't good enough for her. She didn't like my drinkin'; she didn't like the way I run my daddy's farm; she didn't like my *language*. Hell, she didn't like *nothin'* about me. Then one day she got real mad at me, and she left to go to her sister's house. I knew she was going to leave me!'' Roy's voice got louder, angrier. "Me. Who gave her a name and took her in. She was going to leave *me!*"

Suzanne stared, transfixed, at this man who had so terrified her in her early years. She knew beyond any doubt that what he was telling her was the truth.

"But I fixed her," Roy sneered. "I fixed her good! You were the one thing she loved in this world, so I took you away from her."

"Are you telling me the courts gave you custody over my mother?"

Roy snorted. "What courts? That wouldn't have been near bad enough for your ma—even if I'd had a leg to stand on, and I didn't. But she had one awful surprise waiting for her when she came back with her sister to divorce me. She found the farmhouse blown up, and her husband and little girl dead. I was just sorry I couldn't stick around to see the look on her face."

Suzanne paled. "What are you talking about? Why would she think we died in an explosion?"

"Remember little Charlotte? She was just your age, with long, brown hair the same as yours. She and her daddy came through each year to help in the harvest. Migrant workers they was called. Migrant workers who can disappear and no one asks a lot of questions. Well, I rigged the house to blow and burn, then invited them in and gave them lemonade with knockout drops. By the time that house blew, you and me was across the border into Kansas."

Suzanne's words were slow, as if her brain could simply not function anymore. "And my mother? What happened to my mother? You told me she had died in a car wreck. I remember that. I don't remember much, but I do remember that."

Roy shrugged. "Far as I know, she's still alive and kicking!"

Suzanne could feel the wind leave her lungs in a loud whoosh, as though she had been hit in the stomach. *Alive. There is a chance my mother is alive!*

As if reading her thoughts, Roy snorted loudly. "Won't

do you no good, Susie, dear. You ain't gonna be lookin' up no long lost mommie." He raised the Colt up to shoulder level. "I'm afraid I'm gonna have to kill you!"

Suzanne spoke rapidly. "Why didn't you do that when I was five years old? Why did you kill the other little girl in my place?"

Roy lowered his arm. "Because I thought you was worth a fortune. I even had second thoughts after I rigged up my death there in Omaha. I learned you had been placed in that convent, so I went back a few years later and tried to make them give you back to me, 'cause after all, I was your legal daddy and I had the paper to prove it. But some prune-faced nun told me you'd run off. I always did think she was lying to me, but I couldn't prove nothin'. Then after you was all growed up, I saw an article about you in the paper—about your helpin' the police and all. It said you had been adopted from that same convent, and then I knew for certain that nun had lied to me. But it was too late, then. No use makin' an issue of it at that late date."

Suzanne's mind was whirling. She had to keep him talking. It was her only chance. "So. How did you find me? And maybe more to the point, *why* did you find me? Why come looking for me after all this time?"

Roy Cole's eyes narrowed. "You were coming after me, weren't you? I just had to get you first! When I found out you were in Kansas City, I knew it was only a matter of time until you found me. When Clark said you came to the police station, I knew you was getting too close for comfort."

At first Suzanne thought perhaps she had misunderstood. "What did you say?"

Roy grinned. "Surprised you, huh? Didn't think I'd know someone like the butcher? Why, him and me, we're like that." He crossed two fingers and held them up. "He's the one found you for me."

All at once it became crystal clear to Suzanne why she had been feeling such terror. It was the entrance of the man she had thought was her father. The man who had terrorized her as a child. That day in the police station when she had touched Randal Clark, the fear had come because of Clark's association with this man from her childhood nightmares.

Roy stood. "Okay, Susie. We've had our little father-daughter chat." He raised the gun to fire.

Before Suzanne realized what was happening, the front door swung open, and Harry hurled himself into the room, rolling and shooting at the same time.

A surprised look crossed Roy's face as his gun toppled from his hand and he fell to the floor, looking down in amazement at the red stain spreading across his chest.

"Harry!" Suzanne rushed over to the detective as he picked himself up off the floor. Then without any other reason than the need to do so, she threw her arms around his neck. "What took you so long?" She sobbed.

Harry held on to Suzanne, liking the way she felt in his arms, liking the way she was clinging to him. He kissed her cheek lightly. "I'm sorry. We didn't get Jessie's message when we should have. She just told the officers she was a psychic and afraid something was going to happen to you. We had no idea Roy Cole was here." Harry looked over at the form lying on the floor. "That *is* Roy Cole, isn't it?"

Suzanne nodded. "Yes. But he isn't my father."

"I know," Harry answered. "We finally got it all figured out."

Jim came in through the back door. "Everything okay?"

Suzanne untangled herself from the safety of Harry's arms. "Is Jessie with you?"

"Why, no," Jim answered. "Why would she be?"

Suzanne looked back and forth between the two detectives. "Didn't you say she had called you?"

Jim Stahl answered. "Yes, but that was earlier. She told our officer she was calling from a bedroom because she didn't want you to hear."

"Then she must be outside someplace," Suzanne insisted. "She ran out the back door when—" All at once it hit her. There was a reason why Roy had been so unconcerned about Jessie running out like that. He hadn't come alone! She ran over, kneeling beside Roy.

Roy held one hand over the hole in his chest. He smiled up at Suzanne. "I imagine Clark is having a lot better luck than I am. He's probably already cut off your little friend's head!"

Suzanne reached out her hand and placed it on Roy. *Oh, please, oh, please. Let me do it just this once. I have to know where Clark has taken her!*

She could feel the life leave Roy Cole's body. "No!" She pounded on him with her fists. "Don't you die on me, you bastard!"

Strong arms reached down, encircling her, drawing her gently up. "He's gone, Suzanne," Harry said. "There's nothing he can tell you now."

Chapter
Twenty-four

Jessie sat in the passenger seat of the maroon Ford van, her eyes on Randal Clark's face.

"Think you're pretty smart, don't you?" Clark said. "What did you do, hold your breath?"

"If you're so clever, why don't you tell me?" Jessie sassed. He was right. That was exactly what she had done. She remembered feeling Amy's panic at the rag going over her face, and Harry telling them that Clark used chloroform on some of his victims. The instant Clark had grabbed her, she knew what was coming. When he got her to the van, she inhaled as deeply as she could and did not breathe again. She had waited a few seconds, then slumped down as though the chloroform had worked. It was a good plan; however, she hadn't been able to get the door of the van open, and Clark had slammed on the brakes, sending her tumbling. He had reached around, grabbing her by the shirt, forcing her into the front seat.

"And don't think you can get that door open and jump," he said. "At this speed on the interstate you would die immediately."

"So what? Wouldn't that be better than what you plan on doing to me?" Jessie's voice was irreverent, loud and demanding. She had already decided she was not going to let him see that she was frightened. That was what he was used to, and expected.

Clark looked over at the young, brash redhead. "Who the hell are you, anyway?"

"I'm Amy Matthews's sister, that's who I am. I've come to rescue her from you! And I'm going to, too! Just you wait and see."

Randal Clark didn't have much of a sense of humor, but he threw back his head, laughing at the young girl. She had balls. He had to give her that. "What makes you think your sister is still alive? Maybe I've already chopped her into a dozen pieces and floated her down the Missouri."

"I know—" Jessie stopped, catching herself. No. It was better that Clark didn't know about her psychic ability. As long as he didn't know, she might be able to use it somehow. "I just know," she finished. "Sometimes sisters know these things. And besides, I know all about you. You don't throw the girls you kill in the river—you arrange them in some gross way for the police to find."

"Oh, I do, do I? What else do I do to them? Do you know how I make them scream and beg for death before I kill them?" He gazed hard at Jessie, expecting her to recoil in horror.

Jessie tried to remember everything she had seen in her vision, and all that Harry had relayed to her. "I know about everything—the eyebrow, the makeup, the little gouges! I suppose you want a medal for that? Such a brave man, picking on all those helpless young girls."

This time Jessie had succeeded in getting Clark's undivided attention. "How could you know about all that?" he demanded. "None of those facts have even been in the newspaper."

Jessie rolled her eyes. "I have my sources. If you really want to know, then tell me where Amy is."

Suzanne was starting to panic. "Oh, no. Oh, please, God, no!"

Harry held her by the shoulders. "We don't know that Cole was telling the truth, Suzanne. Maybe he just told you that Clark had Jessie to upset you."

"No, Harry. Roy was much too unconcerned about where Jessie went. He didn't even try to follow her, or bring her back. He knew Clark was waiting. I'm sure of it." She looked up at Harry trying to keep from weeping. "I told Jessie's parents not to worry, that I would take good care of their daughter and not let anything happen to her. And look, I've let the butcher get his hands on her! Oh, God, Oh, God, Oh, God!"

"Stop it, Suzanne!" Harry spoke the words sternly. "We *will* find her."

Suzanne saw herself through the eyes of the two detectives. For the first time she fully realized why someone close to a missing person was almost worthless in finding them. Panic sets in. Panic and fear. No wonder her cool detachment was such a valuable aid to the police. She shook her head and took several deep breaths. She would calm down and think what to do. If she kept her head, perhaps she could find Jessie before something awful happened.

"I'm going to drive back out on Interstate Twenty-nine," she finally said, coming to a decision. "If Clark is taking Jessie to the same place he has her sister Amy, we know that he took that route."

"One of us will go with you, darlin'," Jim spoke for the first time. "We radioed for reinforcement on the way over here. I just talked to one of the units outside. One of us can take their police car and go with you, and we'll leave officers here in case Jessie comes back." He turned to Harry. "Your call."

Harry put his arm around Suzanne. "Jim knows the country a little better than I do, Suzanne. He had better be the one to go with you. I'll get back to the station and see what I can dig up on Cole. He might have an address we can check out." He turned to Jim. "Does that sound all right?"

"Yeah. Don't forget to check the computer. I had just started the search for Let Freedom Ring when I was told about Jessie's call. I don't know what might have turned up. Oh, and you might give Ruth a call, if you get a chance. I told her I was on my way home two hours ago.''

Harry's arms went around Suzanne, drawing her close for a brief moment. ''Be careful,'' was all that he said to her.

''You aren't in a position to be doing any bargaining with me,'' Clark spoke harshly. ''I would suggest you watch your mouth, or I'll kill you now. But if you're a good girl, I might wait and let you see your sister first.''

When he spoke, Jessie concentrated hard. A picture of her sister began to emerge in her mind. She was lying down on what appeared to be a cement floor. There was gray tape covering her mouth, and her eyes were wide in fright. *That must be how she looked the last time Clark saw her. He's remembering it now.* Aloud she said, ''Did you leave her any food when you left her, or did you plan on starving her to death?''

Once again Clark's eyes swung around to the young girl sitting beside him. Surprised, he answered truthfully. ''I left her a few candy bars and a jug of water. Of course I intended on coming back in just a day or so. Who knows what condition she is in by now? Dead, more than likely.''

Don't react, Jessie told herself. *You know Amy was still alive yesterday.* ''So where did you put her? How do you know she hasn't escaped by now?''

Clark gave her a contemptuous look. ''I killed my first person when I was fifteen years old. I'm now thirty-eight. I haven't gone all these years without getting caught by being stupid!'' He gave a short laugh. ''No. Your sister is right where I put her. Believe me.''

This time Jessie could see more as Clark thought about where he had placed Amy. It was some kind of a cement box or room. It was buried somewhere, covered with dirt. At least that was something.

''I don't think you're so smart,'' she pushed. ''If you were smart, you wouldn't have left my sister's purse in the Dumpster by your apartment. I'm only fourteen years old, but even *I* would have better sense than that.''

"Yeah, well, it was better than having the cops find it in my apartment, wouldn't you say? I got a tip they were coming after me. I only had a few minutes to ditch the purse and the Dumpster was my only choice, since I could reach it unnoticed from the basement. There was already a police car waiting out front of my building. I had to get rid of it fast.''

"Why did you even take that chance? What did you want with Amy's purse in the first place, that's what I'd like to know.''

Randal Clark looked over at the girl with a strange expression. "Sometimes the pleasure is worth the extra risk. Once in a while I hold the girls I take for two or three days before killing them. At home alone in my apartment, it is so much fun to watch the television blare out about another missing girl, while I'm sitting there fondling all of the personal items from her purse. I know where she is. I know she is alive. I know those people reporting the news would love to know I'm sitting there with all her things.'' Clark reached over and turned the windshield wipers a higher notch to keep up with the increasing rain. "I guess I do it mainly because it gives me enjoyment.''

"Where did you get this van?'' Jessie abruptly changed the subject. "The police don't know about it. They think you only drive a Taurus.''

"In case you haven't figured it out by now, the police don't know jack shit about anything.'' Clark's voice turned hard. "Certainly not about me! I usually keep this van in a parking garage, or at the farm. I hot-wire a new one every six months or so, repaint it, and get tags from a guy I know at a body shop. Stupid damned kids don't always bother turning in their tags when they junk a car. He always has a supply around. They're usually good for a few months, then I get a new one.'' Clark reached over and patted Jessie's knee. "Would you like to know what I did to your sister in this very van?''

His crassness took Jessie by surprise, but she managed

to cover it as she shoved his hand away. "You didn't do anything. You just put her there in the back and drove to the farm. Right? Is that where we are going now?"

"Yeah, little one, we're going to the farm. You're going to buy it!" Clark tossed back his head and laughed at his quip.

"Dumb joke," Jessie said, as she took a deep breath and tried to calm herself. If they were going to the area where Amy was, she had to get help. She also needed to slow Clark down. If Suzanne started after them, she would know to take Interstate 29. Without stopping to think of the consequences, Jessie quickly reached over, turning the keys to "off" and pulling them out of the ignition all in one fast motion. She threw them into the back of the van before Clark even realized what was happening.

"What the hell—!" Clark screamed at her. He grabbed on to her wrist as he brought the van to a stop at the side of the road. "You aren't jumping out, little lady. You can't get away from me. You might just as well learn that right now." With his free hand he hit Jessie hard across the face.

It was the first time in her life anyone had ever raised a hand to her. Jessie's reaction was instant and spontaneous. She swung her hand as hard as she could at his face, returning the slap. She wasn't certain who was more surprised—she or Clark.

The ringing of the telephone awakened Betsy Moore. She looked over at the alarm clock next to her bed, wondering who could possibly be calling her at nine P.M. Everyone who knew her, knew she went to bed at eight o'clock sharp. She grabbed up the receiver. "Yes? What is it?"

"Is this Betsy Moore?" Harry asked.

"Yes, it is. Who is this?"

"Miss Moore, my name is Harry McDermott. I'm a detective with the Kansas City Police, and I'm afraid I need your help."

"*My* help? At this hour?"

Harry glanced at his watch in surprise, double-checking the time. Miss Betsy Moore obviously went to bed with the chickens, because it certainly wasn't late. "Yes, Miss Moore. You're the Registrar of Deeds, and I need you to come down to the courthouse and run through some names for me on possible property ownership. It's an emergency."

Betsy Moore pulled her sixty-four-year-old body up on the edge of the bed. "Certainly not, Detective! I will be at my desk in the courthouse promptly at eight o'clock in the morning. I imagine your big emergency can wait until then!"

Harry just managed to keep his voice polite. "No, ma'am. I'm sorry, but that won't do. I need you tonight. Now."

"And I'm sorry, too, young man," Betsy Moore snapped. "But my job description does not say I have to go out in a violent rainstorm in the middle of the night to accommodate our local police force!"

Harry decided he had better be totally honest. "Miss Moore, you have probably heard of the man known as the Kansas City Butcher. Well, he has taken a fourteen-year-old little girl, and we don't know where. However, we have just come up with the name of one of his accomplices. If that man perhaps owned property, chances are that is where the butcher has taken the little girl. Time is extremely important. Won't you help us out?"

Betsy Moore was already slipping out of her nightgown. "Oh, my goodness. Why didn't you say so in the first place? Of course, of course. I'll get there as quickly as I can."

"You don't need to drive, Miss Moore. I've sent a police car to pick you up. Do you have a pencil handy?"

Betsy fished for her reading glasses on the nightstand. "Yes. Right here. Hold on."

Harry could hear a drawer opening and the rustle of paper. "Yes, officer, go ahead."

"These are the names I would like you to try. Roy Cole,

Floyd Cole, Floyd Webb, Floyd Webster, and Carl Webb. Those are all names used by the same person. Try Floyd Webster first. We know he was using that name recently, so it might be the right one.''

"Yes, certainly. I'll do it as quickly as I can.''

"That's great. If you find anything, tell the officer. He can radio it right to me. That would be faster than the telephone tonight.''

"Yes, sir,'' Betsy Moore said. "And I'll do one more thing. I'll say a prayer for that poor little girl!''

Randal Clark swore under his breath as he felt around in the dark for the keys. Both he and Jessie were on their knees in the back of the van, and even though he had a firm grip on her arm, she had almost succeeded twice in twisting away from him. He didn't dare turn on an interior light, for fear passing motorists might see the girl fighting against him.

Jessie's knee stayed firmly in place over the lost keys as she jerked her body back and forth, making it hard for Clark to keep hold of her and look for the keys at the same time. She could tell by the pressure on her wrist and the frozen set of Clark's face, that she had pushed him about as far as he was going to be pushed. "Oh, look, there they are,'' she said as she reached down and brought up the keys. She handed them carefully to Clark.

Clark grabbed the keys, then twisted Jessie's arm as he reached around in back of her, toward a black toolbox. Jessie's eyes widened as his hand came back with a meat cleaver. Even in the dark, Jessie could see the steel blade glisten. She shrank back against the side of the van, pulling against Clark's hold on her.

Lightning lit up the sky, illuminating the two people struggling in the van, as Clark swung the blade high in the air as though ready for a blow. Jessie screamed and shut her eyes.

At the last second, Clark realized there was traffic coming up on him. He glanced around and saw the lights of several cars almost ready to pass. He pushed Jessie to the floor with his body and lay still.

When the last of the succession of cars had gone by, Clark pulled himself off the girl. "Get up and go back to your seat!" His voice offered no room for discussion on the matter.

"Yes, sir." Jessie's voice was meek.

Twenty miles in back of the van, the police car carrying Jim and Suzanne was in full pursuit, with lights flashing and sirens blaring.

Jessie's scream had ripped through Suzanne's soul like a knife. She had heard it as plain as if the girl were sitting beside her. "Oh, God, Jim. Jessie is looking at some sort of meat cleaver—you know, like a butcher uses." Even as she said the words, their double meaning sent a chill through her. She concentrated hard and watched as Jessie returned to the front seat of the van. "It's okay. He didn't use it. She's sitting back down."

"I thought you had to touch the person to get any type of reading on them," Jim said.

"I know. It's weird," she answered him. "Since the beginning, Jessie and I have been able to tune in to each other. She can read my mind at will, and according to her, that is something new. She has never been able to do that before with anyone. I suppose because we are both psychic it just enhances our abilities."

"Can she read your mind over a long distance? If so, why don't you try sending her a message? Let her know we are coming, but we need to know what route they are taking."

Suzanne nodded. "I have been trying to reach her ever since we left, but she must have been too preoccupied with Clark to get a reception. I'll try again." Suzanne shut her eyes and forced everything but Jessie from her mind. She pictured the words, "we're coming" floating in the air, then she sent them shooting on down the road. It was one device used by psychics. Sometimes it worked, sometimes it did not.

Jim reached over and picked up the microphone on the car radio as it crackled to life. "Stahl here."

Harry's voice came on. "Jim, anything yet?"

"Nothing so far. Suzanne heard a ten-sixty-seven in her . . . uh . . . special way. We are still traveling on I-Twenty-nine. What have you learned?"

"Not much. The computer told us that the slogan Let Freedom Ring was used by a group about twenty years ago who wanted to establish their own little country. It sort of sounded like maybe they were a precursor to our modern-day militia groups. They had purchased various farms around the area, but it was so long ago that the properties have changed hands several times since. I have someone at the courthouse checking on it. She was there anyway, checking on Cole's aliases. Between the two, maybe she will come up with something."

"Ten-four. I remember that now. They were active about the time I first moved to K.C. As I recall, they kept to themselves and the big flap was about their stockpiling weapons, right?"

"Ten-four. I should have something for you before long."

As Jim replaced the microphone, Suzanne had to ask. "All right. I take it you didn't want to go over the air with this psychic business, so what is this ten-sixty-seven that I supposedly heard?"

"A person calling for help," Jim answered. "I thought it damned clever of me!"

Harry had no more than gotten off the radio with Jim, than Jena Karnitz came running up. "You have a phone call in Caswell's office," she said.

Harry worked his way down the hall and entered the quiet sanctuary of his superior's quarters. He picked up the phone, punching the blinking light. "McDermott here. Oh, hi, Bruce. What did you find?" He listened in astonishment to his detective's report. "You're sure? No mistake?"

Harry replaced the phone and sat staring at it in dismay. So he was right! The thought did not give him any pleasure.

Chapter
Twenty-five

As the water reached up past her breasts, Amy started toying with the idea of unscrewing the light bulb, dropping the lamp in the water, and having it over. She was cold, her arms were weak from holding the lamp out of the water, and she was near exhaustion.

As she looked at the bulging ceiling, she knew what she *should* do. She should turn off the light to reduce her risk of shock, and wait in the dark, hoping the ceiling collapsed, giving her a way out.

At the rapid rate the water was rising, it wouldn't be long until it was over her head. Water was pouring in from a dozen places now. Her only hope was .that the ceiling would collapse without killing her, and that she had enough strength to fight her way to the top and crawl out if that miracle occurred. A slim hope. A stupid hope. Why wouldn't she be better off to get it over in one big zap? Besides, if she turned off the light, she would be totally nuts in no time.

Oh, God, she argued with herself, she *had* to turn off the light. Her arms were so tired. One little slump and the light would be in the water. She looked at the opening through which the cord entered her room. Obviously, he had run the wiring in, then wired it to the lamp. There was no way for her to unplug the light. Her only choice was to shut it off.

"You can do it, Amy, you can do it!" She could almost

hear her younger sister prodding her on to try some new adventure. At her sister's insistence, she had learned to swing down from the loft in the barn, ride a horse, and roller blade. She had learned to swim in the irrigation ditch, and paint a canvas with her eyes shut, all because the little tornado known as Jessie, convinced her life was more than books and music. The six-year gap in their ages had never kept them from being close.

"You can do it, Amy, you can do it!" A picture emerged in Amy's mind of Jessie, her long red hair billowing in the wind as she jumped her horse over the corral fence, yelling back at Amy to follow.

Tears spilled down Amy's face, as a trembling hand reached over to turn off the lamp. She had to keep fighting. If she shut off the lamp, there was a chance she might make it. If she dropped the lamp while there was electricity running through it, there was no chance at all. She turned the switch, plunging her watery tomb into darkness.

"Oh, dear God!" Her voice trembled as total blackness engulfed her.

Jessie had ceased speaking to Randal Clark, concentrating instead on watching for any signs she could see along the roadside. With the increasing rain, it was difficult to make out anything. She at least knew they were still on I-29. She also knew Suzanne was in back of them somewhere. She had received her message several minutes before.

Clark took the exit so rapidly, Jessie hardly had time to read the sign. *Vivion Road, Suzanne! Vivion Road!* Jessie rubbed her hand over the moisture forming on the inside of the window in order to get a better look. It was no use. There was nothing to indicate where they were. It was raining much too hard to read the small street signs as they passed. Jessie looked around in frustration. "Where are we, anyway?"

"Almost home, little one!"

"What street are we on?"

Clark looked over at his passenger. "Oh, do you think

maybe your psychic friend can follow us if I tell you that? No, no. She has to touch a person before she does any good. If you're counting on her, you might just as well give it up."

"You're not so smart! How do you know she isn't right behind us?"

Clark reached down and picked the meat cleaver up from the console. He held it up toward Jessie. "I told you to watch your mouth." He turned the blade toward her. "Do you know how this would feel? This little jewel is made from the best tempered steel money can buy. It's all one solid piece, the blade and the handle. And it will split a hair, I'm here to tell you."

"Or a head!" Jessie snapped.

Clark reached over, slapping the blade against Jessie's jeans. "Or a head." He chuckled. "Or a head!"

"I've lost her!" Suzanne cried. "They've turned off of Vivion Road but I don't know where!"

Jim's voice was calm. "Whoa now, take it easy. I'll talk to Harry and see what he's come up with." He reached for the radio, brushing against Suzanne. Once again Suzanne felt frightened, as she had been in the police station when she took Jim's arm. This time she had to act.

"Jim, before we go on, I have to tell you that I see extreme danger for you if you continue. Something bad will happen to you if you aren't careful."

Jim reached over, patting her knee. "Darlin', something bad happens to most people if they aren't careful, doesn't it, now?"

Suzanne shook her head. "No. I mean it, Jim. Maybe you should get out and let me go on alone. I don't want anything to happen to you."

"And neither do I. In two months I'm going to retire with full pension. You surely don't think I'd go getting careless at this late date, do you?"

"No. But it isn't a matter of—"

"Darlin', you don't need to go on. I know what it's a

matter of—it's a matter of keeping a cute little redhead alive. Anything else is beside the point."

Suzanne placed her hand over Jim's arm. "You're a good man. Do you know that?"

"Just don't go spreading it around, dear."

They had been driving in a rural area for several minutes. Jessie could see nothing through the rain. The van tilted and swayed as Clark left the paved roadway, taking a narrow gravel path which seemed to lead into nothing but rows of trees. The rain had washed over the road, making it almost impassable. Several times Clark put the van into low gear, forcing it across roads which were gutted with deep ruts and potholes. Finally, the narrow, flat road began to rise. Jessie realized they were now steadily climbing on a gravel road. All at once it hit her. The gravel road from her vision. The road lined with sunflowers and flowing with blood!

"Where are we?" she screamed as she placed both hands against the window. "Amy! Amy! Are you here?"

Clark grabbed on to her hair, forcing her head back against the seat. "Settle down. What's the matter with you, anyway? Do you think your sister can hear you clear out here?"

Jessie jerked around in the seat. "Let go of me!" She hit against Clark's arm as she struggled to be released.

Clark let go of her hair and grabbed up the meat cleaver. "Sit still and shut up!"

Jessie nodded. "All right! All right!" She could see better now out of the window, as the van slowed, wending its way up the hill. There were sunflowers on both sides of the road, just like in her vision. They were drooping now, their golden heads staring at the ground, but there they were, leading to Amy.

"Turn here, Jim." Suzanne pointed to a side road that led out of the neighborhood where they had been driving for the last several minutes. "I think they were here, and left by this road."

"So you've picked up Jessie again?"

Suzanne looked puzzled. "Not exactly. I seem to be getting a feeling, a hunch if you will, about which road to take. This is how most psychics work. I've just never been able to accomplish it, and I'm not at all sure of what I'm feeling. It isn't anything like what I feel when I can actually touch a person."

"Why do you suppose you aren't receiving any clues from Jessie? Do you at least know if she is still all right?"

At that moment, Suzanne saw through Jessie's eyes the winding gravel path from the first vision she had received from Clark at the jail. The same one Jessie had seen earlier from his cell. There was no question in her mind, but that now Jessie was seeing it for real. It was a pathway leading to horrible evil. Suzanne watched in dread as those same long, black fingers of darkness emerged from the night, wrapping themselves around the van, trying to get at Jessie. "They've reached Clark's place. Oh, God, Jim, I don't know where it is! We have to hurry!" Panic set in as Suzanne realized they would be too late if she couldn't locate that path now.

Up ahead, Jim could see that the gravel road they were on intersected with asphalt paving again. He wasn't positive, but he thought if he took that road it would place him on Highway 169. They seemed to be in the middle of nowhere, with residential streets to the east and south, and pasture lands to the west. To Jim the only logical direction to go was north to Highway 169.

"Darlin', I don't think this road goes anywhere. I'd say our best bet is to go on up to the highway. I doubt that Clark could even get down these roads—they're practically washed away with the rain."

"No, Jim. Stop the car here and let me do a reading. I've got to get a better feel for this. Jessie and I have been so tuned in to one another, I can't believe that I would lose her now."

Jim stopped the police car in the middle of the road. It wasn't likely anyone would run into them. He reached over and shut off the siren.

The flashing lights of the police car made a thousand points of light in the rain that washed over the car. Suzanne stared at the lights for several seconds, clearing her mind, preparing herself for the other dimension. Slowly, she held her arms out, palms up, then took several deep breaths. With each breath she pictured her arms reaching out to Jessie to touch her, to bring her close, to feel the essence of her. *Where are you, Jessie? I need to know. Do you see it, Jessie? There is a lifeline between you and me. From my arm to your arm. Put your arm out, Jessie. I want you to show me the way.*

All along there had seemed to exist an invisible bond between the two psychics. Suzanne couldn't explain it, but she knew that the powers of both Jessie and herself were greatly enhanced when they worked together. Each fed on the other's strengths. *Jessie, picture it. A rope for me to follow. Show me the way, Jessie. SHOW ME THE WAY!*

Jessie tried to close her eyes against the horror she was seeing, but it was no use. Even with her eyes closed, she could see a sea of blood washing down the old road. Instinctively, she knew they were at the place where Clark tortured, killed, and butchered his victims. It was their blood spilling down the road in her visions. And now their souls seemed to cry out to her from the countryside.

Through the jumble of images bombarding her brain, Jessie finally heard Suzanne calling to her. She understood what was needed of her and turned in the seat, extending her arm back toward the rear of the van. She pictured a rope leaving her hand, going back down the road they had just traveled, reaching her friend.

"Now what are you doing?" Clark asked.

"Just stretching," Jessie answered. "You hurt my arm when you jerked around on it."

The dispatcher at the police station motioned for Harry. "You have a radio message from Officer Mullen at the courthouse. He says to tell you Miss Moore found the address."

"Thank God!" Harry said as he picked up the mike.

Chapter
Twenty-six

Amy knew her hold on sanity was slipping rapidly. At any moment she was going to begin screaming and continue doing so until the murky water claimed her.

Water had now reached almost to her chin and was only inches from covering the end of the air pipe, to which she was clinging. The only sound she could hear in the darkness was the distant rumble of thunder, and the gurgling sound of water as it seeped ever higher.

She had finally dropped the lamp, not by design, but by accident. She had no more strength left in her arms. It occurred to her that had she kept the lamp lit, her worries would be over by now.

She thought of her family in Pueblo and said a prayer for them. She fervently prayed they would never have to know what she had gone through before her death. She prayed that her death would not leave Jessie shattered.

Amy had no way of knowing that less than a hundred yards away, her sister was being jerked from a van by Randal Clark.

"Here, Jim! Take this smaller road!" Suzanne pointed to another roadway leading off to the left. She was following a shimmering rope of light, the lifeline between Jessie and herself. It had worked!

The car radio sputtered, startling them. Jim picked up the mike. "Yeah, Harry. What did you find?"

"We've got it, Jim. The address. The farm is located west of the Gladstone area, west of Highway One-sixty-nine. It's going to be a devil to find. The road is a little, narrow, gravel road called Wedermeyer Lane. I'm looking at a map, and it looks like your best shot is to take a little jog on Vivion Road, over through a residential area—"

"We're way ahead of you, buddy," Jim said. "I just caught sight of a sign, and believe it or not, we just turned onto Wedermeyer Lane. How far to the house?"

Harry studied his map. "It's five miles from where you turn onto the road."

"Okay, we should be there in a few minutes, providing I can navigate this road—or what's left of it. How did you come up with the address? Who was the property listed under?"

"Roy Cole was the name he used to purchase the property. I guess he figured after all this time, no one would be around to question him using his real name. Then Miss Moore checked out property held by that militant group twenty years ago, and sure enough, that property had been one of their holdings. It looks like Jessie was right on the money with that one." Both occupants of the car could hear Harry's voice break as he said the child's name.

"We'll get her, Harry," Jim spoke into the mike. "We know she is still all right." He glanced over at Suzanne. "There is someone here who is certain of that."

Jessie stared at the massive, run-down farmhouse. It seemed to tower in the sky as lightning illuminated the area, making it visible in short bursts of light. A shiver of fear ran across Jessie's neck and traveled down her arms. Randal Clark kept a firm hold on her wrist as he forced her to run for the shelter of the porch.

When they got closer to the house, Jessie could see strong bars covering the windows, and a series of locks on the outside of the front door. Clark obviously was taking no chance with intruders. He never loosened his grip on her as he methodically worked his way through the locks, unlocking them one by one.

Jessie tried to spring away as Clark opened the door and pushed her roughly inside, but he grabbed her and threw her spinning across the room, then he flipped on the overhead light.

"What happened to that cocky little brat I picked up a while ago?" Clark smirked. "Not so brave now, are you, little one?" He made a slashing movement with the cleaver. "Are you ready to die? If I wasn't so sick of listening to you, I'd really make you suffer!"

Jessie raised herself to one knee as she looked wildly around the bleak room for another exit. There were two doors leading out of this room, but she did not have easy access to either of them. Besides, judging from the way the windows had been barred, even if she escaped into the rest of the house, she would not be able to get out. No. Her best bet lay with the door they had just entered.

"So where is Amy?" Jessie demanded, still from her crouching position. "You said you would let me see her. Are you a liar as well as a killer?"

Clark's eyes narrowed, menacingly. "I have already killed your precious sister. I cut her a thousand times before she died. She was begging for death by the time I finished with her!"

Jessie stood up, eyeing Clark with contempt. "Huh! Yeah, I guess you *are* a liar, too. Amy is alive. You didn't kill her. You put her in some sort of box, and she is still alive!"

Clark inched closer to the child. "How did you know I did that, little one? Where are you getting all of your information? I think maybe it is time you died." He swung the cleaver high in the air. At the same time, he heard the faint sound of a siren and listened in horror as it got louder and louder.

As they drove into the yard both Jim and Suzanne could see Clark standing on the porch using Jessie as a shield.

He was holding a large knife to the side of her throat.

Jim reached under his jacket for his gun. "Stay in the car, Suzanne."

"Not on your life," she answered him as she opened her car door and jumped out.

"You don't have a chance, Clark!" Jim yelled. "There are more police on the way. You will gain nothing by hurting the child. Let her go."

Clark silently cussed himself for leaving his gun in the van. If he could get to it, then it would be a fair fight. Right now, his only insurance was the girl. "Throw your gun down and walk on up the road or I will slit her throat! Now!" he screamed.

Suzanne came around the car and stood by Jim. "How good a shot are you?" She spoke in a soft voice.

"Not great, anymore," he answered truthfully. "I can hit Clark, though, if that's what you're asking."

"Okay, listen. When I raise my arm, that will be the signal for Jessie to pretend to faint. She will slump down, and you can get a shot at Clark. Do you think that might work?"

"Well, yeah, but how are you—oh! Sure. Give it a try."

"So what's it going to be?" Clark yelled. "Do I kill her or not?"

Jessie! Hear me, Jessie! Suzanne concentrated. *When I raise my arm, pretend to faint. Slump down as far as you can go. Move your hand a little if you understand.*

Suzanne watched as Jessie moved her hand back and forth. "She understood, Jim! Get ready."

It all happened so fast, Suzanne was not even certain that her plan had worked. One second she was raising her arm in signal, and the next instant Jim was firing. Clark dropped the cleaver and slumped to the floor.

Jim and Suzanne ran up on the porch, and Jessie leaped into the older psychic's arms.

Jim held his gun on Clark, who was not moving. "I'm afraid I've only winged him," he said as he carefully handcuffed him to the sturdy porch railing. "I told you I wasn't as good a shot as I used to be."

"We have to find Amy!" Jessie said. "She's buried somewhere around here in a cement box. I saw it when Clark started talking about her."

"Of course!" Jim said, remembering. "That group that was here twenty years ago built a number of cement storage units to hide the weapons they were stockpiling. As I recall, they had about fifteen buried here and there across these hills. It shot the property value all to hell."

Suzanne knelt down by Clark. She touched him on the arm, realizing that he was conscious and aware of what they were discussing. "Which way do we go? Where is Amy Matthews?"

"You go to hell," Clark managed to speak. "You'll never find her."

Even as he spoke the words, Suzanne saw clearly that Amy was north, down the hill. Jessie, reading Suzanne's mind, saw it, also, and took off running.

Suzanne looked at Jim. "If my vision was right, we will probably need a shovel."

"There will be one in the trunk. Standard equipment." He ran over to the police car and opened the trunk, removing a small shovel and a flashlight.

The rain had lessened somewhat as Jim and Suzanne followed after Jessie down the hill, but the lightning and thunder were still fierce. Up ahead they could hear Jessie screaming for her sister.

Jim noticed the gully which had formed from water rushing down the hillside. He flashed his light on ahead, but saw that the gully had stopped. Something was blocking its way, catching all of the water that should have been cascading down the hillside. A sick feeling began to form in his stomach.

"Amy! Amy! Where are you?" Jessie screamed. "I know you're here somewhere. Where are you?"

* * *

Amy decided she must be dreaming. Then she heard it again. It sounded like Jessie! With one hand she felt under the pipe to see if the water had covered it, yet. No. It was still open. She put her mouth up as close to the opening as she could get. ''Jessie! Jessie! I'm here!'' Then she laid her head against the pipe. No. Of course it couldn't be Jessie. She was just hallucinating. Going mad in the dark.

''Amy! Amy!'' This time Amy heard her sister's voice plainly.

''Down here! I'm down here!'' She tried to scream, but couldn't in her weakened condition. ''Jessie! Jessie! Look for a pipe!''

This time Jessie heard her sister's weak cry. She looked down and saw the pipe sticking out of the ground. She dropped to her knees and yelled, ''Amy! I'm here! Are you down there?'' She held her ear to the pipe.

''Yes, Jessie! The water is almost over my head! Get me out!''

Jim came running up and couldn't believe his eyes as he saw Jessie clawing wildly at the ground. ''Are you sure she's down there?'' he said as he pulled her to her feet.

''Yes! Yes! But we have to get her out. The water is almost over her head!''

Jim started shoveling the heavy mud. Suzanne and Jessie both dropped to their knees and began scooping it away with their hands.

Below them, Amy could hear the noise. It was the only thing that convinced her she had not dreamed the whole thing.

Finally, the last of the planking was uncovered. Jim leaned down and called into the pipe. ''Amy. This is Detective Stahl. Listen to me. When I lift this top off, go to the south side—the side opposite the pipe. The top is going to be heavy and if we have to drop it, we'll know where you are. Do you understand?''

''Yes. Okay. But I'm so weak. Without the pipe to hang on to, I'm not sure I can even stand.''

Jessie dropped to her knees. ''You can do it, Amy! You

have to! We can't raise the lid if you are holding the pipe.''

"Okay. I'm letting go now." Amy forced her body through the water away from the pipe.

"All right," Jim instructed, "on the count of three we lift. If it starts to fall, push it toward the north—away from you. One, two, *three!*"

For the first time in two weeks, Amy felt fresh air on her face. Then strong arms were around her, pulling her up, out of the water. The first person she saw was her sister. "Jessie!" She tried to walk, but her knees gave way. She felt Jessie's arm go around her waist, bracing her. "How did you ever find me?"

In the excitement, the girls almost missed seeing Jim Stahl slump noiselessly to the muddy ground. "What is it, Jim?" Suzanne rushed over, kneeling beside him.

"Darlin', I think I'm having a heart attack. I guess your premonition was right, after all."

Back at the farmhouse, even though his shoulder was bursting with pain, Randal Clark finally managed to set himself free from the handcuffs. Stupid, damned police. They should have known what an expert he was with locks. How the hell did they think he got in and out of places so easily? He picked up his knife, got his gun from the van, and started running down the back side of the hill. He had seen the flashing lights of police cars coming up the front way and had no intention of being here when they arrived!

Ahead, he noticed the electrical fence. That was all right. He had hopped over it many times. All he had to do was hold on to the wooden post and not touch the wires. Hell, even if he did slip up and touch them, it wouldn't be much of a shock.

When he got to the fence, in order to free-up his hands, he shoved his gun under his shirt and stuck the dull edge of the meat cleaver into his mouth, holding it tight with his teeth. He reached up to grab hold of the fence post, when all at once the sky exploded with lightning. Electrical charges danced through the air, looking for a point of contact. They found it in Randal Clark's all-steel meat cleaver with which he had butchered dozens of innocent young girls. The jolt knocked him twenty feet into the air. He was dead before he hit the ground.

Suzanne was slipping and sliding, trying to make her way back up the hill to radio for help. She saw a figure running toward her, but couldn't make out who it was until he was almost up to her. "Harry! Oh, thank God! It's Jim. He's had a heart attack!"

"I brought an ambulance, just in case we needed one for Amy." Harry turned around and yelled up the hill. "Down here, boys! Bring a stretcher!" He looked quizzically at Suzanne.

Suzanne nodded. "She's alive."

"Make that two!" he yelled.

Chapter
Twenty-seven

"**S**he's going to be fine," the doctor announced as he came out to the waiting area where Suzanne, Jessie, and Harry were waiting. "Of course she's malnourished, dehydrated, and has lost a great deal of weight. But we have an IV going; she has eaten a little soup; and she is responding nicely." He smiled over at Jessie. "She said she wants to sleep for just a little while, then maybe the two of you could call your mom and dad."

"How is Jim doing?" Harry asked.

"I think he'll be all right, too. His heart attack was brought on by overexertion, and his doctor doesn't think the heart, itself, was damaged too much. You'll be able to see him before long." He chuckled. "I guess he has quite a family. They have taken over the halls outside of the recovery room, and his doctor told me a little gray-haired woman named Ruth informed him that if he let anything happen to her husband, she would personally get his revolver and shoot him!"

"Yeah, that sounds like Ruth." Harry extended his hand. "Thanks, Doctor. We appreciate your keeping us informed about everything." He looked down at his wrinkled, but dry, clothing. "And we also thank your staff for drying all of our clothes. We looked, and felt, like drowned rats when we first got here, tonight."

The doctor smiled, giving a little salute. "No problem. You had all been through enough for one night. We didn't want you getting sick on top of everything else."

The three sat back down. "I have another shocker for you, Suzanne," Harry said. "I've been waiting until we heard how Amy and Jim were before springing it on you."

Suzanne turned to him, puzzled. "What's that?"

"We found your mother."

"You what? Oh, my God! Is this true?"

Harry laughed. "Yes, it's true. Her name is Jean Cole, and she still lives in Oklahoma near the farm she thought had claimed your life."

Jessie jumped up out of her chair. "Hey, wait a minute! I have an aunt named Jean Cole who lives in Oklahoma! She's my mom's sister. But her husband and little girl were killed in a fire about twenty years ago."

"Oh, my God." Suzanne spoke slowly as the true significance of Jessie's words hit her. "We're related, sweetie! Your mother and my mother are sisters. No wonder you sought me out to help you. Psychically, you were drawn to me because of the relationship between the two of us, and probably also because you knew I had some kind of connection to Clark—because of Roy Cole."

"So *that's* why I could always read your mind, huh?" Jessie grinned.

Suzanne nodded. "And that explains why I was able to follow you tonight, even though my own psychic powers do not normally respond except when I am actually in contact with a person."

Jessie sat down on the arm of Suzanne's chair and gave her a hug. "I was wondering how I was ever going to get along without you for the rest of my life. Now I won't have to. And just think! I'm going to be around for years and years to keep nagging you to stop smoking."

Suzanne pretended to swoon. "How will I ever stand it?"

Jessie shrugged. "Take it from me, it would be easier to quit smoking. I can be rather irritating when I put my mind to it. I don't have this red hair for nothing, you know."

Suzanne laughed. "Don't I know! Okay, I'll try. Just for you." A peculiar look crossed Suzanne's face. "Wait a minute. Tell me, your aunt Jean—my mother—wouldn't happen to have hair about the color of yours, would she?"

Jessie nodded. "She sure does. Actually, there are about three of us with red hair in the family."

All at once it dawned on Suzanne that Harry must have already figured out she and Jessie were related. She reached over and took his hand. "So when did you figure all of this out?"

"Truthfully, I didn't figure it out at all. There was no reason for me to think the two of you were related. But when I talked to your mother, I told her you were helping a young girl from Pueblo, Colorado, find her missing sister. And of course she immediately knew it had to be Jessie. The whole family had been concerned about Amy's disappearance. She filled in the gaps for me."

"I think I'll call her and talk to her right now," Suzanne said.

"No. She has already left Oklahoma. She was determined to be here tomorrow. She caught a flight to Wichita on a private jet, then she found a small airline that flies into K.C. early in the morning. She will be here tomorrow." He turned to Jessie. "And so will your parents. Their flight arrives tomorrow afternoon."

"They are going to be so proud of you, Jessie," Suzanne said. "And so am I. You kept your head through it all—even when Clark had you!"

"That place was so horrible. I kept getting all these flashes of the girls he had killed."

"Yes, me, too. There was so much evil surrounding him, that it came to me as long, dark, monstrous fingers, grabbing at me, trying to squeeze out my breath—my soul. When Clark's van started toward the farmhouse, I saw that same evil trying to grab at you from the darkness. It was terrifying for me to watch and be unable to help you."

"You helped me fine. That big jerk was just ready to cut off my head when he heard the siren! And I wasn't

near as brave as you give me credit for. I knew you and
Jim were only minutes in back of us. I'm just sorry we
didn't find the little girl. I wonder what Clark did with
her?''

An astonished look crossed Suzanne's face. ''That's it!
That was what I was trying to remember at the police
station earlier tonight. There *was* no little girl. That was
me in your vision. I knew there was something I was missing, because that child looked so familiar to me. That's it,
of course! You were seeing *me* in the vision where Clark
was killing.''

''I don't understand. Why?''

''Because the land where Clark did his killing belonged
to the man I thought was my father, Roy Cole. I guess,
psychically, you knew I held the key. It had something to
do with a horror from my childhood—someone I witnessed doing evil many, many times.''

''Yes, I see. And this time the evil was coming not only
from him, but from his friend, as well. And my dream
about a little girl being thrown from a car down a long
hill, that was because I remembered about Roy Cole threatening to leave you by the side of the road.'' Jessie giggled.
''Let's see now. *My* subconscious knew *your* subconscious
knew something that you didn't know, right?''

Suzanne laughed. ''You *do* have a way with words, my
little cuz! Whenever I learn to decipher them, we'll be in
business.''

''Oh, I almost forgot, Suzanne,'' Harry said. ''I have a
pile of faxes for you at the station.''

''For me? Who could possibly be faxing me anything?''

''Every time we ran a check on you, everyone wanted
to know how you were. You received a fax from a Detective Botello, in Omaha, saying how much they all missed
you. You received a fax from the *Omaha World Herald*
showing newspaper clippings supporting the work you did
in trying to bring Baxter Underwood to justice.''

''I thought they all hated me for what I did.''

''Nope. Not even close. I spoke with the editor and he

told me their paper had received over three thousand letters defending you.''

"I am totally stunned," Suzanne said.

"I told you that reporter sounded nice," Jessie said. "Maybe now you'll give up trying to be a hermit."

Suzanne looked at Harry and smiled. "Oh, I think I've already given that up, sweetie."

The group heard the elevator door open, and turned to see Jim being wheeled out on his way to the intensive care unit. He saw them and gave a small wave, asking the orderlies to give him a minute.

"Just one minute, no more," a sizable orderly instructed in a tone which indicated there was no room for argument.

Harry patted Jim awkwardly on the arm. "Hey, bud, you gave us quite a scare!"

Jim's voice was weak as he answered. "I told you I had no intention of getting shot, not with two months to go. I just never expected a heart attack."

"The doctor told us you were going to be fine," Suzanne said.

Jim motioned for Jessie to come closer. "How is Amy? Is she going to be all right?"

Jessie beamed. "Thanks to you."

Jim looked pleased as he closed his eyes, drifting off to sleep again.

"That's it, folks," the orderly said. "We have to get him into his room."

"Will you two be all right if I leave you for awhile?" Harry said as he walked Suzanne and Jessie back to the waiting area, his arm around Suzanne's shoulders. "I have another matter I have to clear up tonight."

"Sure, Harry," Suzanne answered. "Jessie needs to go spend some time with Amy, and even though it's late, I thought I would call the hospital in Michigan and leave word for Sister Mary Elizabeth that I'm okay. I want her to know that she absolutely did the right thing not giving me back to Roy Cole, all those years ago. According to what you told me, that must be heavy on her mind.''

Harry leaned over and planted a soft kiss on Suzanne's cheek. ''Okay, see you later, then.''

Chapter
Twenty-eight

The door was slightly ajar. Harry pushed it open and walked into the sterile environment of the autopsy room. Stanley Davis was standing beside the naked body of an elderly, gray-haired woman. He seemed to be combing her hair.

Harry walked over. "Stanley? Isn't it a little late to be starting an autopsy?"

The diminutive medical examiner jumped, startled at Harry's voice. "I'm sorry. I didn't hear you come in." He looked over at the door. "How *did* you get in? I usually make certain the doors are locked when I'm in here alone."

Harry shrugged. "No. It was open. But you haven't answered my question. What are you doing here this late at night?" He nodded toward the autopsy table. "Surely this wasn't an emergency."

Stanley removed his surgical gloves, laying them on a gurney. His smile was easy, relaxed. "No. No emergency, Harry. I was just keeping busy until your boys got here with Clark. I heard what happened and wanted to make certain I was the one here to do the autopsy." Stanley offered a weak smile. "After all, I've been the one on this case since the beginning. Didn't want some upstart finishing it!"

"It's over, Stanley," Harry spoke quietly.

Stanley looked at him and nodded. "Yes. I suppose

we'll all sleep a little better tonight, won't we?''

Harry shook his head. "That isn't what I meant, and I think you know it."

"Oh," was all Stanley uttered. Then, "How did you find out?"

"A lot of little things that didn't add up; no DNA match, the body parts, the investigation being slightly *off* right from the beginning. But the clincher was your wife."

"My wife?" Stanley looked puzzled.

"Yes. You told us your wife did all of the transcribing of your notes and therefore if there was a leak, it could not possibly be coming from your end."

"And?"

"And, as part of a routine investigation of all people who had any dealing with this case, Detective Langston tried to call on your wife."

"Oh," Stanley said, as he pulled a metal stool over and sat down.

Harry pulled a chair over next to the ME, turning it around backward, propping his arms on the back. "Funny thing. Even though your hospital records show a wife listed, your neighbors told Langston they had never, ever seen a woman around. Nor could we find any evidence of a marriage. Why is that, Stanley?"

"Do you really think I would take the chance of ending up like my father? Blasted away because I tried to save my little boys?" Stanley asked the question in a reasonable voice. "Come on, Harry. I'm smarter than that."

Harry looked at Stanley's blue eyes, shining bright with madness. He knew those eyes from another face. "You're Leonard, aren't you? He was your brother, wasn't he? Randal Clark was your brother."

Stanley didn't deny the words. Instead he nodded slowly. "Yes. And a finer brother could not be found anywhere. He did everything for me. He would step in and take the torture that would have been mine. He always turned her wrath on himself, to spare me." He looked at Harry knowingly. "She was crazy, of course. A board-certified lunatic. She had sex with probably every man she ever met, but she came across as such an angel, I'm certain they all thought they were the only one."

"What happened to your mother?"

"Randal killed her." Stanley spoke in an even voice. "I sat at the kitchen table and watched the whole thing. He made her dress up like the whore that she was, then he hacked her body into a dozen pieces." Stanley wiped a hand across his eyes. "I can still remember her face and her voice, pleading—pleading for Randal to stop, pleading with me to run for help. *Run, Leonard! Momma loves you, baby! Don't let him do this! Go, baby! Go for help.* Sometimes I can still hear her voice ringing in my ears. But I stayed right where I was on the chair. I didn't move an inch."

"How did he get away with it? What did he do with her body?"

"He buried it, piece by piece, across Idaho. Then he said I needed a fresh start, in case anyone ever discovered what he had done. In a few months he had enough money saved to send me back east to school. He gave me a new name, forged a school record from a high school in Indiana which he had read about burning down, then told everyone in town I had died on a trip back to see our mother, and the rest, as they say, is history."

Harry looked at the stooped, balding little man who was in actuality about his own age, but who seemed years older. He had to ask his next question. "Did you help Randal kill any of those girls, Stanley?"

"No, no, no. *I've* certainly never killed anyone, Harry! You know me better than that. When I cut on people they are already dead!"

"How long have you known Randal was the butcher?"

"I knew from the first body I saw. It was the eyebrow. Like mother's. Her father caught her wearing makeup when she was fifteen, and sliced off her eyebrow. Not just the hair, he scarred her up pretty bad. She wouldn't leave the house without drawing it in.''

God, Harry thought, it's a never-ending cycle. From parent to child, to their child, and on. It never stops. "Why didn't you turn him in, Stanley? How could you let him keep killing over and over and over? Didn't you feel some responsibility?''

Stanley's head tilted up with a look of astonishment. "My responsibility was to the brother who watched out for me all those years. This time *I* had to save *him*!''

"Whose blood did you turn over to the FBI and Genericode for analysis?''

"Just a bum's. A dead bum with no police record, and nothing else to distinguish his blood from the blood of anyone else. I had always told Randal if he ever got in trouble, to insist a doctor be the one to draw blood for any DNA profiles. He insisted, and I was right there. It was just that easy.''

"And the body parts at Randal's apartment? That is the part I can't understand at all. Why *try* to implicate your brother?''

Stanley threw back his head and laughed. "Well, that just shows how much smarter I am than you, Harry. Too much evidence, especially when it turns out not to *be* evidence, makes it easier to get someone off than just about anything. Wasn't I right? Didn't Caswell have to release my brother? And if worse came to worst and it went to trial, why, you boys would have been laughed out of court! Randal understood, after I explained it to him.''

Harry hated to admit it, but more than likely Stanley Davis was right. Clark's attorney would have screamed that the evidence had been planted, and it would certainly have looked like it to any jury if it couldn't be explained. To Stanley he said, "Maybe not so smart, after all. That was the part which kept bugging me. Where would anyone come up with fingers and toes that had been removed because of gangrene? The only answer I could come up with was a teaching hospital of some kind. Perhaps stolen from a lab as a lark by one of the medical students. And of all the people associated with this investigation, *you* were the only one who that might apply to.''

''Mother used to hold us after she had beaten us, did you know?'' Stanley ignored the spiel Harry had just delivered, lost in another world.

Harry's answer was soft. ''No, Stanley. I didn't know.''

''She would come into the bedroom and grab us and hold us tight. She would cry, and say, *Forgive me, Father, for I know not what I do. Forgive me, Father, for I know not what I do.* She was very religious. Never missed a Mass that I can remember. Sometimes she would pray for days about not hurting us, especially Randal. But then in the blink of an eye, she would lock him in the bedroom with her, and I could hear Randal's screams as she tortured him, hour after hour.'' Stanley looked at Harry with vacant eyes. ''I've always wondered which was worse—going through the torture, or listening to it.''

Harry stood up. Looking at his longtime associate, he figured they both must have been equally bad. ''You know I have to take you in, Stanley.''

Stanley put both of his hands up as though to push Harry away. ''No. Not yet. Randal needs me. I won't let someone else cut on him. I have to wait for him. I have to tell him I'm sorry for what I have to do to him.'' Stanley stood and walked over to the corpse lying on the table. ''It's important that they know you care for them.''

Before Harry could stop him, Stanley hopped up on the autopsy table and lay down by the dead body. ''I'll be right here when you need me, Harry. Just let me know when they get here with my brother.'' He began caressing the old woman's face. ''Now, don't you worry. I'm not going to hurt you. Why, you won't feel a thing.''

Chapter
Twenty-nine

Suzanne's eyes swept over the people exiting the small USAir nineteen-passenger plane. She spotted her mother the instant she started down the stairs, her red hair glistening in the sunlight.

Suzanne stood behind the roped-off area, impatience getting the better of her as she watched this woman whom she had not seen in twenty-two years, walk toward her. She stepped over the roping and sprinted across the pavement, skidding to a stop in front of the tall, beautiful redhead.

"Mother?" Every word that Suzanne had rehearsed in preparation for this meeting went flying out of her head.

Jean Cole's eyes swept over the younger version of herself standing before her. Her eyes widened in disbelief at the daughter she would have known anywhere. Except that her daughter's hair was brown while her own was red, the resemblance was undeniable. She dropped her purse and grabbed her daughter. "Susie! Oh, God! It really is you!"

All of Suzanne's doubts left her as she tumbled into her mother's arms. "Momma! I remember you! Oh, my God, I remember you!"

Tears streamed down their faces as the two women clung together, drinking in each other's features.

"All this time you were alive!" Jean said. "I have blamed myself a thousand times for your death, and all the while you were alive!"

"The same is true for me," Suzanne said. "Roy told me it was my fault you had died in that car wreck. He said you were trying to get away from my *witchcraft*. All these years I have felt responsible for your death. I think I believed him in part because I could remember telling you something bad was going to happen when you left."

Jean wiped tears from Suzanne's face with gentle hands. "Oh, my darling child. If only I had taken you with me that day. You have no idea how many times I have relived that dreadful choice." The two women entered the terminal and sat down on the nearest seats, hands clasped.

"I left you with a neighbor," Jean said, "the day I went for help, because I thought it would be better for you. My oldest sister, Alma—your aunt—lived close by, near Tulsa. I knew she and her boys would help me leave Roy. I was frightened of him and what he would do to us if we didn't have some backup getting away." Jean pressed her daughter's hand. "I didn't take you because I wanted to spare you hearing me tell the family about how horrible Roy was. I thought—it's bitterly funny now—but I thought it wouldn't be good for you to hear me ranting and raving about him."

"What about Zero, Momma? What part did the dog have in all this?"

Jean nodded. "A big part. The day Zero was killed is the day I left. It all came to a head that awful day. Roy was such a horrid man. He had taught Zero to chase old man Collins's pickup truck when it came by our farm. That morning you were playing in the yard with Zero. I don't know for sure exactly what happened, but I think Zero jumped up on you, or something. You were wearing a new dress I had made for you, and so you got after Zero and told him to get down. That's all, Susie. You did nothing else. But right about then, old man Collins came down the road and Zero took off after the truck and was caught under the wheels."

Suzanne's head bobbed up and down. "I remember that! I remember screaming for Zero to come back."

Jean patted her daughter's hand. "Yes. Well, Roy had to blame someone for the dog's death, and he had seen you make Zero get down off your new dress. Roy was always a little frightened of you and your special power, always giving you trouble over it. He decided you had sent Zero under the wheels of the truck on purpose, which was ridiculous. He knocked you down and tore your pretty dress off of you. I don't know what he might have done, but I heard your screams and came running. I hated him then. He had killed every ounce of gratitude I might have felt for his marrying me. All I could think about was getting help and getting away."

"Is my father still alive? My real father?" Suzanne asked the question, then wondered if perhaps that subject would be best not broached. "If you'd rather not talk about it, that's okay."

Jean brought Suzanne's hand up to her cheek. "Oh, my darling girl. Yes. Yes, your father is alive. We didn't want to throw too much at you right away. His wife passed away two years ago, and we have been seeing each other again. I hadn't seen him since the day I stormed into his office at Washburn College twenty-some years before, accusing him of killing you. Of course I really was blaming myself, but I needed to lash out at someone."

"Roy told me last night that my father didn't want you and didn't want me. He said all you were concerned with was saving your reputation. Of course I didn't believe him."

Jean turned her eyes down from her daughter's face briefly. How could she explain that horrible time? "Susie, your father had a wonderful, kind, and loving wife. She was stricken with multiple sclerosis, though, and almost totally helpless. I came to work for them my freshman year at college. Your father, Stephen, and I fell in love. We hadn't planned on it happening, and we both understood that nothing could ever come of it. When I found out I was pregnant, I didn't know what to do. Stephen talked about divorce, but we both knew that wasn't the answer.

I could never have stood the pain which that would have caused Muriel, his wife.''

"How did you ever wind up with Roy?''

"I know this probably seems impossible to you now, but at one time, Roy Cole seemed like the answer to my prayers. I knew I was not going to give you up for adoption. I did not even consider that option. I wanted you—more than life itself! I came home for a short visit and ran into Roy again. His father had just died, leaving him the farm. Roy had always wanted me. He had never made any bones about that. One evening I went to a movie with him, and afterward I told him about you, and my problem. He asked me to marry him, and it seemed the perfect solution to everything.''

"I only remember him as mean and nasty. It's hard for me to think of him as having any redeeming features.'' Suzanne shuddered at the thought of her beautiful mother in Roy Cole's arms.

Jean smiled. "Truthfully, Roy didn't have many redeeming features. He was lazy, stupid, and a brute of a man. I soon learned to stay out of his way as much as possible. When you came along, I devoted all of my energies to seeing that you had the best childhood possible. I suppose part of the blame for his vile behavior has to rest on me, because I quit trying to make our marriage work. I began shutting Roy out. I couldn't stand for him to touch me, and I didn't like him touching you.'' Jean stopped talking as huge sobs engulfed her. "He knew exactly how to hurt me the worst! He knew the one thing I loved in this world was you, so he made me think you had died in the fire, along with him.''

"I can't believe he killed two innocent people just to get back at you.''

Jean shook her head in dismay. "I know. I just learned about that last night when your Harry called.''

"*My* Harry?'' Suzanne asked.

Jean's moist eyes twinkled as she gazed lovingly at her daughter. "I don't know—that's what the man said. He all but called me *Mother*! And as I understand it, you don't have 'the touch' with him. From everything I've read on the subject, that means there is either hate or love greater than the psychic force.''

Suzanne leaned over, kissing her mother's cheek. ''It's true. I know it sounds crazy, since we only met a few days ago, but I do love him. And I know you'll love him, too. He and Jessie are waiting at the car for us. He said we should have some time together, without the two of them.''

''And how is my little fireball of a niece? I had no idea she had the gift, also!''

''Also? Is there someone else in the family 'cursed' with this gift?'' Suzanne's smile let her mother know she did not really consider it a curse.

''Yes. I did some research when you began telling me things about people you had touched.'' Jean laughed. ''I remember the shocked look on the minister's face one day when he came to call, and you told him where he had just been! I don't believe he wanted the world to know he had been in bed with the widow Perkins!''

''Oh, my! How old was I when that happened?''

''About three. Right after that, I talked with as many people in the family as I could, and guess what I discovered!''

''What?''

''Your great-grandmother Ula had the gift—the second sight. It was reported in old town records that she even had the touch of healing.''

''You're kidding! How wonderful! I can't wait to tell Jessie.''

''And I can't wait to show you off to our family! You already know about your aunt Martha, Jessie's mother. She is the youngest sister. Then there is your aunt Alma, who has more sons than any of us can count, and who are all anxious to meet you. Aunt Joyce and her family live in Denver, your aunt June lives in Kansas, and there is one of my sisters who is gone—''

"Vera," Suzanne interrupted. "She was a teacher and died in a scuba diving accident, right?"

Jean nodded. "Yes. But you'll want to meet her children. Everyone is so excited! We've already planned a big reunion in Pueblo as soon as Amy is back on her feet. We talked to the entire family last night."

Suzanne stood up, pulling her mother to her feet. "I can't believe I've found you." She folded her mother in a tight embrace.

"I know, sweetie," Jean said. "It's a miracle!"

Suzanne smiled at the name, remembering.

Epilogue

"If you could read my mind at this very minute, what do you suppose you'd discover?" Harry asked as he began unbuttoning Suzanne's white silk blouse.

"Hmmm. Let me see now. You're thinking that was the longest wedding dance you've ever attended."

"No."

"You're thinking what a fabulous crime-fighting aid your new wife will be."

"No."

"You're thinking you drank too much champagne and you want to go to sleep."

Harry's large hands caressed Suzanne's neck as he slid the silk blouse from her shoulders. "No."

Suzanne shivered as she locked her arms in back of Harry's head, bringing his mouth close to hers. "Harry," she whispered seductively. "I have a news flash for you."

"What's that?"

"A person doesn't have to be a psychic to know what you're thinking right now!"

"Is that so?"

Suzanne pulled him down on the bed. "Yes, that's so."

The scars on her wrists, throat and chest told the story. Somehow Audra Delaney had survived a brutal rape ten years ago, but with her memory of her attacker shattered. Then the unthinkable happens: she hears his voice on the radio, and now all she lives for are dark dreams of revenge.

She was his one loose end—the only one who got away, the only one who can still destroy him. All he has to do is find out her name, so he can silence her forever.

Soon, they're racing neck-and-neck, stalking each other in a world of shadows and evil, where it will take all of Audra's strength and the unexpected ingenuity of a child genius to survive . . .

DEAD EVEN

A gripping novel of psychological terror

EMMA BROOKES